CINNAMON SKIN

CINNAMON SKIN

The Twentieth Adventure of Travis McGee

John D. MacDonald

1817

HARPER & ROW, PUBLISHERS, New York

Cambridge, Philadelphia, San Francisco, London
Mexico City, São Paulo, Sydney

All characters in this book are fictional,
and any resemblance to persons living or dead
is purely coincidental.

Dedicated to our special group of Kiwis, with love

A man's life is dyed the color
of his imagination.
>   Marcus Aurelius

CINNAMON SKIN

one

There are no hundred percent heroes.

Every man can be broken when things happen to him in a certain order, with a momentum and an intensity that awaken ancient fears in the back of his mind. He knows what he must do, but suddenly the body will not obey the mind. Panic becomes like an unbearably shrill sound.

I was trying to explain this to Annie Renzetti, the trim, tidy, and loving person who had been an essential part of my life for many months. It was late June, summer season at the resort she manages, the Eden Beach near Naples, Florida. We were down on the beach, at the quiet end, beyond her personal cabaña, sprawled on huge beach towels. It was difficult for me to carry on any kind of complex discussion and keep looking at her at the same time, especially when she was using a tiny white bikini to set off her golden-dark tan. I had never before been seriously involved with a short, slender, dark-haired woman. My taste had run to tall blondes with long long legs and good shoulders. Maybe in my ignorance I had thought the little ones too fragile. Found out they are not. At least this one wasn't.

"Did it ever happen to you?" she asked.

"Not really, but I have been so close I know that somewhere, sometime, it *could* happen. We have a lot of myths in our society, Annie."

"Please remember you are the only person in the world who is allowed to call me Annie."

"I will never forget. I think the myth that has humbled Meyer is one of the worst: the myth of the unbreakable hero. I told him some stories. I thought one would make the right impression on him.

"A long time ago, in one of the wars we didn't win, I had a company commander who was the best I ever saw. Quiet and competent

and humane and tough. When bad orders came down, he'd find ways
to sidestep them without getting himself or any of us jammed up. He
took all the risks we took, and he tried to keep the risk factor down.
He took damned good care of us, and when we lost people, it really
hurt him.

"One day we had to go through a patch of Asian jungle which had
a leech out at the tip end of almost every leaf and twig, swaying,
waiting for something full of blood to walk underneath. The captain
hadn't been in leech country before, but the company had. There are
two good ways to get them off: touch them with a lighted end of a
cigaret or slide a sliver of bamboo under one up to the head end and
give a little flip and he'll come off. After you've flipped about ten of
them off, you begin to get the hang of it. The thing I hated most
about them was the way they would crawl through the eyelets on
your boots and fasten onto you through your socks, swell up huge,
and then get mashed by the pressure of the boot as you walked."

"Hey, look!" she said, and showed me the goose bumps on her
upper arm.

"Where was I?"

"I won't even tell you."

"Oh. Anyway, it was really a heavy fall in there, and they were
coming down faster than you could get them off. And if you tried
pulling them off, of course you left the jaws embedded and they
would fester. So we broke out of the column and looked up and ran
to where there were open places in the trees overhead, where they
couldn't fall down and you'd have time to get rid of the ones already
on you. But the captain didn't know the routine. He stood there,
pulling them off, faster and faster, thrashing around, and finally he
began screaming and running, falling down and jumping up, screaming and running. He was a good brave man, but this little thing came
at just the wrong time and place; maybe it resonated with something
in his childhood. It broke him. Also, it destroyed his authority over
the company. He began to make mistakes. And one of them got him
killed about three weeks later."

"How awful!"

"A couple of days after the leech business, one of the company
clowns did an imitation of the captain fighting off the leeches. I
decked him."

"I'm glad."

"Strange thing, the clown got killed in the same weird skirmish
that got the captain killed. The captain read the map wrong, and we
went down the wrong trail."

"But you couldn't make Meyer understand what you were telling him."

"I told you how it was. We knew Grizzel was a dangerous psychopath with nothing to lose and that he was probably on his way to see us. Meyer had never seen me bring in outside help before. So when Grizzel came up behind Meyer, spun him around, jammed that derringer into his gut and announced that they were both going to come over to the *Busted Flush* and visit me—and it would be the last visit Meyer would ever make and I would ever get—Meyer said he looked back into that man's crazy eyes and saw something moving back in there, something without soul or mercy. He read his own death. He saw there was no hope. He turned into a robot, doing only what Grizzel ordered. He was broken and he knew it."

"But he saw Grizzel fall dead, Travis! Didn't that . . . ?"

"Maybe it helped, but not much. It's been a year. We all miss the old Meyer. That's why we cooked up this Toronto lecture thing. We had to be careful. If he'd suspected it was a put-up job, he'd have refused the invitation to lecture up there. His old friend Aggie Sloane helped us arrange it, after she flew down and saw Meyer looking so dwindled and withdrawn. She has a lot of clout. She talked one of Meyer's friends, a man named Pricewater, into backing out of a speaking engagement up there in Canada and asking Meyer as a special favor to fill in for him. The man pled illness."

"Then I don't understand about the niece."

"That was another plot to get Meyer out of his shell. We phoned her. I told her about Meyer. She was hurt that he hadn't come to her wedding in April and had just sent regrets and a check and the usual best wishes for happiness. And so she said she and her new husband would fly over as soon as she could take some time off. So of course Evan and Norma Lawrence arrived the day before Meyer had to fly up to Toronto for the two-week lecture series. So he insisted they live aboard his cruiser while he was in Canada. One of the captains from Charterboat Row is taking them out on day trips aboard the *Keynes*. We had two great schemes, and they just happened to overlap. Anyway, he'll be back here July sixth and they don't have to leave until the tenth. After that Aggie is going to send him off to cover something or other for her newspapers. She told me that any kind of depression can be cured if you move a person around enough."

"Let me see, I keep moving you back and forth between Lauderdale and Naples. Feel depressed?"

"Let's move up to your place and see if there is anything wrong with me that needs fixing."

"Oh, no, you don't! I'm a career woman, and there is my career sitting right over there, all two hundred rooms of it, dying for lack of attention."

"Annie, we've been out here in the blazing sun, and we're going to have to take showers anyway. Florida has a serious water shortage. Why waste a good shower?"

"I have got to learn to start saying no to you."

"Why?"

She rolled onto her elbows and looked down into my eyes. She pursed her lips and raised her thick dark brows and said, "Now that is a very good question. A *very* good question indeed. Why should I start that?"

So we picked up our gear and climbed the steps to the shallow porch of the manager's cabaña, up on pilings six feet tall. We had half a bottle of red wine left from the previous evening, and I mixed it half and half with club soda and lots of ice, for tall spritzers. She dimmed the daylight in the bedroom by pulling the draperies almost across. We sat on the bed and sipped the spritzers and grinned at each other. Finally we set them aside, and I took all of her out of her scraps of bikini, admired her every inch at close and loving range, and in due time, with knowing effort, set her to hooting and whimpering and finally sighing deeply and long.

I did not know the relationship was in any difficulty until after our showers, after we were dressed and I was ready to drive back to Lauderdale and she was ready to go back to work. It was a banquet night for some fraternal order and she wanted to watch it very closely, as it was their first arrangement at the Eden Beach.

I said, "When can I come back? When can you drive over? Seems to me I've asked before."

"It's pretty damn convenient for you, Travis."

"I'm not sure how you mean that."

"I'm not really sure either. It just seems to me you're kind of a lucky chauvinist."

"Now hold on! We are pretty damn convenient for each other, if you want to put it that way. I wouldn't exactly call you unfulfilled, lady."

"Bragging about your work?"

"Jesus, Annie!"

"I'm sorry. I'm trying to hurt you, I guess, but I don't know why."

"I thought we got on together pretty well."

"We do, we do. Of course we do. Maybe it's some kind of chronic guilt. I used to have the guilts when I worked for Ellis and lived with him. Everybody is supposed to have the right to live as they please these days. Oh, hell, I know what it is, but I hate having to try to explain it to you."

"Please do."

"We've talked a lot, Travis. That's been such a big part of us, all the good talk. And you've told me about the loves you've had and the way you lost them. But . . . I sense a kind of reserve about you. You seem to be totally open with me, but some part of you is holding back. Some part of you doesn't really believe that you are not going to lose me also. So you cut down on the amount of loss by not getting as deeply involved as . . . as we could be involved. Do you understand?"

"I'm trying to. I'm not holding back. I don't think I am. I tell you I love you. Maybe oftener I should tell you?"

"It isn't words or deeds, dear. We're never part of each other. We are each of us on the outside of the other person."

"And this is no time for a bawdy comment."

"No, it is not!"

"Are you talking about marriage, for instance?"

"No, dammit! But I would like it if we lived closer together and saw each other oftener."

"Hell, I wish you'd pick up your life savings, separation pay and all that, and move aboard the *Flush*."

"You know better than that. I really really *love* it here. I'm doing one hell of a job. It shows in the figures I send in, and in the appreciation they're giving me. I'm just about the best manager in the chain. I like working with people, finding the way to approach each one to make him or her do a better job, to motivate them. Because of me this resort hotel is clean and profitable and fun."

"Okay, already. Why can't you just settle for what we have? I think it's a little better than what most people settle for."

She sighed and leaned against me, then reached up to kiss the side of my chin. "Okay, McGee. I'll try, but something about us hasn't quite meshed yet. Maybe it never will. Who can say? Run along. Drive carefully. Phone often."

two

The fifth of July began with heavy rain from a tropical depression in the Atlantic east of Miami, a warm rain accompanied by random gusts of wind.

By ten in the morning, the rain had diminished to a misty drizzle and Meyer's stubby little cruiser, the *John Maynard Keynes,* had left the gas dock at Pier 66, Fort Lauderdale, proceeded under the bridge, past the cruise ships tied up at Port Everglades, out the main channel and past the sea buoy, and had headed on an east-southeast course, the blunt bow lifting with the chop, mashing out small sheets of spray each time it fell back.

An old man in a condominium apartment facing the sea was looking out his sixth-floor window at the time of the explosion and was able to fix the time of it at precisely 10:41 Eastern Daylight Time.

A cabin cruiser was inbound from Nassau, heading for the channel and wallowing a little in the following sea. It was the *Brandy-Gal* out of Venice, Florida, owned by a Mr. and Mrs. Simmons Davis. Mrs. Davis was in one of the two fishing chairs, the one on the starboard side, and her husband was at the wheel up on the fly bridge. They both testified that when the two cruisers passed each other, a slender dark-haired woman in an orange string bikini had waved and Mrs. Davis had waved back. They had both seen a bulky man at the wheel and a blond man in the cockpit, coiling and stowing a line.

Mrs. Davis said she remembered being amused at the unusual name on the cruiser, the *John Maynard Keynes;* she knew that any mention of Keynesian economic theory tended to make her husband very cross. And she remembered thinking that the chunky little cruiser did not take the chop very well, and that if it were hers she would head back to the Inland Waterway. Also, she thought it seemed to ride too low in the water.

She estimated that it was two hundred and fifty to three hundred feet from the *Brandy-Gal* when it blew up. It was there, and then suddenly the only visible thing was a white bright glare, larger than the cruiser, with small objects arching up out of it. There was a sound she described as being both sharp and heavy, a kind of cracking *whump* that made her ears ring, and she felt heat on her face. Simmons Davis wheeled the *Brandy-Gal* about and went back in a hopeless search for survivors. He knew he was in eighty to a hundred feet of water. He rigged a small spare anchor to an orange float with ample braided nylon line and flipped it overboard. Then he and his wife, using scoop nets, picked up the few floating bits of debris. Half a scorched life ring. A soiled white cap with a blue bill, part of it still smoldering. The lid from an ice chest.

He called the Coast Guard on his radio and reported the incident and then headed in, with his wife, Brandy, vomiting over the side.

An anonymous call was made to the Fort Lauderdale police a few minutes after the explosion. The call was recorded. It was a muffled male voice, heavy and deep, with an accent which could have been Spanish or Portuguese.

"The Liberation Army of the Chilean peoples hass executed the pig dog Doctor Meyer. Death to all who geev help to the fascist military dictatorship."

I knew nothing about it until I got back to Bahia Mar a little after six that Monday evening. I was walking from the parking area over to Slip F-18 where my houseboat, the *Busted Flush,* is tied up, when Captain Johnny Dow came trotting up to fall in step with me and say, "Hey, they got Meyer."

I stopped and stared at him. "What do you mean?"

"Hell, they blew him up."

"In Toronto?"

"What do you mean, Toronto? In that stupid-looking little cruiser of his. Out past the sea buoy, this morning. They blew him up and took the credit."

"Who is they?"

"One of those bunches of terrorists. You know. The red army of liberation, truth, and justice. One of those."

Suddenly I felt hollow and sick. "Johnny, don't you know who was aboard the *Keynes?*"

"How should I know? I just got back from Key West."

I explained it to him patiently. "Meyer is doing a series of lectures at a seminar in international banking at Queen's College in Toronto. His niece and her husband were on vacation. They were living aboard for the two weeks he'd be gone. And Meyer had arranged with Hack Jenkins to take them out fishing or cruising if they wanted to go, because neither of them could operate a boat. Hack was free because his boat is having the engines replaced."

Johnny Dow looked stricken. "I knew about the work he was having done on the *HooBoy*. Jesus! What they say, it was one hell of a big explosion. Anybody aboard got blown to little tiny bits. Jesus! I better go see Hack's wife. This is terrible, Trav."

He went trotting off through the light rain. I unlocked the *Flush,* checked out my alarm system, and heard the phone ringing as I went in. "Did he get back early?" Annie asked. "Tell me he didn't come back early, please."

"No, dear. He's due to give the last lecture tomorrow, and he's booked on a flight that gets into Miami tomorrow night at eight."

"They said on the news that a woman on another boat saw three people aboard Meyer's boat before it blew up. And I thought—"

"No, the third person was a captain from Charterboat Row here. A friend of both of us. I think you met him once over here. Hacksaw Jenkins. Hack."

"Oh, yes! That big rubbery guy that looked like a Japanese wrestler. With the very nice little wife. How terrible! Didn't you hear any of it on the news on the way back?"

"I avoid news whenever possible. I was playing tapes all the way across."

"Have you got a phone number for Meyer?"

"I know what hotel he's in. I could call him, but I don't know what to say. It's very sad and very ironic, Annie, after all the trouble we went to, trying to get Meyer out of the dumps."

"Look, let me know how it goes. Let me know how he reacts. I love that funny old bear."

"I'll be in touch."

I didn't have to phone Meyer. As I was unpacking toilet articles, he called me.

"Travis? A reporter from the *Miami Herald* tracked me down. Is it true? They're dead?"

"I didn't know a thing about it until about fifteen minutes ago. Johnny Dow told me. He thought you were aboard."

"Would that I had been," he said. It was not dramatics. He meant it.

"What can I do here?" I asked.

"I don't know. I can't think. What is there to do anyway? Where have they taken the bodies?"

"Meyer, from what I hear it was a very big explosion. Very violent. Out past the sea buoy. Out in the open ocean. Who handles your insurance?"

"I can't think. You know him. Tall."

"Sure. Walter. So he probably knows about it by now."

"Before I phoned you, I checked with the travel desk here at the hotel, and I can't get out any earlier than the flight I'm already booked on tomorrow."

"I'll pick you up. Ten after eight. Anybody I should let know about it?"

"There's an address book in the . . . oh, dear God, that's gone too, of course. Anyway, under Amdex Petroleum Exploration in Houston I had the name of her immediate superior. Hatcher, Thatcher, Fletcher . . . one of those names. Travis, what I don't understand is this grotesque nonsense about Chile. I was in Santiago for one week, three years ago. It was a small conference. Yes, we were invited to make recommendations to the military government about controlling inflation. And they took the recommendations, and their inflation is under control, unlike the situation in Brazil, Argentina, and Peru. It was a small international conference: Britain, France, Canada, the U.S.—a dozen of us. I didn't write the final report or any part of it."

"Meyer, listen. It's a crazy world. You were there. You got on somebody's hit list."

"And so Norma and Evan and Hack die. Can you find whoever did it?"

"There are going to be lots of very competent people trying to find whoever did it."

"They never seem to find terrorists." His voice was lifeless, dulled by loss.

At ten o'clock the next morning, local time, I got through to a brisk switchboard person at Amdex in Houston.

"You had a woman working there, a geologist named Norma Lawrence."

"Sorry. There's no one here by that name, sir."

"Look, I *know* she worked for Amdex. She was on vacation."

"Oh, you mean Norma Greene! Miss Greene."

"Okay. Sure. I want to talk to her boss."

"That would be Mr. Batcher. Sorry, but he's out of the country, sir. If you want to leave a message, we expect him Friday."

I sighed with moderate exasperation. "Who on your team there, besides Mr. Batcher, would be interested in being informed that Norma Lawrence, your Miss Greene, is dead?"

"Oh, God! No! To whom am I speaking?"

"My name is McGee. Travis McGee. An acquaintance. Her uncle suggested I inform her employer. That's what I'm doing."

"Mr. Dexter will want to know the details. He should be in any minute now. Where can he reach you, Mr. McGee?"

I gave her the area code and the number. She said she was sorry about the whole thing, and I said I was too.

"Automobile accident?" she asked.

"Explosion on a boat."

I heard her gasp, "Geez, you know I heard that on the news this morning and didn't make the connection. I mean I didn't listen to the name, you know? Her and her new husband and a fishing guide? The news said it was maybe some kind of Cuban terrorists. Why would they—oh, Mr. Dexter just came in. Shall I ring him now?"

"Please."

In a few moments he said, "Mr. McGee? What can I do for you."

"Hardly anything. Mrs. Lawrence's uncle suggested that I call her employer and say that she was killed yesterday in an explosion aboard a boat off Fort Lauderdale, along with her husband and a local charterboat captain."

"Lawrence? Norma Greene Lawrence?"

"That's right." There was a silence that lasted so long I said, "Are you there? Hello?"

"Excuse me. That's a terrible shock."

"I was trying to get hold of Mr. Batcher. I didn't think you'd know her."

"Mr. McGee, this is a small company. A little over two hundred people. The smartest thing we ever did was take on Norma Lawrence when she'd been out of Cal Tech a year. We hired her away from Conoco. She's . . . she was going to be one of the best geologists in the business."

He said something else, but a sudden rumble of thunder drowned him out.

"Didn't hear you. Sorry."

"I was saying what a loss it is. What happened?"

"It looks as if somebody put a bomb aboard, some nut trying to kill her uncle. But he was in Toronto. They were going to dive at the site this morning, but the weather is very bad: eight- to ten-foot waves out there, lots of white water. There was a marker buoy at the site dropped off by a pleasure boat, but it was washed loose during the night."

"I don't know what to say. Maybe her uncle would know what her personal estate arrangements are. We have an insurance program, of course. And there would be other funds payable to her, or her estate."

"I'll have him get in touch. What's your whole name?"

"D. Amsbary Dexter," he said. Hence, I supposed, the Amdex. His company. I wrote down his addresses and phone numbers, and he thanked me for calling him. He said it was a terrible thing, and I said it certainly was. He had one of those thin fast Texas voices. Not a good-old-boy voice, a hustler voice. Hurrying to sell you.

By nine o'clock Tuesday night, in the very last of the watery daylight, I was heading back toward Lauderdale from the airport in the Mercedes station wagon I'd borrowed from the Alabama Tiger's highest-ranking girl friend, the one who has charge of his floating playpen while he is back in Guadalajara having his big old face lifted again. Wind gusts whacked the occasional rain against the right-hand windows. Meyer sat damp and dumpy beside me, radiating bleakness, speaking only when spoken to.

"Were they annoyed you didn't give the final lecture?"

"I was there. I'd taken their round-trip ticket, hotel room, and food. I gave the talk. Only because it was easier than not giving the talk."

"The weather has been rotten."

"Um."

"The tropical storm has moved closer and picked up a little. But they don't think it will reach hurricane force."

"Uh huh."

Conversation wasn't working, so I tried silence. After fifteen minutes he said, "These last few months I've gotten into the habit of watching television."

"Meyer!"

"I know, I know. A laxative for the mind. Thinking makes lumps in the mind. Bad memories make lumps. Television flushes them away. At five o'clock, alone there aboard my boat, I've been able to get a rerun of *MASH* on one channel and then switch to another rerun on another. Old ones. Trapper, Hawkeye, Radar, Hot Lips. You know, the introduction has stayed almost exactly the same. The helicopters come around the side of the mountain. Then you get a shot from on high of the hospital complex. Then an ambulance, a closer shot of the choppers, and then people running up a hill toward the camera. In the left center of the screen a young woman runs toward you, slightly ahead of the others. You see her for four and a half running strides. Dark hair. Face showing the strain of running and her concern for the wounded. A pretty woman, maybe even beautiful, with a strong, lithe, handsome body. She is in uniform. A gleam of dog tags at the opening of her shirt. I've thought about her often, Travis. That shot of her was taken years ago. She's probably in her thirties now. Or even forty. I wonder about her. When they filmed that introduction she had no way of knowing that she would be frozen there in time, anxious and running. Does she ever think about how strange that is? Multiply viewers times original episodes and the countless reruns on hundreds of stations, and you can see she has been looked at a billion times. What do you pay a person to be looked at a billion times? How many thousand miles has she run? It's the fly-in-amber idea, plus a paradox of time and space. Maybe she never thinks of it these days. Or yawns when she sees herself. Last night I saw her again, late, in a Toronto hotel room. And she became Norma: dark hair and vitality. Now she is caught in some eternal time lock. Death is an unending rerun until the last person with any memory of you is also dead."

I had not heard him say this much since that bloody June day when Desmin Grizzel had so totally terrified him that he had, in his fear, violated his own image of himself. I did not make any response because I wanted him to keep talking. I was afraid that anything I might say would make him clamp shut again, like an endangered clam.

"I went through the long list of all the things I should have done and didn't do," he said. "Go to the wedding. Or at least pick out a present and send it instead of a check. She was my very last blood relative. It's like a superstitious fear, having no one left in the world directly related to you by blood. As if you had started somehow to disappear. She wasn't at all pretty, but being in love made her beautiful. I noticed that. And I haven't been noticing much lately, have I?"

"No. No, you haven't."

"In that sense, to that degree, Desmin Grizzel won after all. All my life, until this last year, I have always noticed everything. Noticed, analyzed, filed. I watched people, understood them, liked almost every one. If he killed that in me, then he killed me, because he killed that part of me that made me most alive. And I let it happen."

"No, Meyer. There wasn't any way—"

"Be still!" he said with a surprising vehemence. "I've been dwelling on my sorry image, how I sat on the floor like a dumb pudding, peeing in my trousers, while I watched a maniac start to kill the best friend I ever had. In some kind of inverted fashion I fell in love with that image of Meyer. Oh, the poor dear chap! Oh, what a pity!"

"But—"

"So today in that aircraft I took a longer steadier look at myself. I saw my face reflected in the window beside me. One can become weary of shame, self-revulsion, self-knowledge. I am an academic, damn it. I was not intended to become some sort of squatty super-man, some soldier of misfortune. It was not intended that I should be unafraid of sudden death. Curiously, I am not afraid of the prospect of my own demise. Plainly I shall die, as will you and everyone we know, and I do not think that a fact worth my resentment. Life is un-fair, clearly. One must hope that the final chapter will be without too much pain. It was his terrible eyes and those four barrels on that strange handgun he had. Something inside me broke into mush, into tears and pee and ineptitude. But it does not signify!"

"I tried to tell—"

"I did not listen. I was too enchanted with my humiliation, with how I had failed my adolescent dream of myself as hero. There was a child on the airplane, directly across the aisle. The seat beside me was empty. I smiled at her and did finger tricks, and she giggled and tried to stuff her head under her mother's arm in shyness. She finally came over and sat beside me, and I told her a story about a cowardly goblin who refused to go out on Halloween and scare people because he was too fat and too shy. Partway through the story I realized I was telling a story about Meyer the Economist. It made the ending easier. They had a meeting of the Goblin Council and called him in and told him not to worry. There had to be room in each pack of goblins for a cowardly goblin who stayed home in the cave. Other-wise, who would count all the others as they came back home after their adventures? So there is room for me: counting goblins, includ-ing my own."

"There always has been—"

"No, Travis. Not for the Meyer of the past year. No room for him at all. But for this Meyer? Why not? I am not the same as I was be-fore the incident, I am less naive. Is that a good word?"

"I think so."

"You have always been less naive than most of us, Travis. You are a different sort of creature, in many ways. But you are my friend, and I don't want to lose you. I want you to help me. Somebody blew up my boat, and with it all the artifacts of my past and my last close relative. I want to find that person or those people. And kill them. Is that an unworthy goal?"

"It's understandable."

"You dodge the question."

"You want a moral judgment, go to Jerry Falwell. Anything you really want to do, I will help you do. And it *is* nice to have you back, even in slightly altered condition. Okay?"

I glanced over at him and saw in the angle of a streetlight that he was smiling. It was a fine thing to see. Utterly unanticipated. I had thought this would be the end of him. Instead, it shocked him out of it—not all the way out, but far enough to lead one to hope.

"I keep remembering that Sunday evening aboard the *Flush*," he said. "They were really in love, weren't they?"

three

The evening had not been awkward because Evan Lawrence was not the kind of man to let that happen. I guessed him at about forty, ten to twelve years older than his bride. He had a broad, blunt face, brown sun-streaked hair, snub nose, crooked grin, the baked look of an outdoor person, and large fan-shaped areas of laugh wrinkles beside his eyes. He was perhaps five-ten, hardly an inch taller than his wife, but broad and thick in chest and shoulders. In repose, Norma was almost homely. Narrow forehead, long nose, an overbite and a dwindled chin, long neck. But her eyes were lovely, her long hair a glossy blue-black, her figure elegant, her movements graceful. In animation, and when she looked at Evan, she was beautiful.

Evan asked Meyer a dozen questions about how he had made the meat sauce. He asked me fifty questions about my houseboat. We went through several bottles of Chianti Classico while we ate the ceviche I'd made and then had the spaghetti al dente with the meat sauce Meyer had brought.

In the warmth and relaxation after dinner, Evan told us how he had met Norma. "What I was doing, I was down there in Cancún, gone over to Yucatán to visit with my friend Willy, and I was putting in my time helping him sell off some time-sharing condos. He had some he couldn't move at what he needed to make out, which was one hundred big ones, so he'd taken to selling them off in one-and two-week pieces for three and six thousand, people buying those same weeks for life and Willy explaining how they had tied into the big vacation computer so the pigeons he was selling to could like exchange with some other patsies who'd bought the same two weeks on maybe the coast of Spain or Fort Meyers, Florida. I had no work license, so when I sold stuff, Willy had to slip me the pesos in cash and keep it off the books. I can always sell. I'm a scuffler, and there are always things to sell and people to buy them, so I'm home anywhere. Good thing, the way they keep moving Norma around the shaggy places of the earth.

"One day what I was doing, I was taking the pickup to Mérida to get some things that had come in that Willy had ordered way back, and ten miles from anywhere I came onto this beat old Dodge pulled way over on the shoulder and this tall pretty girl trying to open the hood. So I pulled over and walked back and I said in my best Texican, her hair being so black, '¿Tiene una problema, Señorita?' She just spun around and give me the glare and said, 'Problema? Me? No, I just enjoy standing out here in the hot sun breaking my fingernails on this son of a bitching hood latch.' And right there it was love at first sight, on my part, not on hers.

"Opened the hood for her and looked in and right there looking back at me is a granddaddy rat, biggest damn thing I ever saw, big as a full-growed possum. We both jumped back, and he ducked down and hid someplace under the engine. I looked around, real careful, and I see he had chewed on the insulation on the wiring to the starter motor. So I had Norma get in and start it while I jumped the contacts with a screwdriver. When it caught and roared, old mister rat he went charging off into the brush. What had happened, she'd stopped to walk over to a formation that looked interesting, and chunked at it with that hammer she's got at all times, and came back and the car wouldn't start. Just a click when she turned the key. I led her into town to a garage I'd been before, and we went down the street and sat at a sidewalk place and drank cold Carta Blanca for the half hour it took them to rewire where old rat had chewed. I didn't find out for a long time how important she was down there, being borrowed by the Mexican government."

"Hey, it wasn't all that big and great!" she said. "I had a Mexican friend at Cal Tech, Manny Mateo, and he became an engineer with Pemex, the government oil company. They thought they had a new discovery field just west of Maxcanú, way to the north of the Bay of Campeche, and from the initial geophysical survey work it looked as if it might be a particular kind of formation I've had a lot of luck with. So Pemex arranged with Am Dexter to borrow me, and I went down there and we ran two more sets of computer tests and I finally picked a site for the test well, crossed my fingers, and went back to Houston. It took about nine weeks."

"Did they make a well?" Meyer asked.

She shrugged. "Just barely. It's a long way from their big fields and their refineries. It's a discovery well and a new field, but the porosity is bad. It makes the MER pretty low when you are so far from . . . excuse me, MER is Maximum Efficiency Recovery rate, and they figure it at seventy barrels a day, which would be a two-thousand-dollar-a-day delight in Louisiana but isn't so great down there. They'll try again a thousand meters to the north where, according to the core samples, they should hit the formation higher."

"She talks like that a lot!" Evan said proudly. "Isn't she something else entire?"

Norma flushed. "All geologists talk funny."

"I kept after her," Evan said. "She finished up and went back, so did I. Every time she'd look around, there I was. So along sometime in March she gave up, and we got married in April. Meyer, we sure wish you could have come to the wedding. That was a handsome check you laid on us, but you being there would have been a better present."

"It would, really," Norma Lawrence said. "People in this family are always missing ceremonies." She sounded wistful, and her eyes filled with tears.

Meyer touched her lightly on the arm and said to me, "Remember three years ago when we were in the islands, and I came back and found a three-week-old telegram about my sister's funeral?"

"And I was with a crew up in western Canada and didn't know either, until a week later," Norma said. "Her friends in Santa Barbara said the church was almost full. She had a lot of love from a lot of people. And gave a lot of love. And she was so damn proud of me."

She got up abruptly and went over to the window ports and looked out at the marina in the dusk of the year's second longest daytime. Evan went and put a thick arm around her slender waist, murmuring to her. She leaned her cheek on his shoulder, and soon they both came back to the table.

He poured her some wine and touched glasses with her and said, "Here's to your never having another gloomy day, Miz Norma."

We all drank to that. And Evan Lawrence began telling stories of things he'd done. They were disaster stories, all funny, all nicely told. There was the time he had tried out for the University of Texas football squad "as a teeny tiny hundred-and-sixty-five-pound offensive right tackle, fourth string, and next to those semi-pro freshmen they had on there, I was five foot nothing. Big old boy across from me, looked forty years old, kept slapping my helmet and I kept getting up, thinking, Well, this wasn't too bad, and then all of a sudden there were voices yelling at me and I came to and I was standing in the shower with my gear on, shoes and all, and everybody mad at me."

And then there was the time he "got a job with a crazy old rancher just north of Harlingen. Old Mr. Guffey had tried to buy a Japanese stone lantern for his wife's flower garden and they wanted a hundred dollars for one. Made him so mad he got an import license and imported thirty tons of them. Nine hundred of the forty-pound type and four hundred sixty-pounders. I slept in a shed on his place, and they'd wake me up before dawn to eat a couple pounds of eggs, load lanterns into the pickup, and take off by first sunlight going up and down those crazy little roads, selling stone lanterns. Living expenses plus a ten-dollar commission, payable when the last one was gone. They's *never* going to need another Japanese stone garden lantern down in that end of Texas. I got bent over with muscle from lifting them fool things in and out of the pickup. Finished finally and got paid off, went into Brownsville to get the first beer in three months, woke up behind the place with my head in a cardboard box, no money, no boots, no watch. I lay there thinking it was a funny place for a fellow with a B.S. in Business Administration with a major in marketing and a minor in female companionship to spend a rainy night."

And later on, he said, "Good old friend of mine, he said there was good money to be had traveling with the rodeo. See a lot of new places, meet pretty girls, people clapping hands for you and all that. He said I should do the bull riding, because I didn't have any roping skills or such. First time I stayed on more than three seconds and got me any prize money, the bull he tore up my left hind leg so bad, I was on crutches a month, but they let me take tickets. Prettiest girl I saw there looked like John Chancellor in drag, and she borrowed my old car, totaled it, and walked away without a scratch."

"Didn't you ever have a *good* job, Evan?" she asked him.

"You mean like making lots of money? Oh, hell yes, sweetie. I worked better than a full year in Dallas, selling empty lots and lots with tract houses on them, out in the subdivisions, working for Eagle Realty. Had me a hundred forty thousand in savings, after taxes and living expenses, and this fellow told me that what I had to have, I was making so much, was a shelter. So he sheltered me. What he sold me was a hundred twenty-five thousand Bibles at one dollar each. He was to hold onto them in a warehouse for a year, then start giving twenty-five thousand of them Bibles away to religious and charitable organizations, and on the inside of the Bible it said, plain as day, Retail value seven fifty. What that meant was each year I'd be giving away a hundred and eighty-seven thousand dollars' worth of Bibles, and half that would come off my tax as a charity deduction. He said it was all legal and I'd be doing a good work. After he was long gone there was a piece in the paper about him. What he was was a Bible salesman, selling fifty-cent Bibles for a dollar each. I went to find the warehouse and look at my Bibles, but the address for the warehouse was pastureland. Honey, I made lots of money several times here and there, and what I needed and didn't have was one smart wife to help me hold onto it long enough to get it spent wisely."

There was a lull in the storm when we got back to Bahia Mar. I parked and locked the station wagon, took Meyer to my place, then took the car keys back to Wendy aboard the *'Bama Gal.*

"Stay with Meyer," she told me. "Stay close to him. Don't let him be by himself too much."

When I got back to the *Flush* I found Meyer fixing himself a very stiff arrangement of Boodles gin and ice. "Sleep insurance," he said. I fixed one half that size for myself, and we went up to the topside controls, under the shelter of the overhead there. He swiveled the starboard chair around and stared through the night toward the place where, for years, the *John Maynard Keynes* had been berthed. He hoisted his glass in a half salute. "Damn boat," he said. "Bad lines. Cranky. Not enough freeboard."

So we drank to the damn boat.

In a little while, in a very gravelly voice, Meyer said, "I feel gutted. Everything was aboard her. All my files and records. Copies of all the papers I've had published. All the speeches I've given, except the ones I updated and took to Toronto. Letters from the long dead. From my father. From old friends. Photographs. My professional library. Unanswered letters. My address book. I feel as if, on some strange level, I've ceased to exist. I've lost so many proofs of my existence."

"Safety deposit box?"

"Yes. A few things there. Passport, birth certificate, bearer bonds." He swiveled the chair back around so the dock light angled across the right side of his face. "It's so damned senseless! I had nothing to do with the overthrow of Allende. What is that word used by the agencies? Destabilization. When I was in Santiago, the military was busy returning to private ownership the hundreds of companies nationalized by Allende and badly run by Allende's people. Who is most hurt by hyper-inflation? The old, the poor. So I helped them as much as I could. We devised and recommended the controls, enough controls to put a leaky lid on inflation without stifling initiative. Nobody in Toronto had ever heard of that group. What do they call themselves?"

"The Liberation Army of the Chilean People. Two men will be here to talk to you in the morning. They were here this afternoon. I couldn't give them much help."

"Who has jurisdiction?"

"Hard to say. State of Florida. Coast Guard. Federal agencies. The State Attorney's people are investigating, but they aren't what you'd call eager."

"Can we find out, Travis, the two of us?"

I tried not to show reluctance as I said, "I promised you we'd give it a try."

He was still there when I went to bed. He'd made a fresh drink. He knew how to lock up. After I turned the bed lamp off, I kept thinking about Meyer. The fates were trying to grind him down. And almost doing the job.

The hard rains had begun again. Soon I heard water running in the head, saw a light under the door. Then it went out. I knew he'd sleep.

I reconstructed from memory the bilge of the *John Maynard Keynes,* the twin engines, the shafts and gas tanks—gasoline, not diesel. I marked the mental spot where I would place the heavy charge, right where the heat of it would turn the two gas tanks into additional explosive force, going up simultaneously with the charge, blowing the boat to junk and splinters. Perhaps it had been detonated by a timer. But how could whoever planted it be certain the boat would be out in relatively deep water when the timed instant arrived?

Had it blown at the dock with that much force, it would have taken the neighbor vessels as well, and a lot more than three lives. People who have tried to put bombs on airliners have used timers or fuses that worked on reduced atmospheric pressure. A bomb aboard a little pleasure boat couldn't reasonably be hooked up to the depth finder.

Interesting problem. What does a boat do out in deep water that it doesn't do at the dock? Answer: It pitches and tosses. Very good, McGee. So you use a battery and you get a very stiff piece of wire or leaf spring and you solder a weight to the end of it. It will not bend down to touch the contact, closing the circuit, firing the cap that fires that charge, until it has started oscillating in rough water. That would be efficient, because the whole device could be self-contained and would take only a moment to place below decks. It could have been placed there while they were gassing up at Pier 66.

What if out in the channel somebody came from the opposite direction, throwing a big wash? Okay, so it was a little more sophisticated, perhaps. It had a counting device, a cogwheel arrangement. On the twentieth big lift and drop, or the fiftieth, *bah-room!*

And maybe it had been stowed aboard weeks before Norma and Evan arrived. Maybe a fake factory rep inspecting the new sniffer Meyer had installed had brought it aboard back in January, tucked it into the recess aft of one of the tanks.

When the mind starts that kind of spinning, sleep becomes impossible. So I wrenched my thoughts away from explosives and thought about Annie Renzetti, about all her sweetness and unexpected strength. I reinvented her, bit by bit, portion by portion, and went trotting down after her, into sleep.

four

The next morning came with a black sky low enough to touch, and about the time I heard Meyer in the shower, the two men from Washington returned. The big natty one with the white hair and red cheeks was Warner Housell, and he called himself a staff person on Senator Derregrand's Anti-Terrorist Committee, and the terrier type with the hairpiece and the hearing aid was Rowland Service, a specialist from the Treasury Department.

They both carried dark brown dispatch cases with brass hardware. I told them Meyer would be out in a few minutes, and would they like coffee, and they said they would, no sugar no cream. They were less friendly with each other than they had been the previous afternoon.

Meyer came out wearing a bathrobe and a headache, and after I had introduced him, he poured himself some coffee and put a chip of ice in it so he could get to it quicker.

Warner Housell asked the questions. Since he had last called on me, he had briefed himself on Meyer's career, and he was properly respectful. He just took a few quick dabs at Meyer's background and then said, "How did you get involved in the Santiago conference?"

"I was invited by the chairman. Dr. Isling from the London School of Economics. I imagine there was some sort of selection process, but I don't know what it was. It was an interesting group."

"Had you been associated with any of the members before?"

"Only very indirectly. Good people. Academics with a good sense of what is practical, of what might actually work."

"Are you aware of and have you expressed any opinions in your speeches or your writings about the way the military regime treats dissidents?"

"I've expressed no opinions except to friends, like Travis McGee here. Yes, I've been aware of the reports of violations of human rights."

He turned to me. "Can you recall any such opinions expressed by Dr. Meyer?"

"Not in his exact words. We've discussed what he calls the Shah of Iran paradox. When you crush a rebellion by killing people who are trying to overthrow your government and install their own, at what point are you violating their human rights, and at what point are they violating yours? The Shah let Khomeini escape to Paris. And Batista let Castro leave the country. At what point on the scale are people dissidents, and at what point does it become armed rebellion?"

Meyer nodded at me approvingly. Warner Housell took notes.

"Now then," he said, "are you aware of any threat on your life as a result of the Santiago conference? Any threat, no matter how indirect?"

"I didn't expect any, so I really wasn't being observant. No strange letters, phone calls, confrontation. Nothing."

"Mr. Service, for reasons of his own, considers this a fruitless line of interrogation. Your turn, Mr. Service."

Rowland Service took out a small notebook and, in silence, leafed through page after page, his forehead furrowed. It is a tiresome device.

"What is your source of income, Dr. Meyer?"

"Please, I do not like doctor used as a form of address except for brain surgeons and such. I am used to being called Meyer. My income comes from lecturing, from consultant work, and from dividends, interest, and capital gains from my investments."

He snapped his ferret head around to stare at me from those two pale close-together eyes. "And you, sir?"

"Me what?"

"What is your source of income?"

"A little of this and a little of that."

"Impertinence makes me uncomfortable, McGee."

"Me too, Service."

Housell broke in. "Please, let me explain what he's trying to establish—"

"Damn it, I'll ask my own questions!"

"*After* I explain the background. Two organizations in Washington have contacts within the underground groups in Chile, with information contacts arranged through our embassy. The regime has an information network as well. Mr. Service here spent most of yesterday and yesterday evening drawing a complete and total blank not only on the so-called Liberation Army of the Chilean People but on any antipathy toward any economist who attended the Santiago conference three years ago. Things have quieted down a great deal there. There has been enough economic progress to make people look with more favor on the generals. Within the context of everything those groups know, the attack upon Dr. Meyer here is incomprehensible to them. And so the—"

"I'll take it," Service said. "The way we see it, that phone call claiming responsibility was a cover story, intended to mislead. It is far more likely that the explosion was connected to the drug traffic that has proliferated along the Florida coast."

Meyer set his coffee aside and stared at the man. "Drug traffic!" he said incredulously. "*Drug* traffic! My niece was a respected geologist who worked for—"

"Don't get agitated. She checked out clean as a whistle. We are wondering about her husband"—he turned a page in his notebook and read off the names—"Evan Lawrence, and the boat captain, Dennis Hackney Jenkins, a.k.a. Hacksaw Jenkins."

"Not likely in either case," I said. "Evan Lawrence came over here with his wife from Houston because she wanted to have him meet her uncle, her only living blood relation. Hacksaw was a successful charterboat captain. He had a long list of people who wouldn't fish with anybody else. He had a talent for finding fish. He kept that fishing machine of his in fine shape at all times. He was booked solid every season at premium rates. Once upon a time he was a professional wrestler. Once upon a time he spent a year in a county jail. He was raised down in the Keys. There are dozens and dozens of Jenkinses there, all related to him. He settled down when he met Gloria. He was fifty a couple of months ago. I went to the birthday party. They have three sons. The youngest is fifteen. Neither Hack nor the kids would be into drugs in any way, shape, or form."

The ferret looked bleakly at me. "We'll check all that out, of course."

The big florid staff person said, "Please forgive my temporary associate here. He has an unfortunate manner."

"I'm here to do my job," Service said, "not beat the bushes for votes."

"Do it elsewhere," Meyer said.

They both looked at him. "What was that?" Service asked.

"That was the end of cooperation. No more questions and no more answers. End of interview. Leave."

"I know all about you high-level experts," Service said angrily.

"Next time you come sucking around the government for a consultant contract, maybe you'll find—"

Housell stood up abruptly. "Come on, Rowland, for God's sake. You're acting like a jackass."

"And you don't know the first thing about interrogation!" Service yelled.

Housell led him off, still protesting, and turned to smile apologetically at us. The door closed. The bell bonged as they stepped on the mat at the head of my little gangway to the dock. Meyer went over to the galley and poured himself fresh coffee. I saw the cup tremble slightly as he lifted it to his lips for a cautious sip.

He sat and frowned down into the cup. "I wanted them out of here so I could think. They were a distraction."

"An incompetent distraction?"

"That too." He sipped again and set the cup aside. "Of course it could have something to do with drugs. Somebody cheated somebody or turned them in, and a bomber was hired and he hit the wrong boat. But the anonymous phone call rules that out. The caller knew my name. I'm thinking out loud, using rusty equipment, Travis. Forgive me."

"Keep going."

"The phone call came about eight minutes after the explosion. So the caller knew it was going to happen and had a vantage point where he could watch for it and then make his call. So the explosive had to be placed just before Hack took the boat out."

"I'd agree with that."

"If the caller knew that much about what was going on, wouldn't he have known I wasn't aboard?"

"Reasonable assumption."

"Then the call was intended to deflect attention from the real motive and the real victim. Somebody wanted to kill Hack, or Evan Lawrence, or Norma. So there was one victim and two innocent bystanders, not three."

"Hack Jenkins?"

"It's possible, I suppose," he said. "I keep wondering why he wanted to go on out into that chop."

"While you were in Toronto, Hack took them outside after fish. Your niece developed a taste for it. She and Evan were good sailors. Some of it was in fairly heavy weather, so I guess Hack learned how much the *Keynes* could take, and he had some confidence in the boat. If he had word there was something working a little way out into deep water, I think Evan and Norma, especially Norma, would have urged him to take a shot at it and then come running back in if it started to get a little too rough."

"She really liked it?" he said, eyebrows raised.

"Hack put them into some small tarpon about two days after you left. She hooked a forty-pounder that jumped into the cockpit green, smashed a tackle box, and flipped on out again, and she managed to keep it on the line and bring it to gaff. She told me all about it, with lots of gestures, lots of energy. So, I can understand his heading out past the buoy."

"Evan liked it too?"

"Whatever Norma wanted was fine with him."

"It seemed like a good marriage," Meyer said. "Never knew what hit them. Hell of a phrase, isn't it? Nothing can happen so fast that there is not a micro-instant of realization. Each nerve cell in the brain can make contact with three hundred thousand other cells, using its hundreds of branches, each branch with hundreds of terminals, and with electrical impulses linking cell to cell. Ten trillion cells, Travis, exchanging coded information every instant. The brain has time to release the news of its own dissolution, time to factor a few questions about why, what, who . . . and what is happening to me? Perhaps a month of mortal illness is condensed into one thousandth of a second, insofar as self-realization is concerned. We're each expert in our own death."

And I knew that strange last statement was correct. We're experts. We get it done the first time we try it. And we spend too much time thinking about it before we do it.

"Hack's two older boys are back in town," I said. "They're waiting for the sea to flatten out and one of these evenings, about seven thirty, all the charter boats will go out and they'll drop a wreath on the water, and the Reverend Sam John Hallenbee of the First Seaside Baptist Church will give the memorial service on a bull horn, consigning to the deep and so on."

"I'd like to have that done for Norma and Evan too. But all her friends are in Houston. I'll have to go over there and see what shape her affairs are in. I would suppose I'd be her heir, but I'm not sure."

"Want any breakfast?"

"Thanks. I don't think I could keep it down yet."

"Why don't you get dressed and we'll go talk to one or both or all of the Jenkins boys."

"And Gloria," Meyer said. "I have to face that. She's going to feel bitter toward me. I asked Hack as a personal favor to take Norma and Evan out in the *Keynes* a few times. He said he was glad to do it. With the *HooBoy* laid up, he felt restless unless he could get out on the water once in a while."

He went trudging off to put on some clothes. He didn't have much choice. All his treasured old shirts and pants and jackets had blown up along with his boat.

five

Dave Jenkins was twenty-two, and he was a guide down in the Keys, an expert at fly-rod fishing for tarpon, at stalking the wily permit, at outsmarting bonefish. I had heard he was beginning to pick up a reputation after surviving the early attempts of the locals to run him off. They play rough down there. He had come up as soon as he heard. And Bud Jenkins, the twenty-year-old, had come down from Duke University. He was there on full scholarship.

Hack and Gloria lived in a two-bedroom frame bungalow on a county road a long way west of the city. They had an acre of flatland, two big banyan trees near the house, a pond with Chinese white geese, and an electrified fence around the pond area to keep the predators away from the geese. There were almost a dozen vehicles parked in the drive and in the yard, several of them the big glossy pickups that charterboat captains favor, with tricky paint jobs and all the extras. A gabble of small children was racing about in the mud. Miss Agnes, my ancient blue Rolls pickup, looked odd parked with the modern machines, like an old lady in a bonnet at a rock concert.

The small house was packed with people. I could see them through the windows, moving around. The intense competition of the fishing folk was dropped whenever tragedy struck.

There was a shallow front porch with a slanted roof, an obvious afterthought. Two steps led up to the porch level. As we approached the steps, the screen door burst open and Rowland Service, the T-man, our recent visitor, came out at a dead run, with big Dave Jenkins so close behind him it took me a half second to realize, as I was stepping back out of the way, that Dave was running him out, with one hand on the slack of the seat of the pants, the other on the nape of the neck. Service's eyes and mouth were wide open. Dave gave him a final giant push and stopped at the edge of the steps. Service landed running, but leaning too far forward for balance. He made a good effort, though, and galloped about thirty feet from the steps before diving headlong into the wet grass.

Warner Housell, the staff person, came sidling out, carrying both dispatch cases and trying to look inconspicuous. An ingratiating smile came and went, over and over, very swiftly. Dave made a feint at him and stamped his feet. Housell made a bleating sound and sprang off the porch and trotted out to where Service was getting up, dabbing at the mud stains on his knees.

"Hey, Trav," Dave Jenkins said. "Meyer."

Housell and Service got into their economy rental. Service was apparently talking angrily and Housell was shaking his head no. They drove off.

"What happened?" I asked.

"They came a couple minutes ago. The big one was trying to hush up the little one, but the little one, he asked my mom if maybe Daddy was blowed up on account of he was mixed up in some kind of drug action. He asked her a little bit mean and a little bit loud, and I got my hands on him before one of the other men tried to kill him. It broke her up some. Miserable little scut. Drugs! It took Daddy seven months to set aside enough for the engine work on the *HooBoy,* so he wouldn't have to borrow at no high rate. Drugs? Daddy was dead against it. Remember, Trav? He came on those three bales of pot floating out there near Sherman Key over a year ago, and he picked them up and brought them in and turned them over to the narcotics guys. He had no charter aboard. Who was to know? Mom said he hadn't even had a taste of booze since he got born again twenty years ago."

"Is there any chance of talking to Gloria?" Meyer asked.

"This wouldn't be too good of a time, not right now. She's in the bedroom with a couple of her women friends, and they're in there praying and crying and hugging."

"Does she blame me?" Meyer asked.

Bud came out of the house in time to hear Meyer's question. "I don't think she's thought of it that way. I suppose she could get around to it in time," he said. He was the small-boned son, the one who was most like his mother physically, with delicate features and steel-rimmed glasses.

"Just tell her, when you get a chance, that it appears as if somebody was trying to make it look like a terrorist act," Meyer said. "There would be no reason to go after me. And nobody has ever heard of the organization that claimed credit. It was a cover for something. We think that if they were in close enough touch to make the phone call so soon after the explosion, they must have known I wasn't aboard. They were after somebody else. After one or both of the Lawrences, or after Hack."

Both boys shook their head, and Dave said, "Nobody would up and kill my daddy. Maybe by accident if it come to a fight, something like that. He was sometimes mean. But not planned ahead. Not that way. Mom said he really liked that couple, liked showing them places along the Waterway, liked putting them into fish. But he kept saying what a terrible boat you had, Meyer, and how much work it needed."

Bud said, "If they ever find out, I think they'll discover that somebody came over from Texas, following that couple, and killed them, and it didn't matter to them who else they killed in the process. Maybe it was somebody who didn't like the idea of your niece marrying that man. Or maybe it was something to do with the oil business, something she knew that somebody wanted covered up for good. If you get any clue at all, me and Dave and Andy would be most grateful to know who did it. Dave and Andy and me wouldn't like it to be one of those things where it takes three years to come to trial, and finally they call it second-degree, and then there's a bunch of appeals and the guy gets out a couple of years later. We'd surely like the chance to save him the fuss of waiting around all that time for his trial."

I looked at their eyes. Hack's eyes looking out at me. The same amber brown with golden glints, one pair behind lenses, one pair squeezed by the wrinkled squint of a few thousand hours searching the sun riffles for fish sign. A fierce independence.

"What we find out," I said, "you'll get to know."

There was a look of satisfaction diluting the intensity, and Bud said, "We'll tell Mom it doesn't look like it was anybody after you, Meyer."

On the way back to Bahia Mar, Meyer said, "I never really got to know Norma. One summer I stayed out there in Santa Barbara with my sister, Glenna, for a couple of weeks, helping each other remember things, good and bad. I think Norma must have been about fourteen. She was in a school for exceptionally gifted children, and that summer she was going on some sort of series of field trips with a batch of kids. Overnights, with sleeping bags. She had a rock hammer and a closet full of labeled samples. Her eyes danced and shone with the pure excitement of learning things. Her world was four and a half billion years old, and she had a vocabulary newly full of strike-slip faults, cactoliths, andesite, and monzonite, and she made tilting slipping shapes with her hands to show us how the mountains came about. Strange the way how a bright young brain, exposed to a certain kind of knowledge at just the right time, bends in the direction of that knowledge, sops it up, relishes it. Glenna concealed her dismay at having her only child aimed toward a life of bounding from crag to crag with a lot of rough people, carrying a rock hammer, a sample bag, and a chemistry set. I thought I would get a chance to know her better, after Toronto. Did you see much of them?"

"Not much. They came aboard a few times. She was picking up a good tan. He had a tendency to burn. The obvious thing about them was they were in love. There was between them a . . . I don't know the word for it. . . ."

"An erotic tension?"

"Right. Tangible. You could almost see it. Like smoke."

"I didn't realize she would ever get to be so handsome," Meyer said. "She was in fact a very homely young girl, all knees, elbows, and teeth. Glenna thought it would be useful for her to have a profession, and she told me Norma would probably end up in the world of academe, taking students on geology field trips. I'm talking around and around and around what I'm trying to say."

"Take your time." We were at a light. I looked over at him. He was scowling.

"Travis, suppose a drunk came across the center line and killed the two of them while I was in Toronto. It would be the same degree of loss. The obligation would be the same. To go to Houston and . . . tidy up. So, in that process, which I want to accomplish by myself, I may or may not come upon anything which might be related to what happened. If I do come upon anything, I'm not sure I'll take the right steps. Do you understand?"

"Of course."

"You'd come help out if I come upon anything like that?"

"Gee, I don't really know. I have these tennis matches with the ambassador's daughter, and I've been thinking of getting my teeth capped. You know how it is."

"I'll pay all expenses."

"For Christ's sweet *sake,* Meyer!"

"I'm sorry. It's just that I'm not at home in the world the way I was. The same as it would be, I suppose, for a person who had been in a coma for a year."

"You holler, I'll come running."

When the big swells flattened in a couple of days, they were able to anchor a work barge out beyond the sea buoy, and divers went down and located what was left of the *John Maynard Keynes*.

It wasn't much. The heavy metal parts of the old cruiser were scattered over a half acre of sloping sand, mud, and weed, with a lot of the stuff already covered or partly covered by sand drift. All the lighter stuff was gone—wood, paper, flesh, plastic, and bone—pulled up and down the coast, in and out of the pass, by tides and currents. From the amount of damage done to the metal remains—engines, anchors and chain, refrigerator, galley stove, wheels and rudder, hatch frames, and transom rail—the borrowed expert estimated that the amount of explosive used was from four to six times the amount necessary to kill three people aboard and sink the vessel. He called it "interesting overkill." Because of the submersion in seawater, his tests for the kind of explosive used were inconclusive. He found nothing which could have been any part of a detonating device.

All the Bahia Mar boats that could make it, and were interested enough to make it, went out in a twilight procession. Meyer and I dropped our separate wreath for Norma and Evan on an outgoing tide. The minister brayed words of destiny and consolation over the bull horn. We bowed heads for the final prayer and headed back, in convoy, with the running lights winking on in the gathering darkness, moving aside to let the *Royal Viking Sea* come easing out, a giant hotel, golden lights aglow, full of holiday people on their way to the islands and the tour buses.

After I was properly secure again at Slip F-18, with the phone and electric plugged back in, we went out and ate and came back to the *Flush* and went topside into the warm bright night, leaned back in the deck chairs up on the sun deck to look at stars too bright to be totally obscured by the city glare and the city smog. But we could smell the smog underneath the scents of the sea, a sad acid, mingling burned wine and spoiled mouse.

"I keep thinking I'll look something up and suddenly realize that I can't," Meyer said. "I don't even have a picture of her. There was a wedding picture, a Polaroid print she had duplicated."

"I think they can make a print from a print. In fact, excuse me for stupidity. That's what they would have to do. So somebody else will have a print and you can get another made."

"Somebody in Houston," he said. "Very probably. You know, all the pictures I had of the *Keynes* were on the *Keynes*."

"I'll look in the drawer where I throw pictures. There's probably one there, if you want it."

"I can't get used to being a guest. I want to have a boat and live on it just where I've been living all these years."

"We can go shopping, if you want."

"Not yet. That is, if I'm not getting on your nerves."

"So far you're only a minor irritation."

"*Somebody* around here must have taken pictures of Norma and Evan."

"Sure. But who? They'd be in tourist shots, mostly by accident. Of course there was a very fuzzy picture taken by the woman from Venice, the one that was reproduced in the paper two days after the . . . the accident."

"Maybe if we call it the murder, it will be more accurate."

I went below and looked for the old newspaper, but it had been tossed out.

So on Saturday morning, I called a man I knew in the city room of the paper, Abe Palinka, and asked about the photograph. Abe checked and called me back.

"What it was, it was one of those little tiny negatives from one of those little Kodak cameras that take the cartridge. It was on Kodacolor, and maybe you know you get a pretty dim-looking black-and-white off of that, worse in repro in the paper, but Clancy thought it was good enough to use because it was like, he said, dramatic: the scene before it went boom. What we did, we got a rush job on development, made a set of prints, picked the one we wanted, made a black-and-white, and sent the rest back to the lady—got a pencil?—Mrs. Simmons Davis of eight four eight Sunrise Road, Venice, three three five nine five. How come you haven't given me any kind of a hot lead in a hell of a while, McGee?"

"Nothing has been going on."

"I bet. Okay, if that's what you want me to believe."

"Thanks, Abe."

I dialed information for that area and got the Davis number. After the fourth ring a low, warm, husky, slightly-out-of-breath voice said, "Hello?"

"Mrs. Davis?"

"This is Brandy Davis."

"I'm calling from Fort Lauderdale. My name is McGee. Travis McGee."

"Mr. McGee, when I hear the name of your city, why, my stomach just sort of rolls right over. It's been five days now, but the whole thing is just as vivid in my mind as if it happened five minutes ago. Excuse me, I'm a little out of breath. I was just locking the door when I heard the phone, and I ran back."

"I don't want to hold you up."

"I was just going to the drugstore is all."

"What I'm calling about, a dear friend of mine owned that little cruiser."

"I heard he was out of town when it happened."

"That's right. And the pictures he had of his boat and of his niece all were blown up with the boat. We saw the one you took they used in the paper. . . ."

"That was a terrible job they did! My goodness. They paid me twenty-five dollars for the right to use it. I wish they hadn't said who took it, even. I take much better pictures than *that!*"

"I would think so."

"What I did, you see, I took two. It was an uggo little old boat and so I wouldn't have taken any at all except that Sim and I, we collect weird boat names, and you need a picture to prove it. I guess our, or at least my, favorite this cruise was a Miami motor sailer we saw in Nassau called *Estoy Perdido*. Meaning, I Am Lost. Well, I took two because it looked to me, looking through the little finder, that a wave slopped up and maybe hid part of the name on the transom just as I clicked it. But it turned out they both came out with good shots of that fancy gold lettering. You mean that poor man would like a picture of his boat and his niece?"

"He would indeed."

"I got them back in the mail day before yesterday, and I took them right down to the camera shop and ordered an eight-by-ten of the best one, the one that was nearest when I took it. That usually takes forever, but I do have the small prints the newspaper made up, or had made up. Maybe you think it's a little creepy, me ordering the enlargement, but nothing like that ever happened to me before, never in my life. I have no need for these two prints, so I'd just as soon put them in the mail to you when I go to the drugstore, okay?"

"You're very kind." I waited while she got a pencil, then gave her the address.

"Aboard the *Busted Flush?*" she said. "Maybe I should come over and take a picture of *that!* What is it?"

"Kind of an old barge-type houseboat. Fifty-two foot, two diesels. It'll go six knots if the wind isn't against it."

"It sounds quaint. The name is really odd. Does it mean . . . some kind of broken toilet?"

"No. A poker hand. That's when—"

"I know poker. I know about a flush and a straight flush. And I know how, like in stud, a hand can get busted."

"I had a black card face down and four hearts showing."

"You mean you won a whole houseboat on—"

"No, I won a pretty fair pot on that bluff and kind of by accident let the hole card show after I'd pulled the pot in and everybody else had folded. From then on they kept staying in, to keep me honest. And I had a lot of good hands."

Her voice dipped a half octave. "You sound really kind of adventurous, Mr. Travis McGee. Maybe you could sort of whip over here and pick up the prints in person? I'm getting a little stir crazy with Sim away at one of those weird conferences about setting up trusts in Liechtenstein."

"It certainly sounds like an attractive idea, Mrs. Davis, and I would really take you up on it like a shot, but on Monday I'm being fitted for a new prosthesis."

"Uh. Well, maybe some other time," she said briskly.

"The other one never hurts at all," I said.

"How nice for you. I'll put these in the mail right away. Nice to talk to you. Goodbye, Mr. McGee."

Meyer flew to Houston on Sunday and phoned me at four o'clock on Monday afternoon, the twelfth. His voice sounded tired.

"A progress report. Or a no-progress report. The traffic in this city is monstrous. They are maniacal. I've checked out of the hotel and moved into Norma's apartment. Want to write this down?" After he gave me the address and phone number, he said, "It's quite nice. It's a rental, in what they call a garden complex, nothing over two stories, jammed in close but angled very cleverly to give the illusion of privacy. All her stuff is here, so I thought it would be easier to work if her lawyer set it up for me to move in. She left a will, leaving everything to me. It's dated soon after Glenna died. She was probably going to change it again in favor of Evan. They were married on a Saturday, the seventeenth of April. He may have moved in here with her before then. Probably did. I've started going through her papers. Her lawyer is pleasant enough. It's a small firm. He handled her tax matters and apparently advised her on investments. Windham, his name is. Roger Windham. Did I say he seems pleasant? I'm probably repeating myself. I find I seem to get tired easily. There's a lot to do.

Windham thinks she had some things in a storage warehouse somewhere. And a lockbox at the bank where she did her checking. He'll have to arrange with the tax people about opening the safety deposit box with them present."

"Want me over there yet?"

"Not yet. I'll get the chores done, and if anything comes to light that might be a hint as to anybody wanting to kill her, then, if it wouldn't be too much trouble . . ."

"Come off it! That Mrs. Davis is mailing me one print each of the two pictures she took. She took them because of the name. They collect boat names."

"It still seems like a bad dream. There's a picture of her parents standing with me somewhere in front of a lot of trees. It's in a silver frame on her dressing table. I haven't any memory of its ever being taken. I usually remember things like that."

"Meyer. Get some sleep tonight."

"Did you tell them about my mail?"

"I forged your name on the change of address card. It's coming here. Today you got a fat publication from the Federation of Concerned Economists, a bill from American Express, a catalogue from the Vermont Country Store, and a bank statement. Also, I talked to Irv. There's a thirty-one-foot Rawson made in Panama City, Florida, moored over at B-Eighty. Apple-pie shape. They went out of business a few years ago because they made them too good. GE diesels, air, recording fathometer. The old couple that lived aboard, he went into the hospital in March, and then into a nursing home, and he died last week, and she is looking to sell privately before she puts it in the hands of a broker. She wants thirty days to move out and go back to South Dakota. She's talking fifty-eight five. Walter says you'll get thirty-nine or forty out of the insurance."

"I don't want to think about it yet."

"It's a good price and a roomy hull."

"When I do get another boat, I'll have to think of a name. I couldn't call it the same thing."

"Well . . . stay in touch."

So I walked over to B-80 and met the old lady from South Dakota. She showed me the boat. She was proud of it. She said she knew one of them would have to die, sooner or later, and they had each hoped it would be themself instead of the other one. "But George won, I guess," she said. "Tell your friend how nice it is, how nice we kept it."

six

When I got the mail on Wednesday, there was a buff envelope with Brandy Davis and her address embossed on the flap. It was heavy stock, with a bright yellow tissue lining, and the two prints were inside, with no note or comment.

I glanced at the two prints just long enough to see the transom and the name and the stubby vessel tilting under a lead-colored sky, white crests rolling on a dishwater sea.

When I was back aboard the *Flush* I looked at them more carefully in bright sunlight. The first print showed the *Keynes* at fifty or sixty feet, going away, and the second at about a hundred feet. Assuming an average six knots on each vessel, they were diverging at about fifteen miles an hour, or a little better than twenty feet per second. So about ten seconds after the second picture was taken, the three people were blown to bits: the tall slender woman with the brand-new tan and the vivid orange string bikini, standing at the starboard side near the rail, one hand braced against the bulkhead, waving and smiling, teeth white, black hair snapping in the wind; the burly figure of Hacksaw Jenkins at the sheltered wheel, in silhouette against the sea beyond the windshield, Greek captain's hat on the back of his head; and Evan Lawrence, bent over so far in the cockpit, working on a line, that in the first picture only his back and denimed rump showed, then caught in the second picture beginning to straighten up, beginning to turn.

I accepted it as Evan Lawrence, the man with whom I had broken bread, drunk wine, told the tales. And suddenly it was not Evan Lawrence. In the act of starting to straighten up, starting to turn, it became a different person, younger, not as broad, with skin that took a better tan, hair longer, tangled, sun-streaked. Once it became someone else, I could not by any exercise of imagination or will turn it back into Evan Lawrence. But it did turn into somebody I knew from somewhere. I looked at the line of the brow, and the slant of the jaw as seen from the back, from off to the left side. The print was sharp. There was a glint of something on the left wrist, a watch or a bracelet. I found the magnifying glass in the drawer, but I couldn't make it out. I looked at the hand, then, and I could make out something very specific. The pinky and the ring finger of that left hand were stubs little better than a half finger long.

And then I knew who it was. Along Charterboat Row he was known universally as Pogo, God only knows why. Maybe because he was as cheerful as that immortal possum. Meyer had once pointed him out to me as an example of the perfectly happy fellow. He had a functioning IQ, Meyer guessed, of seventy-five. He loved the sea. He grew terribly excited when fish were being caught. His body seemed to thrive on cola and junk food. He could sew bait, rig lines, net little fish, gaff big fish, wash down the boat, clean up the mess, serve the Coke and beer, swarm up to the tuna tower to search the sea for fish sign. He was cheerful, smiling, quick in his motions, polite to everyone. His face had a fat bland look at odds with his tough body. He had a little thin high voice. He filled in when any one of the captains needed a hand for a day or a week. They paid him off in cash. He had some learning defect which kept him from ever being able to read and write.

I walked down to Charterboat Row and found the *Key Kitty* with her cockpit hatches open, Captain Ned Rhine staring gloomily down at an electrician working in there.

Ned gave me a beer and we sat on the side of the dock and talked about the memorial service with the wreaths, and how Gloria was bearing up, and how his wife said Gloria would probably get married again someday. Nobody would ever guess she had those three hulking sons.

"Seen Pogo around?" I asked casually.

"Come to think of it, no. Maybe not for a week. Got something for him to do?"

"If he's available. Where does he stay anyway?"

"Here and there. Here and there. After Roy got hisself all busted up that time last year when the kid ran into his truck, Pogo slept aboard the *Honeydoo* and worked mate while Stub was taking the contracts Roy had set up. For a while there I think he bunked in the supply room at Castle Marine until it got sold. Pogo is okay. He does a better job of work than some brighter people around here I could name. And he isn't ever grouchy."

I changed the subject, and a little later I unchained my bicycle and rode over to Pier 66 and walked out to the gas dock. I don't buy fuel there, so I don't know the attendants. There were two on duty, a narrow-faced redheaded man in the office and a young Cuban with a shaved head filling the tanks of a Prowler from Georgia. The redhead had been on duty the morning of the fifth.

They remembered gassing the *John Maynard Keynes* only because it had blown up soon afterward, and the police had questioned them after somebody reported having seen the *Keynes* at their gas dock at about ten that morning.

They had noticed the woman in the string bikini but not much else. There were three people on the boat. Or maybe four. It had been a busy morning. The woman had paid cash. She had gone below to get her purse. Ninety-five gallons of regular. A hundred and twenty-nine dollars and twenty cents. She'd asked for a receipt.

"Sure, I've seen Hack Jenkins around," the redhead said. "I remember wondering what he was doing with that boat instead of his own."

Neither of them knew anybody called Pogo who worked around the docks over at Bahia Mar. As all the charterboat captains would customarily buy fuel at Bahia Mar, that wasn't unexpected. Every large marina seems to acquire its own village of regulars.

As I biked on back to Bahia Mar, I kept tugging at the minor improbabilities, hoping something would come loose. Norma Lawrence had not impressed me as the kind of take-charge lady who would jump up and pay the bills. It would be more likely she would get the money from her purse and give it to Evan to pay the bill with. And why had Evan stayed below when they went out past the sea buoy into the chop building up from the offshore storm? That was when the customers were *always* on deck, holding on, peering into the wind like dogs leaning out of car windows.

I carried the bike aboard and locked it to the ring I had bolted to the aft bulkhead, under the overhang, unlocked the *Flush*, and went into the lounge, into the air-conditioned coolness that chilled the sweat the ten-speed generated.

So, what if Evan Lawrence wasn't aboard for the big bang?

It was an idea that offended my emotional set. A very likable guy with a good grin, a man of warmth, of funny stories, a newly wedded man in love with his wife. And if he hadn't been aboard, and hadn't made known the fact of his survival, then it was a possibility he had engineered the explosion and made the anonymous call to deflect any possible suspicion.

So if he was that sort of man, he would have left a special scent along his back trail. I did not know enough about him, and neither did Meyer. Dinner aboard is not an excuse for an inquisition. He had seemed open about himself, but I could recall no talk of family. Funny stories of things which had happened to him here and there along the way. How they had met. How he had pursued her. Strange jobs he had held. Nothing more than that. They were in love. And there was that physical attraction so strong it was tangible, a musk in the air.

In the evening I went over to Charterboat Row during the interval after the customers have had their pictures taken with their fish, that time when the boats are cleaned up, the gear put back in shape, the salt hosed off. I had some heavy work I wanted done, and I was looking for Pogo.

Finally Dan List, skipper of the *Nancy Mae III,* told me I might try the construction shack over behind that big sign I had seen which said SHOREVIEW TOWERS, 200 Elegant Condominium Apartments, $165,000–$325,000, Ready For Occupancy Soon. Model ready for viewing. Phone so-and-so for appointment. But the construction cranes had stopped when the structure was about four stories high. They stood silent against the sky, like huge dead bugs. Somebody had run out of something essential: money or time or life. One of those things.

There was an old man in a blue uniform living in the construction shack. In the fading daylight I could see the cot in there, neatly made up. The old man had a big belly, and a badge, and a revolver in a black holster.

"You see that half-wit Pogo, friend, you tell him the only reason he should come back here is to get his stuff. It's in a suitcase and a cardboard box. What clothes he owns and those filthy dirty picture books. I'm only filling in until they can get somebody for next to nothing, like they paid Pogo. I'm a licensed security guard, and my old lady is nervous alone at night in the apartment while I'm here in this stinking heat to keep vagrants and Haitians and trash from sneaking into that there building and messing up. You tell him he doesn't show up soon, I'm putting his stuff out in the weather. There's no agreement we got to store it for him. You tell him that."

"Is there anything of value?"

"There's a gray metal lockbox. It's locked and there's no key I could find around here. And the little television set I'm using, to keep from going nuts. The picture starts rolling and there's no way to stop it. You just have to wait until it stops. Feels like it would pull your eyes out on sticks."

He kept slapping the black leather holster. It was shiny from being slapped ten thousand times. It was a habit that could get him killed. I said if I saw Pogo, I'd tell him.

Even when a missing person is reported, nothing much happens. Local police forces have higher priorities. Nobody would report Pogo, and I saw no reason why I should. There would be a lot of interviews, a lot of forms to fill out. Transients flow back and forth across the country, and up and down the coasts. They are of little moment. They become the unidentified bones in abandoned orchards. Dumb, dreary, runaway girls are hustled into the dark woods, and their dental-work pictures go into the files. As the years do their work, shallow graves become deep graves, and very few of the thousands upon thousands are ever discovered. Burial without the box, without the marker, hasty dirt packed down onto the ghastliness of the ultimate grin. Old Fatso would eventually pry open the box, take anything of value, and destroy the rest. The trash truck would pick up the suitcase and the cardboard box, sodden with rainwater. And years down the road somebody would say, "Hey, remember that Pogo that used to work around here? Kind of a dimwit but a good worker?"

And somebody else would say, "Guess that was before my time."

Nobody remembers very long any more. Like the half owner of the *Nancy Mae III,* which Dan List skippers. Three seasons ago, as a defensive lineman for the Dolphins, he made thirteen sacks in the regular season before they smashed his knee. And now I can't remember his name. Six-five, about two fifty-five, quick as a weasel. And I can't remember any part of his name.

Intimations of mortality often make me lonesome. I went back to the *Flush* and stretched out and called Annie Renzetti on the new private line that rings in her office and in her beach bungalow over there in Naples. Four rings and hang up. If she was alone she could catch it on four rings. If not alone, she could call me back. If she wasn't in, nobody else would answer that line. It was known to be private.

I tried again at nine fifteen, and she answered from the bungalow. "How's with you, Annie?" I asked her.

"This day has just about flattened me, love. They start arriving tomorrow before lunch."

"Who?"

"My convention, dummy. Did you forget? Fifty-three specialists and their wives, or husbands, or special close friends. Proctologists."

"I forgot it was this week."

"By Monday afternoon when they all leave, my smile is going to feel as if it was nailed to my face. Tomorrow, early, some computerized little snit from company headquarters will be here to double-check my arrangements. This group doesn't strike bargains. They want it nice. They'll get it nice. Management wants them back here every year. What I have paid out for beef you wouldn't believe. Lobsters and clams are coming by air express. Orchids for the ladies. A really good trio in the lounge. And by the time they arrive I will have personally inspected every room, every suite, every bath towel, tested every light bulb. The thing I resent, Trav, is their thinking they have to send somebody down to backstop me. I've proved I'm a damn good manager here. I get the printouts from the whole chain every month. I'm always in the top ten on the ratio of gross profit to gross sales, percentage occupancy, personnel turnover. They hired me to manage so they should let me manage, right?"

"Right!"

"My, my, my, how I do go on. Why should I take it out on you?"

"I'm your friend. Remember?"

"But if you were thinking of driving over about now . . ."

"Forget it?"

"Yes. Look me up after the convention. I fought it, you know. I don't think we should have conventions here, even in the slack season, even at top rates. I've had to turn away reservations good old customers wanted to make, just to accommodate these . . . these . . ."

"Careful."

"Are you okay, love? You sound kind of down."

"Lonesome, sort of. Meyer phoned from Houston. He got permission to stay in her apartment while he takes care of the details. He sounded depressed, but he seems to be coping. But I know something he doesn't know, and I don't know whether I should tell him. I'm going over there soon. Maybe tomorrow."

"Whether you should tell him what?"

"I won't go into how I found out, but if only three people were blown to bits on Meyer's boat, one was his niece, one was Hacksaw Jenkins, and one was a local retard, an itinerant worker everybody called Pogo, actual name unknown."

"What do you mean, if only three?"

"The photo taken showed three. Maybe Evan Lawrence was below. But I have the queasy feeling he was on shore. I have the feeling that maybe he was where he could watch the *Keynes* and push a button on a transmitter. I have that feeling in spite of believing he was not the kind of person to do something like that. I really liked him. He had a good face, good laugh lines. You know?"

"I know what you mean. How would he arrange to stay ashore?"

"I don't know. Back out at the last minute. Plead an upset stomach. And Hack would have picked up Pogo to help with the fishing because he'd be busy at the wheel out there in that chop. The Lawrences had been living aboard for almost two weeks. Time enough for him to poke around in Meyer's files and pick up enough information so he could make a convincing phone call about the Chilean connection."

"But what are you going to do?"

"Annie, I can dig into his life and find out if he was what I believed him to be. If so, he blew up too. If the back trail is rancid, he didn't die, and we have a new kind of ball game."

"In either case, you'll have to start in Houston, and you'll have to tell Meyer what you are thinking, won't you? So no need to worry. Tell him the whole thing."

"He's had so much—"

"Look. Trust him to be able to accept that immortal truth, dear, that life is unfair. And unpleasantly abrupt at times."

"It would be a lot easier to talk this all over if you had your head on my shoulder, and my left arm around you, and—"

"Hush. Please hush, McGee. I'd be of no use to you at all."

"Let me be the judge of that."

"No way."

"And so I am separated from my own true love by fifty-three proctologists?"

"That's one way to put it. Say hi to Meyer for me. Extend my love and affection and sympathy and so on. And phone me from Houston or wherever you may be—but not before Monday night next, which will be . . . the nineteenth. Look, if things turn ugly, don't take any dumb chances, okay?"

"No dumb chances."

"I had sort of an idea. There's a place on the waterway where they are condominiumizing boat slips: in other words, selling the slip itself with the dock, pilings, and overhead roof, like for forty or fifty thousand for a slip big enough for the *Busted Flush*. I haven't worked out the arithmetic yet, but I suspect that I could talk management into letting me invest in that as an adjunct facility to the Eden Beach. Then we could work out a lease arrangement, a sort of contract with you, to have a kind of permanent party-boat setup whereby the guests at the hotel here could sign up ahead and there could be sightseeing cruises, or cocktail cruises, or maybe even dinner cruises if we could work out the service details. What I mean to say, it could be a very nice little living for you, dear. It wouldn't be a killing but it would be steady, and you would practically be your own boss. And we would . . . see each other oftener."

"And I wouldn't be charging around taking dumb chances?"

"Something like that."

"On the dinner cruises, could I wear one of those great huge tall white chef's hats?"

"Don't be such a bastard, McGee."

"Look into your heart of hearts and see if you can really see me doing that."

"Hmm. . . . Oh, shucks. No."

"Thanks anyway for the concern."

"You're welcome indeed. Good night, McGee. I love you."

seven

On Thursday morning as I was washing up after breakfast, Dave Jenkins came by to see me. Old-looking for twenty-two. Burned to a brick bronze by the summer sun down in the Keys. Muscles rolling under the parched hair on his big arms. Sloping powerful shoulders, just as Hack had.

You have to wait the locals out. Nothing is done without a reason, and sooner or later they either get around to it or change their minds and leave. The quickest way to change their minds is to press them to find out what they want.

He looked around the lounge and said, "Changed it some."

"You haven't been aboard in a while."

"I guess I was about fourteen. You and Dad arm-rassled to a draw, maybe forty minutes, with the sweat popping out and one or the other of you groaning from time to time, your faces like beets. He was a little bit stronger, and you had a little bit better leverage, having a longer arm."

"I remember."

"Then it was Meyer stepped in and called it a draw, and you both fell off the chairs and lay on the floor there, panting like dogs in the summertime."

"I remember it well. Want a beer?"

"I won't ever forget it, not ever. I'd never seen anybody ever rassle my dad to a draw, arm rassling or any other kind. Little early for me for a beer, I guess."

"Carta Blanca?"

"Well, not all that early."

He drifted out to the galley with me, and I took two cold ones out of the locker and uncapped them. We went back into the lounge, and he dropped into a chair and took long swallows, wiped his mouth on the back of his brown hand. "Real good. Thanks. You and my dad were friends."

"Pretty good friends."

"I come onto something, I don't know how I should handle it, and there's nobody I can rightly ask. I don't want to bring Bud in on it. He's back up at Duke in that summer program. Andy's too young. And I can't ask Mom."

"What's it all about?"

There was a long final hesitation, and then he shrugged and sighed. "Like this. I've been building up a fair trade down there below Marathon, but it's nothing like Dad had here. I've been over his list for the season coming up, and he's booked nearly solid. I know his kind of fishing. I can do it, but not as good as he did. He could smell fish. The *HooBoy* would be mine to use or sell, whatever. I went prowling around among the charterboat guys, trying to find out if I could make some kind of a deal for his boat plus the bookings. Everybody acted just a little bit funny. You know? There was something going on I couldn't figure out.

"So I went over to the boatyard, to Dalton and Forbes, where the engine work is being done. And they acted funny over there too. It'll be ready in one more week. I climbed up the ladder and went aboard her. I looked at the work sheets. The work is all paid for. Thirty-eight thousand dollars' worth, and he paid in cash."

"To rebuild a couple of old diesels?"

"Rebuild, hell. A new pair of high-speed jobs, with every kind of booster you can think of. They reinforced and cross-braced the whole front end of the hull. High-speed props. New controls. Outside it isn't changed. It was always just a little bit underpowered. He could have gone bumbling around in it, looking the same as always, but when anybody jammed those throttles forward that thing would take off like a big-assed rabbit."

"Isn't that a displacement hull?"

"No. It's kind of a modified deep vee, and they've put a new kind of step thing on the hull that will pop it right up into planning position. I remember when it was new, if we were heading downwind and he gave it full throttle on both engines, and we had a lot of room ahead of us, it would get up onto the plane and scoot. But it took too much gas to get it there. Jerry Forbes told me they think it will do a little better than forty knots once they get the step adjusted just right. I don't even like to think about it. He told Mom he had to get five thousand together to get the engines rebuilt. I've been through his papers, and there's nothing there to show where any thirty-eight thousand came from or where it went to. What do you think was going on, Trav?"

"Did they enlarge fuel capacity?"

"Bigger tanks, and they set them so the center of balance is a little more forward of where it used to be. When he got that boat, I was six and Bud was four and Andy wasn't born yet. We were so proud of the *HooBoy*. It was so pretty!"

"Your father was a good man, Dave. He had lots of friends. He worked hard. You could trust him."

"So where did a good man get thirty-eight thousand cash money?"

"Have you looked around at the charterboat people along this coast and in the Keys lately? There's a lot of big new vans and pickups. Lots of gold jewelry. New television with big big screens. Brand new washer-dryers. And little trips over to Freeport for shopping and gambling, and maybe a visit to the branch of the Bank of Nova Scotia."

"Certainly I've looked around. And I've thought about it. Fellow I knew down in Marathon had him a fast little runabout, like a California boat. Cigarette hull and power assists so he could do up to eighty-five, he claimed. He was clearing ten thousand a week running coke from a mother ship. One time they waited for him and tried to corner him. They had three boats not as fast as his. But he tried to get away around the end of a reef, and he cut it a little bit short and turned himself and his pretty boat into a ball of flame rolling for fifty yards along the night water. Friend of mine saw it happen. We're not talking about people like that coke dealer. We're talking about my dad, Dennis Hackney Jenkins, Hack. We're talking about lying, and cash money, and why'd he have them turning the *HooBoy* into a bomb."

"Look. I don't want to be in the position of making excuses. He'd just turned fifty. Men do funny things when they come up against a birthday with a zero on the end of it. They wonder if their life is pointless. They wonder what other kinds of lives they could have led. Don't judge him. A man can be tempted. Few ever get caught, and the ones that do get out on bail, and cases don't come to trial for years. The U.S. Attorney's office in Miami has a nine-year backlog of dope cases."

He stood up abruptly. "Thanks for the beer. He wasn't like that. You know it and I know it. And I'm going to find out what the hell was going on." And out he went. Blind loyalty. It made me wish my life had been different and I'd had some sons. Sure, McGee. What you want are the full-grown variety, big and sturdy and loyal and true. But you never wanted what came in between: diapers and shots, PTA and homework, yard mowing, retirement programs, Christmas lists, mortgage interest, car payments, dental bills, and college tuition. You made your choices, fellow, and you live with the results. And if in the end there is nobody to give a single particular damn when you die, that too is part of the bargain you made with life. And maybe that was what Annie was trying to tell me a couple of weeks ago.

If Dave Jenkins was as shrewd as I judged him to be, he would take delivery on the *HooBoy,* put it back on Charterboat Row, and start filling Hack's commitments to his clients. Certainly Hack wasn't working in a vacuum. Sooner or later some information would turn up. Somebody would come around. Charter fishing was sick. Money was tight and getting tighter. A lot of them were out there after the square grouper, as the bales of marijuana were called. Hack, or whoever would run the transformed *HooBoy,* could make $10,000 a trip, out and back to the mother ship, some rust-bucket freighter chugging around out there, sixty miles offshore.

I decided to look him up when I came back from Houston, find out if anything at all had happened. But I wouldn't look him up to do any arm-rassling. He looked as strong as his father, and his arms were longer. After a match with him, I would have to brush my teeth with my left hand for a week.

On Friday the sixteenth, Eastern Airlines took me from Miami to Houston by way of Atlanta. I went first class, I told myself, for the sake of the leg room. At six-four I am not the right size for tourist. But I probably went first because I like first. If I did a lot of flying, I'd probably find a reasonably good way to wedge my knees into the tourist-size seats. But flying seldom, I tend to treat myself to the best. I had alerted Meyer, and he met me at the gate and led me with my underseat case out to the lot to his rental Datsun, which seemed even smaller than tourist class.

He said I had best not talk to him in the noontime traffic. I soon saw what he meant. We came whining down the Eastex Parkway at sixty-four miles an hour, because that was the average speed of the dense stampede in which we were enclosed. It is a fact of highway life that each heavily traveled road establishes its own cadence. The great pack of candy-colored compacts, pickups, vans, delivery trucks, taxicabs, and miscellaneous wheeled junk flowed in formation, inches apart, through the gleam, stink, grinding roar, and squinty glitter of a July noontime, through a golden sunshine muted to brass by smog.

What the traffic consultants seem unable to comprehend is that heavy traffic makes its own rules because nobody can nip in and pull anybody over to the side without setting up a shock wave that would scream tires and crumple fenders for a mile back down the road. California discovered this first. It is probably a more important discovery than est or redwood hot tubs.

In such traffic there are two kinds of maniacs. The first is the one who goes a legal 55 and becomes like a boulder in a swift stream. The stream has to part and go around, finding the spaces in the lanes on either side, getting impatient when they can't find the spaces, finally cutting out somebody else and making them so cross that a few miles down the road they actually nudge another car. Hence the plague of car wars. At times I have had a fleeting sympathy for the fellow in Dallas who ran such a station wagon off onto the median strip, hopped out, dragged the offending driver out of his vehicle, and flipped him into the fast traffic. Murder by impulse. Rage unconfined.

The second maniac is the one who tries to go nine miles faster than the flow instead of nine miles slower. This type is often bombed out of his mind on booze, cannabis, crazy candy, or marital disagreements.

Once you have the concept of the pack making the law, driving the urban interstates is simplified. You maintain just that distance from the vehicle ahead which will give you braking room yet will not invite a car from a neighbor lane to cut in. You pick the center lanes because some of the clowns leaving the big road on the right will start to slow down far too soon. You avoid the left lane when practical because when they have big trouble over there on the other side of the median strip, the jackass who comes bounding over across the strip usually totals somebody in the left lane. When you come up the access strip onto the big road, you make certain that you have reached the average speed of all the traffic before you edge into it. Keep looking way way ahead for trouble, and when you see it put on your flashing emergency lights immediately so that the clown behind you will realize you are soon going to have to start slowing down.

Meyer did well, hunched forward, hands gripping the wheel at ten o'clock and two o'clock. We traversed the interchange onto the loop interstate 610, heading west. The average speed moved up to a little above seventy. He took the first exit past the junction of Interstate 10, headed west again, turned south at a light, and after a couple of miles turned into the main entrance of Piney Village, a misnamed development of clusters of town houses and duplexes in stained wood with some stone facing, set at odd angles on curving asphalt to manufacture illusions of privacy. Berms added variety to flatness, and new trees struggled. The architect had been crazy about step roof pitches, a manifest insanity in the Houston climate. Meyer meandered left and right and left, pulled into a driveway barely longer than the orange Datsun, and parked with the front bumper inches from the closed overhead garage door, killed the motor, and exhaled audibly.

"Very nervous traffic," I said. "You did good."

"Thank you. Lately I seem to get along better by focusing on just one thing at a time, pushing everything else out of my mind. Driving a car, shaving, cooking eggs. The other day I was adding figures on a pocket calculator and I suddenly lost track of what I was doing." He frowned at me. "I was adrift all of a sudden, and I had to reinvent myself, find out who I was and where I was and what I was doing. Like waking from very deep sleep. Strange."

He got out and I followed as he went to the door of D-3 and unlocked it. In the hallway, he pushed a sequence of numbers on a small panel, and a voice came out of the grill and said, "Identify, please."

"Meyer here. Two eight two seven five."

"Thank you," the grill said, after a short pause.

"Security," Meyer explained. "All these places are hooked up to a central control. When we sign out, they'll be listening for sounds of break-in or fire or whatever."

It was a two-level town-house apartment, with two bedrooms and bath off a balcony, with kitchen, bath, and a studio-workroom under the bedroom portion. The two-story-high living room had a glass wall at one end, with sliding doors that opened onto a small garden surrounded on three sides by a seven-foot concrete wall, and a fireplace at the other end. The furniture was modern and looked comfortable without being bulky. The colors were mostly neutral, but with bright prints on the wall, bright jackets on the bookshelves. It had the look of being well-built, solid, efficient, and impersonal.

"Norma lived here alone before she got married, and Evan moved in with her. She was the first occupant after this unit was finished. She rented it on some complicated lease-purchase arrangement whereby she paid six hundred and twenty-five a month, and two hundred of that went into an escrow account against her decision to purchase for sixty-five thousand when her two-year lease was up. It will be up in October. These places are now going for ninety to a hundred, so I guess she made a good decision. There's a big shopping mall about a mile away, and it's close to a very direct route into the middle of the city."

He said it would be easier if I stayed in the place, and he assigned me the bedroom on the left. I unpacked in about seventy-five seconds and went down, and he said we could eat at the mall. He checked out over the security intercom and locked up.

We drove to the metallic acres of mall parking lot. Meyer said it was going to get up to a hundred and five again by midafternoon. It was the fourth day of the heat wave. A lot of old people were dying, he said. They didn't dare leave windows open because the feral children would climb in, terrorize them, and take anything hockable. Their windows were nailed shut. They sat in heat of a hundred and twenty with their bare feet in pans of water, fanning themselves, collapsing, dying. They couldn't afford the cost of air conditioning or, in many cases, the cost of running an electric fan. From where they died, from anywhere in the city, the giant office towers of the seven sisters of the oil industry were invisible.

We walked through the cool shadowy passageways of the mall, lined with the brightly lighted shops. The tiled pedestrian avenues led to Sears, to K-Mart, to J. C. Penney. There were fountains and benches and guide maps: "You are here." Thousands shuffled through the mall in coolness, children racing back and forth, dripping ice cream. It is contemporary carnival, an entertainment of looking at shoe stores, summer clearance sales, of being blasted by the music coming out of Radio Shack, of trying to remember the balance already committed on the credit card account. There was a public service display of security equipment devices, with uniformed officers answering questions. Uniformed guards stood in boredom in the jewelry stores. Young mothers with tired and ugly expressions whopped their young with a full-arm swing, eliciting bellows of heartbreak.

He led me to a narrow fast-food place with a German name, and we went to a table for two way in the back. He recommended the wurst, the kraut, and the dark draft. So be it.

Then I had the feeling he had run down. He had preplanned the airport pickup, the ride, getting me settled, taking me to the mall. But it ended there. He had no key for the rewind.

"How is it going?" I asked.

"Going?"

"Cleaning up her affairs."

"Well, there is a will. Everything comes to me. She didn't get around to changing it. She previously changed the beneficiary when my sister died."

"Is there much involved?"

"It—it seems to be complicated."

"Okay. So you don't want to talk about it. Okay."

"No, Travis. It's not that. I don't want to compromise what you might think by telling you in advance what I think."

"In advance of what?"

"I made an appointment for us with Roger Windham."

"Her lawyer?"

"At three o'clock in his office in the Houston Trust Building."

"Let's cover a couple of things first," I said. "Take a good close look at this." I handed him the Kodacolor print.

He looked at it and gave me a puzzled look. "So?"

"Take a closer look at the man's hand."

His eyebrows lifted in surprise. "Good Lord! I remember Pogo telling me how he lost those fingers. He was boating a mako, and a loop in the wire leader slipped around his fingers just as the shark shook his head for the last time. Nipped them right off. Now I can see that it really is Pogo. In the picture in the paper I thought—"

"So did I. Then I wondered if maybe Evan Lawrence had been below when that woman took the picture. I tried to check it out. I went to the gas dock over at Pier Sixty-six. I went from boat to boat along Charterboat Row. Here is my best guess. Evan Lawrence was handy. He caught on quickly. There was no need for the expense of a mate aboard when Hack took Evan and Norma out. In the rough chop out beyond the sea buoy, Hack would want to stay at the wheel. So when Evan couldn't make it, he hired Pogo. Norma was hooked on game fish. If Evan wasn't feeling too great I don't think she would have stayed ashore in some motel room just to hold his hand, even if it was a belated honeymoon. So with no proof at all, it is my belief that Evan didn't get blown to bits. He seemed like such a hell of a nice man, it's hard to take the next logical step."

"He arranged to blow up my boat."

"Exactly. And living aboard for a couple of weeks, he had a chance to go through your papers and come up with that Chilean connection to use as a red herring. Why did you jump on the idea so quick and easy, Meyer?"

"You'll know after you hear Windham."

I waited until it became obvious he wasn't going to say any more. So then I gave him the next chapter, about Hack Jenkins giving the boatyard, Dalton and Forbes, thirty-eight thousand in advance to turn the *HooBoy* into a fifty-mile-an-hour bomb, and it would be finished within a week.

"Young Dave came to me with the information. He was very upset. Couldn't see his daddy mixed up in drug running."

"Can you?" Meyer asked.

"I don't know. I don't know what pressure could have been brought to bear against him. Maybe he was tired of seeing his friends making it big. But the thing that bothers me there is that his friends make out pretty well using the same old slow fishing machines, just by knowing their way around the area."

"It doesn't sound like Hack. He was about the best in the whole marina," Meyer said. He shrugged. "On the other hand, these are the days when people are turning strange. Doing things they never thought they would do."

The food was better than I had any right to expect. Walking back through the mall to the exit nearest our part of the parking lot, we passed one shop which sold computers, printers, software, and games. It was packed with teenagers, the kind who wear wire rims and know what the new world is about. The clerks were indulgent, letting them program the computers. Two hundred yards away, near the six movie houses, a different kind of teenager shoved quarters into the space-war games, tensing over the triggers, releasing the eerie sounds of extraterrestrial combat. Any kid back in the computer store could have told the combatants that because there is no atmosphere in space, there is absolutely no sound at all. Perfect distribution: the future managers and the future managed ones. Twenty in the computer store, two hundred in the arcade.

The future managers have run on past us into the thickets of CP/M, M-Basic, Cobal, Fortran, Z-80, Apples, and Worms. Soon the bosses of the microcomputer revolution will sell us preprogrammed units for each household which will provide entertainment, print out news, purvey mail-order goods, pay bills, balance accounts, keep track of expenses, and compute taxes. But by then the future managers will be over on the far side of the thickets, dealing with bubble memories, machines that design machines, projects so esoteric our pedestrian minds cannot comprehend them. It will be the biggest revolution of all, bigger than the wheel, bigger than Franklin's kite, bigger than paper towels.

eight

Downtown Houston seemed an empty place on a Friday afternoon. Bulky skyscrapers faced with granite and marble stood in a kind of gloomy silence in the golden smog. There was light traffic, few pedestrians, few stores, a broad deserted public square. Meyer ducked down a ramp into an underground parking garage.

Once we left the garage, I realized why there were so few pedestrians out on the streets. The underground tunnels were cooler and busier. We missed an important sign and had to double back to an intersection before we finally found the elevator bank for the Houston Trust Building.

The law offices of Sessions, Harkavy and Windham were on the twenty-seventh floor. We waited ten minutes on plastic furniture looking at sections of newspaper before Roger Windham's secretary, a rangy graying redhead, led us back to a small conference room.

Roger Windham was waiting for us. He was tall, in his early thirties, with red-blond bangs, a ragged reddish mustache, pale blue eyes that looked red and irritated. He was in shirt sleeves with a conservative tie, perfectly knotted. I wondered how many ties you could find in downtown Houston when the temperature was over a hundred.

I saw Windham trying to put a label on me as we were introduced, and as we sat in three chairs at the end of the conference table. I manage to look out of place in an office. Too much deep-water tan, too much height, too many knuckles, too many fading scars of past tactical errors and strategic mistakes. Had I come to repair the wiring in the overhead ducts, he would have had not a glimmer of curiosity about me.

Windham opened the folder in front of him, closed it again, and sighed. He scratched a freckled wrist. His shirt sleeves were turned back, midway up the tendoned forearms of the tennis buff.

"As I understand the situation, Mr. McGee, you are here as a friend of the deceased's uncle."

"And someone," I said, "with a lot of curiosity about how it happened to happen."

"You're not alone," he said tiredly. "I'd handled Norma's legal affairs and advised her on financial matters for probably four years. The longer I knew her, the better I liked her. I must confess to a certain bias in this whole affair. I did not realize what a complete damn fool I had been until all of a sudden I discovered that she was in love with Evan Lawrence, he had moved into her place with her, and they were going to be married. She was one hell of a woman. I didn't know how far I'd fallen for her until . . . it was too damn late. I wasn't planning to tell you this, Dr. Meyer—"

"Please, I am just Meyer. McGee is Travis. You are Roger. We're talking personal things, so it will be easier without formalities."

"Okay. Let me give you the financial picture the way it was before she went to Mexico. She was very bright. I guess you knew that already, Meyer. She got her degrees at a tender age. Am Dexter, who is wise in the ways of geologists, snapped her up six years ago. He hired her away from Conoco and talked her into a long-term contract, with a smaller royalty override than she was maybe worth then, and certainly smaller than she was worth at the time . . . at the time she died."

It was hard for him to say. His throat worked. It was something he didn't like to swallow.

"Anyway, even being paid less than her market value, she was able to accumulate a substantial amount after living expenses and taxes. I had her tax returns done here in the firm. I tried to talk her into investing in private drilling programs with people in the industry, people she knew and respected. I told her it would be a good tax shelter for a single person with her income. But she was not interested in manipulating money and making it grow. She wanted to tuck it away and forget it. So three years ago I had her open a discretionary trust account at Houston Bank and Trust and empty her savings accounts into it. The trust officer, Phyllis DeMar, consulted with me about what we should recommend to Norma. We put her into growth stocks, because it was not appropriate for her to invest for income. And we put her into tax-frees. It made a suitable portfolio."

"Very sound," Meyer said.

Windham turned the open folder to where both Meyer and I could see a page of columns of figures, and then he came around the table to lean between us and point to the appropriate places.

"This is a summary printout made by the Trust Department. It shows the contributions in this column, withdrawals in this, and the total value of the trust based on market value of the holdings, at the end of each month since the account was established.

"As you can see, the total value of the account reached a peak of three hundred and fifteen thousand, seven hundred and twenty-eight dollars and forty cents on the last day of February this year. There were no more contributions made after that date. In the period from March first to June fifteenth, three and a half months, the account balance was drawn down to this figure here, which is approximately what is in the account today, nine thousand three hundred and something.

"Though it was a substantial amount for her to have saved, it is but a tiny driblet of the money that surges through the banks in this city. In each case she authorized the sale of the securities, signed the authorization, and deposited the checks in the account she maintained at First National. Then she cashed a large number of checks over that time span. As she made me and the Houston Bank and Trust co-executors, I was able to get access to the checking account records. The summary is on this next sheet. This column here is normal account activity: charge accounts, bills, etc. These are the checks she cashed. One hundred and fifty-two, all in the fifteen-hundred- to twenty-five-hundred-dollar range. About ten a week. Two every working day. But because she was on field trips from time to time, the incidence had to be higher than that when she was in town. She went around to branch offices of the bank. She evidently wanted to accumulate cash without attracting any kind of attention. And it worked."

"What do you *think* was going on?" Meyer asked. "Take a guess."

Windham went back to his chair and slouched into it, leaning his chin on a steeple of long fingers. "My bias comes into the answer. Where did this Evan Lawrence come from? Maybe she married some kind of con man, or somebody given to harebrained schemes to make a million. Even though Norma wasn't interested in money for its own sake, she was a very smart woman. She had a good mind. Could she have been cheated?"

"Probably," Meyer said. "She was deeply in love. Trust becomes very important then. You suppress doubts for fear of offending the loved one. Her man and her work, they were the important things in her life. If he asked for a loan, made a plausible sales pitch, she would have given it to him."

"But why such stealth?" Windham said. "If she had doubts, she knew she could come to me for advice."

"Tell him, Travis," Meyer said.

I didn't want to, because I knew it was going to have a very ugly effect on Roger Windham.

"It was a very violent explosion," I said to him.

"I read the reports. I know. Explosions are the big thing lately. How many school kids can you kill with a car bomb?"

"There were no identifiable remains. In fact, there were no remains at all. None recovered. Not of anybody aboard."

"I read that—at least a hint of it—and I couldn't believe it. Or understand it."

"Nobody aboard ever knew what happened to them. Existence suddenly stopped," I said.

"Her friends," he said, "decided we'd have a memorial service for them in a week or so. For there to be a funeral, there has to be something to bury."

"We had a little ceremony in the Atlantic off Lauderdale, out off the sea buoy," Meyer said. "The other boats were there because of Captain Jenkins. But we brought our own wreath and floated it out on the tide at the same time. Our wreath was for Hack Jenkins and Norma and Evan Lawrence."

"I'm glad that happened," he said.

"But now," I said, maybe too loudly, "Meyer and I are ninety-nine percent certain only three people were blown up out there—Norma and Hack and a harmless little guy who worked mate part time."

Windham shook his head and knuckled his tired reddened eyes. "What are you trying to tell me?"

"Evan Lawrence had some time to work it all out. The happy couple were living aboard Meyer's boat. In the Miami area you can buy anything in the world. Anything. A bazooka and a case of antitank grenades. Russian land mines. Persian whores. Chinese poisons. All you need is enough cash. He had access to Meyer's professional files aboard the *Keynes*. He could have picked up enough about Chile to be able to fake the terrorist claim on the phone. We have *identified* the third person on the boat as the hired mate. Evan was handy enough so that Jenkins would never have hired the mate if Evan had been along to help with Norma's tackle and bait. When they gassed up, Norma paid the hundred and something in cash out of her purse to the man at the pumps. Had Evan been there, she would have given it to him to give to the man. Had Evan been aboard, he would have been up on deck when they went out past the buoy into the wind and the chop. And what is more conclusive, Roger, is the way the money fits into the whole pattern."

He didn't say anything. He did a strange and touching thing. He bent over slowly, all the way over, to rest his forehead against the shiny dark wood of the conference table. His red hair was thinning at the crown. It gave him a vulnerable look.

We said nothing. In time he straightened up. "I guess I knew it somehow," he said in a flat voice. "Maybe I knew it when he shook my hand. After the wedding. He pumped my hand and beamed at me and told me how happy he was. All that great warm grinning. She was right there, his big left paw resting on her waist in ownership. He looked at me in . . . in a *jolly* way, as if we shared some kind of joke together. I guess he was laughing on the inside at the way he'd gotten Norma to spirit the money out of the trust without letting her faithful old adviser know about it. Or laughing about how it was all going according to plan."

Meyer said, "Maybe at that time he already planned to kill her in such a way it would look as if he had died too. But he wouldn't have had the details worked out. They didn't know they were going to live aboard my boat while I gave talks in Toronto."

"But they seemed to be so much in love. Both of them," Roger said wonderingly. "Do the police believe any of this?"

"There's nothing yet to tell them," Meyer said. "We've got no basis on which to try to trace Evan Lawrence. No personal papers. No fingerprints. Nothing. Just some little stories he told about his past. We're going to look into his past, provided those stories weren't lies."

"If only Mr. Dexter hadn't loaned her to Pemex," he said. "You know, when I found out about the money, about her taking it out of the trust account, that's when I knew why she was avoiding me after she married Evan Lawrence. I'd told her that she ought to come in and chat about the changes that ought to be made in their wills. But she was elusive. It wasn't a matter of any great urgency, I thought. I just wanted to see her and talk to her. She was an honest person. She was doing something without telling me, taking that money out. She really didn't *have* to tell me. It was her money, after all. But she didn't want to come in and *not* tell me. Sorry about nattering around like this, thinking with my mouth open. I just have the crazy feeling I lost her three times, when she got married, when she died, and—now —finding out maybe she was killed. I really think she liked me. We always found a lot to laugh about together. I just didn't make a move when I should have. And she happened to be in the wrong place at the wrong time, and there was Evan Lawrence, grinning away, putting those big hands on her."

Meyer said gently, "I never really got to know her. I should have made the effort. But she had a very busy life. We all think of the inconvenience of making an effort. We're all going to do the right things a little later on. Soon. But soon slides by so easily. Then we vow we'll try to do better. We all carry that little oppressive weight around in the back of our mind—that we should be living better, trying harder, but we're not. We're all living just about as well as we can at any given moment. But that doesn't stop the wishing."

We went down into the tunnel system and found the underground garage and paid the ticket on the way out. He was silent on the way back to Piney Village, apparently concentrating on his driving, but I sensed that things were moving about in the back of his head, where his little personal computer works on equations.

As soon as we were inside, he announced his return and the voice of the security office made its metallic acknowledgment. I stretched out on the couch near the fireplace. Meyer stood by the glass wall and looked out into the little garden.

Finally he came over and sat near me. "Once Windham arranged for me to stay here, he asked me to go through all the papers and documents I could find to see if I could learn anything about Evan Lawrence. The only traces of him were some old clothes, a pair of work shoes, and some love letters from Norma to him."

"With addresses?"

"Without the envelopes. From the contents I think they were sent back here from some field trips she went on. All the rest of her papers were professional documents, in those files there in the office alcove. Reports, surveys, daily drilling reports. Field maps. Computer printouts. All apparently in good order. How do we look for him?"

"We can start with a picture of him."

"There isn't one here. Not one. I thought there would be wedding pictures at least."

"There probably are. She would have invited her friends from the company to the wedding. People who go to weddings take their little cameras and take shaky shots of the happy couple. And they would not have thrown them away."

"Yes, you mentioned that before. I'd forgotten. I seem to be forgetting too many things this year."

nine

On Saturday we drove out to a commercial area where Amdex Petroleum Exploration was located. It was out Interstate 10, east of town, past Jacinto. Hurricane fencing and barbed wire enclosed a yard full of big trucks and incomprehensible hunks of machinery. There were two long prefab steel buildings. Even at nine thirty in the morning it was sickeningly hot. The guard on the big gate let us in and told us to park over near the first building. Meyer parked between a white Continental and a row of big rugged-looking trucks.

We walked through a shop area, the machines silent, work floor empty, air stale. The offices were at the far end of the first building, partitioned off and air conditioned. Beyond the reception area, two men and several women worked at the keyboards of data processing units, green figures glowing on the small screens. Fanfold paper came out of two high-speed printers that clattered and roared as the paper piled up in the waiting tray.

Mr. D. Amsbary Dexter came hurrying out of the larger office in the rear. He had met Meyer, of course, and seemed glad to see him. He looked me over with that quick appraisal of my financial condition which all hustlers learn before they leave grade school and decided I was worth only a small portion of his attention.

He shook hands, then trotted ahead of us into his office, waving us in, waving us toward the chairs. "Come in, come in." He perched a haunch on the corner of his desk, a smallish wiry man, going bald, fishing in his shirt pocket with yellowed fingers for a cigarette. He had faded eyes, full of a nervous alertness, and a sore-throat voice.

"Meyer, I have to ask you for a favor. I talked to our lawyers. And I've cleared this with Roger Windham. He doesn't see any estate tax consequences here, because even if the trust account were intact, there is enough coming in from the employee insurance, and enough pay and royalty interest due her, to more than take care of the tax. Apparently, all she has otherwise is that old van of hers, professional library, the furniture, and so on. There's two four-drawer, gray-steel, fire-resistant, legal-size filing cabinets in that little office setup of hers in the apartment near the stairs. We bought them, and they are on our corporate inventory. They hold work papers which she created as a part of her employment contract with us, and thus belong to us. Most of the work papers are case histories, but there are quite a few which involve acreage we still have under lease."

"I went through the files, Mr. Dexter. Her personal papers are in one drawer, half of one drawer. Once I remove those, you're welcome to the files and the rest of the documents."

"I appreciate your attitude. If it's convenient, I'll have some men over there tomorrow afternoon to pick up the filing cabinets."

"Have them bring a letter from you, explaining ownership. Just in case anybody ever asks."

"No problem. Now then, gentlemen, what was it that you wanted to see me about?"

Meyer signaled me with a glance, and I said, "We wonder what opinion you formed of Evan Lawrence."

"Opinion? Well, he seemed very likable. Everybody around here took to him right away. I thought he was maybe a little bit old for her, ten or twelve years, I guess, but on the other hand she was beginning to get a little long in the tooth. Pushing thirty. Reaching the point where if she wanted kids she'd have to hurry. Maybe I resented him a little. He was marrying a successful woman. Someday she was going to be my best geologist. Maybe someday she would be a legend in the drilling industry. I mean she had that capacity. And I thought marriage might send it all down the drain. Children and a husband and all that. Of course, now all my worries seem ridiculous. What did I think of him? A very relaxed cat. A drifter, I think. And just by the way he listened to you, he could make you feel important and interesting."

"She's a big loss to your company?" I asked.

"I'm going to miss her. A lot. Unless you know modern oil and gas exploration, it's hard to describe her talents. An old friend birddogged her for me when she was with Conoco. I hired her six years ago after talking to her for an hour. We worked out a contract.

"What the public doesn't know is that there is just too damned much information available when you try to make an exploration decision. Old wells, core samples, old geophysical surveys, producing wells, geological surveys. It's a big fat confusion because of so much raw data. Norma helped move this company into computerized data processing and into electromagnetic mapping from the air. I've got the airplane now, loaded with electronics. We do some contract mapping with it to help pay the rent. Norma got into remote sensing analysis too. That's where you get a computerized image analysis of satellite photographs. She worked with a good programmer until they finally developed the software to tie all the random information together, all the way from the history and the geophone records from the charges and the thumper trucks to core analysis.

"The thing is, she had a knack of sensing what was pertinent information and what was junk. With all the pertinent data in the computer, it could draw you a map of the subsurface structures that was clean and pretty, without anomalies that give you questionable areas. Norma put us out front of a whole mob of little exploration companies. She could take the series of computer maps and go into a trance, dreaming of what the earth was like at that place once upon a time, and she'd put down a little red circle with an N inside it. Her mark. Drill here. Or she would throw the whole thing out. There's no big demand for dry holes, she'd say.

"Hell, we got a lot of other benefits from the data processing. We never lose track of a lease rental payment. We're right now revamping the software to catch up with the changes in the WPT. We got all the payout status reports up to date. And we do our own econometric studies. But keeping track of all the nuts and bolts is housekeeping. Using computer technology to process information about what might be a couple of miles underground, and draw maps of it, that was her contribution, and she came in for a percentage of every well after payout, a certain percent for the ones she worked on and smaller for the others, and for the development wells based on her original recommendation. Having that engineering under her belt gave her a practical base for all the rest of it."

"I understand her percentages stop now?" Meyer said.

"You sound like you disapprove. You don't understand the picture. I'm not running a farm team to train people for the seven sisters to snatch up. It's all spelled out. She came in with her eyes open. The longer good people stay, the more they make. If they quit, their percentages go back into the pot. If they retire, they keep the percentages until they die, provided they have at least fifteen years in. In case of accidental death, there's the insurance, and the percentages keep on going for the full calendar year following the year of death, payable to the heirs. So you'll make out okay. Not to worry."

Meyer seemed to swell visibly. He said in a very quiet gritty voice, "I never approve or disapprove of practices with which I am not familiar. I would suspect that when a person becomes contentious and defensive about a given practice, without cause, then there could be reason to doubt either its efficacy or its morality. I did not come here to learn how I would 'make out,' as you put it. I came here to see if you could give us any useful information about Evan Lawrence. Mr. McGee and I are quite convinced he killed my niece. If we are ever to find him, we must learn more about him."

Dexter stood up from the corner of his desk and stared at Meyer and then at me. "Jesus H. Jumping Christ!" he whispered. "Killed Norma? For the money? Jesus, if he stuck with her, in ten more years she'd be spilling money on the way to the bank. Talk about killing the goose!"

Then he made a funny little bow to Meyer.

"Excuse me. I had you all wrong. I thought a band of nuts tried to blow you up but got Norma and her husband by accident. I thought you were here to find out how much you were going to get. In my line of work, there are a lot of people who spend all their time trying to find out how much they are going to get. They generally get less than if they spent less time thinking about it. What did that husband do? Blow up a stand-in?"

"Good guess," Meyer said. "No part of any body was recovered. In a photo taken moments before the explosion, from another boat, Norma and Captain Jenkins are recognizable and the third person has been identified, but not officially, as a hired mate. Authorities can find no trace of any such terrorist organization. Of course, there could be an international organization with a compulsion to kill economists, an urge I would find understandable, if not sympathetic."

Meyer startled me. It was almost the very first glimmer of humor I had detected in a year, and it came at an unexpected time and place.

"But you do have more to go on than what you've told me?"

"Just behavior patterns. But convincing," Meyer said.

"I think I told you what I know about the husband. A pleasant guy. Maybe not very motivated. Maybe twelve years older than Norma, maybe less. He seemed like the kind of person who makes lots of friends and has lots of contacts. A salesman type. He had a good laugh. I decided he'd make a pretty good husband for Norma. That is, if she had to have a husband."

"Any distinguishing marks or characteristics?" I asked. "We had dinner with the two of them aboard my houseboat, and we can't come up with anything. Maybe five ten and a half or eleven. Close to two hundred. But pretty good shape. Brown hair, receding a little. Green eyes, I think. Nose a little crooked. Plenty of tan. Good teeth."

"Big hands on him," Dexter said. "Real big. Thick wrists. Big bone structure. Spoke some Mexican."

"We know how they met," I said. "If he swindled her out of her money and killed her, he'll make himself hard to find. We want to go down his back trail and see if we can turn up anything. We need a good picture of him. We thought maybe somebody at the wedding took some."

He called a plump woman in from the outer office and asked her. She remembered that one of the women in the office had taken a lot of pictures of the ceremony. Her name was Marlane Hoffer, and she lived with a friend in a little apartment in the Post Oak area. She went out and typed the name, address, and phone number and brought it in and gave it to Meyer.

Marlane was on the third floor of a new nondescript apartment building a block off Westheimer Road, behind the Galleria development area. Marlane's friend checked us through the peephole lens and rattled the lock chain. He was a big man with long hairy legs. He wore short running pants and an unbuttoned yellow shirt. A slab of brown belly bulged over the top of the running pants. He had a big head and a lot of brown hair and blond beard.

As soon as he let us in he turned and bawled, "Marl! It's the guys about the pictures. Marl!"

"Okay, okay," yelled a voice from behind a closed door.

She came out in a few minutes in a floor-length white terry beach robe, her hair turbaned in a blue terry towel. She was a small woman with a pert, friendly face. The friend had gone over to an alcove off the living room and was stretched out watching automobiles racing somewhere, noisily.

She spoke over the roar of engines. "*I* want to go down to the pool, but *he* says it's too hot. Here's the pictures I took. I didn't do so great with them. What I got, it's this Pentax *he* used to use until he got a Nikon, and he never explained all the buttons so I could understand."

We stood and looked at the pictures together. There was one where she had evidently tried to get them both in a closeup. It was an outdoor shot, under some trees. In that picture Evan was looking directly into the camera, with a slightly startled expression. Norma was beyond him, out of focus.

"It was in this sort of garden out behind a restaurant, a really great place to get married. The food was absolutely delicious, and I kind of busted loose on the wine. They said it was Spanish champagne, but what do I know? Look, take the whole thing. She was my friend and now she's dead and I don't want her picture around, okay?"

"If you're really sure you don't . . ." Meyer said.

"You can bet your ass I'm sure. You, being her uncle, I can understand how you'd want pictures. But she wasn't one of my best friends, you understand? It's a hell of a thing, dying on a honeymoon. But there you are." She whirled and yelled, "Can't you turn that shitty noise down?"

"You don't like it, go out in the hall!" he yelled.

We thanked her and left. Through the closed doors, as we walked toward the stairs, we could hear her squalling at him and him roaring back.

I made sure we had the negatives, including the one of Evan. "Now we find a good lab," I said.

On Monday morning we brought the four color prints back to the condo at Piney Village. The professional lab had done good work on the eight-by-ten enlargement. The Pentax lens had done the original good work. It was unmistakably Evan Lawrence, every pore, blemish, and laugh line. He was half smiling, startled, one eyebrow raised. The lab had put them in gray portrait folders.

Meyer sat at Norma's desk in the little office she had fixed up. The file cabinets had been taken away.

Outside, the rain fell in silver-gray sheets out of a gunmetal sky. A tropical disturbance had moved in off the Gulf, a rain engine that had broken the heat wave. All over the city the body and fender shops were accumulating backlogs.

I leaned against the angled drawing board, one foot on the rung of the stool she had sat on when she worked at her maps, my arms crossed.

"One thing we know is that he left almost no trace of himself here," Meyer said. "He lived here for almost three months. No possessions. No personal papers. Just some rough cheap chain-store clothing. This was going to be his home. It isn't normal that he should leave so little hint of himself."

"You said there were letters she wrote to him when she was out in the field. No hints in those? No clues?"

He frowned. "When I found them I thought he was dead too, and it seemed a terrible invasion of privacy. I threw them out, and then I retrieved them and put them with her personal papers. I just scanned a couple of them quickly. There's about a dozen, I think. She was very much in love."

He went off and found the letters and brought them back to me. "Travis, I don't think I want to read them. If you wouldn't mind . . ."

There were twelve of them, written on whatever paper was handy at the time. Yellow legal sheets, office memo paper, the blank backs of obsolete printouts. She wrote in the hasty scrawl of a busy person, using abbreviations, leaving out words. She talked of her work but without the technical details he would probably not have understood.

They were all dated and could be divided into small batches. Apparently she wrote frequently when she was out in the field. Three consecutive days in March, four in April, two in mid-May, and three in June.

Darling, having dreadful time today with a ranch woman who refuses to believe we will repair their land when we're through. Kept coming out, whining about the ruts and how we were scaring her animals. We were using some new equipment, and I had to make certain it was placed just where I had marked the aerials. If, when all the reports are in, we decide to try to make a well, she will really go out of her mind.

Miss you so much I can't believe it. I think of your hands touching, and I feel all weak and dizzy, and I forget what it is I'm supposed to be doing here. I can close my eyes and look into your eyes and see my whole life there. You can never ever love me as much as I love you. I never thought I could feel like this, not in my whole life. I never thought I could feel this kind of physical hunger for someone. Tomorrow night I will be home, darling, and we will be together, and I will be in your arms, and we will make it last and last until I go out of my mind.

That erotic strain ran through all the letters, those written before the marriage and those written afterward. It was a very strong physical infatuation. I could guess that she had been a shy person, not pretty, uncertain in any kind of sexual relationship, dedicated to her work. At twenty-nine, awakened by Evan Lawrence, she wanted to catch up on everything she had missed, and from the letters she was making a pretty good try.

But I was after hints and clues. What about the money? What kind of a man was Evan Lawrence?

I came upon a comment in a June letter that puzzled me.

When we talked the other night, Evan, I guess I seemed too nervous about the arrangement. I'm sorry. I didn't mean to sound that way. It's just that I've been so damned orderly all my life. Oh, I've taken big risks in my work, but not in my personal life. I pay every parking ticket on time. I know you are amused by that, and maybe you are a little irritated by it too. I agreed, and I'm not going to back out. The only thing is, we have to turn it around by April of next year. You say we will, so okay. And, darling, I can understand how just as a matter of personal pride, you want to make a contribution to our future. But it really doesn't matter that much to me. I don't think of things like that. I love you just as you are, and it would not matter to me if you had five million dollars or twenty-eight cents. I trust you with my life and everything that goes with it. Now it is Cinderella time, and I am yawning, and this gasoline lantern in the van is hurting my eyes and attracting every bug in Louisiana, and tomorrow is the day when we'll find out—not for sure but for maybe—if we want to keep this lease. If we want to keep it, we have to start making a hole in the ground by August at the latest.

I marked the passage and took it over to Meyer. He read it carefully. "So! She filed a quarterly estimate in addition to the deductions they took from her salary at Amdex. And she would have to pay the estimate plus last year's tax on April fifteenth. She was telling him that she had to have the deal consummated, whatever it was, and get enough money back so she wouldn't be caught short when tax time rolled around. He had some kind of scheme and he talked her into letting him have the money quietly and secretly so he could, perhaps, double it."

"That makes her sound like a dummy, Meyer."

"What could she say to him? 'No, thanks. I don't want you investing my money. I don't trust you. You're not smart enough, Mr. Lawrence. I earned it and it's mine.' Think of all the ways he could have worked on her, and then see if you really want to call her a dummy."

I told him it was probably the wrong word to use, and I went back to my reading and rereading of that highly personal mail. I marked a few short passages and finally, when I was certain there was nothing else, I read each one aloud to Meyer.

You must have lots and lots of friends, darling. Don't they know where you are living? It seems odd that you don't get any mail or phone calls at all, only from my friends—or I should say our friends.

And, in another letter:

I don't know what I did to make you so angry. I wasn't jealous. I was just curious. I want to know what every minute of your life has been like. If you don't want to talk about her, I'll never bring it up again.

And finally:

I don't care how beautiful Cuernavaca is, darling. Anywhere we can be together will be wonderful enough. I just can't run out on Am Dexter at this point. Can't we just begin to make plans instead of being so abrupt? In two years I could arrange to be as free as a bird. But I don't really know how well I would adjust to being unemployed. I shouldn't have brought this up in a letter. Don't be angry with me.

Meyer shook his head and sighed. "So he was going to double her money and they would then live forever in Mexico in peace and luxury. And it is a fair guess he was married before."

"Where does all this leave us?"

"Only a little better than nowhere at all. I've been trying to reconstruct some of the history he told us that night aboard the *Flush*. He worked on time-sharing sales with somebody named Willy in Cancún. He has a degree in Business Administration from the University of Texas. He worked for a Mr. Guffey, a farmer living north of Harlingen, selling Japanese stone lanterns. He worked for Eagle Realty in Dallas. He worked in a rodeo for a short time. Can you remember anything else?"

"Not a thing."

"Where do you think we should start?"

"You're the academic type, Meyer. So you go to Austin, and I'll go to Dallas."

ten

On Monday afternoon in Dallas, I found Eagle Realty with a certain amount of difficulty because it had no sign. They had just moved into larger quarters, into a new building, and the sign hadn't arrived yet.

The car rental woman at the airport had been helpful in getting me to the general location, north of I-30 and east of the North Tollway, over in the vicinity of Southern Methodist, but once I was in the area I had to ask three times before I finally found it near a giant shopping mall, a long low building with lots of windows, faced with pale stone and redwood, with a big carved golden eagle over the double doors in front. Something had been there first and had been torn down. Heaps of rubble were shoved to the back of the raw lot, waiting to be trucked off. They were starting to pave the parking lot. Some very small trees had been put into the planters, and a man was watering them.

I pushed my way into the air-conditioned reception area, where a man in khakis was slowly stripping transparent plastic from the reception-area chairs and couches.

A big nervous young woman came trotting back to the reception desk, stared at me, and said, "Thank God! At last!"

"At last what?"

"You're from the electric, aren't you? My God, you've got to be from the electric!"

"I'm from Florida."

"If you're here trying to sell something, I can tell you that you are going right back out that door so fast—"

"I'm not selling anything, buying anything, or fixing anything."

She finally smiled. "Then you're not going to be much good to us, are you? Honest to God, I'll quit before I get involved in moving the office again."

"I'm trying to find out a couple of things about a man who used to work for Eagle. His name is Evan Lawrence."

"Doesn't mean a thing to me. Not a thing. How long ago?"

"I'm not too definite about the date."

"We get a big turnover on salesmen, especially the last few years. You know how it is. The old personnel records are on floppy disks, and unless somebody comes from the electric and gets that back office juiced up, nobody is ever going to read them. We've got four tabletop IBMs back there, with data-processing programs and printers, and our information about current sales and rentals is all on the disks, and we can't run anything because the current keeps cutting out."

"Who's around who's been here the longest?"

"Well, I guess that would be Martin Eagle." She reached toward the phone. "Who will I say?"

"McGee. Travis McGee from Fort Lauderdale."

She picked up the phone and said a very ugly word. Her face turned red. "Now the effing phone is effing well dead too. You wait here."

She trotted off. The man uncovering the furniture was chuckling and shaking his head. She came back and beckoned to me, and I followed her to Martin Eagle's big corner office with a view of the rubble piles and a corner of the mall and ten thousand automobiles winking in the heat waves. She waved me in and closed the door.

Martin Eagle looked over his shoulder at me and smiled and nodded and turned back toward the perforated section of white wall where he was hanging trophies and credentials on little hooks that fitted into the perforations.

He hung a framed scroll which said in Olde English that Martin Eagle was Junior Chamber of Commerce Man of the Year. It was dated three years ago.

"You think it's maybe too close to the award from the city? What do you think?"

"I guess it would depend on how much you are going to hang there."

"Good thinking. McGee, is it? Call me Marty. I don't know if I should hang all this shit or not. Look, I got the top of the desk covered. Maybe I shouldn't even hang that JC scroll. They gave it to five of us that year. I was the third runner-up. All this stuff could be, you know, ostentatious. But you take doctors. They hang stuff all over.

Gives the patients confidence, I guess. I'm doing the same thing. Eagle Realty gives you a fair deal, buying or selling. That's the only thing I've ever learned about this business. You screw somebody, it comes back to haunt you. Even when you don't screw somebody, it comes back to haunt you. People don't listen and people lie. What am I doing in a new building anyway? In these times. You want to know why? We got too big for the old place and we were going to stay right there, all packed in, no matter what, and they decided to tear down the whole block and put up another gigantic building. So here I am. Wait a second. I want to put up this little shelf thing and put some eagles on it. I've got a big collection of eagles. Pottery, silver, stone, wood. You wouldn't believe how many I've got at home. Everybody knows I collect eagles, and there you are."

He put four eagles on the little shelf and stepped back and made a little sound of satisfaction and went around his desk and sat down and gestured toward a nearby chair.

"It's going to look okay in here when we get organized," he said. "Nice building, don't you think?"

"Very nice, Marty. My name is Travis McGee."

"Trav, my friend, you have given me invaluable advice about my wall over there. I am in your debt. What can I do for you? Like a good price on a nice little house? Why live in Florida when you can live in Texas like a human being? Bring the wife around. In a week we'll have our new slide show deal going and it will be computerized. The way it works, a man says he can spend from eighty-five to a hundred and five thousand. He wants at least a half acre of land. He's got to have two bedrooms. Okay, we save a lot of time by showing the slides before we go out driving around in traffic. What can I do for you?"

He was a jolly man with a happy face. Dark hair combed all the way forward and then curved off to one side and sprayed into place. He was carrying a little too much weight, but he looked comfortable with it. Fawn-colored slacks, white shoes, yellow sports shirt with a little eagle embroidered over the left pocket. Gold chain around the neck and the right wrist. Gold watch on the left wrist. Gold ring on the right-hand pinky, with an eagle on it.

"I wanted to ask a couple of questions about a man who used to work here."

"I'm telling you, Trav, we try to screen them all as well as we can, but these days it's a real burden. A man fills out an application, and it costs you real money to check out all the references he gives you. What I do, and sometimes I'm sorry, I size them up myself. We have a little chat. Take for example yourself. If you wanted to work here, I'd say okay. I'd teach you the ropes, help you get the licenses. But I wouldn't let you handle any cash money until I was damn well sure you were okay. I'm telling you that over the years we've had some bad apples. They float around like used car salesmen. But we've had some real good ones too. Who are you looking for?"

"Evan Lawrence."

"Evan? Evan Lawrence?" He shook his head slowly. "No, that doesn't ring any kind of a bell at all."

"He said he worked here for at least a year, and he made quite a lot of money selling tract houses and lots for you."

"Listen, anybody who makes money for me, I remember. Because when they make money, I make money. A year, you say? Trav, my friend, somebody is kidding you, or you are kidding me. What did this fellow look like anyway?"

I took the portrait folder out of the small leather portfolio, stood up, and leaned over and handed it to Marty Eagle across his big new desk.

Still smiling, he flipped it open.

All expression ceased. The blood drained from his face, leaving a yellowish cast to his tan. He seemed to stop breathing. Suddenly he looked alarmed, heaved himself up, and trotted to his personal executive washroom and slammed the door. I heard him in there retching, heard the water running, the toilet flushing. When at last he came out there was a gray tired look about him. There was a water stain where he had dabbed at his yellow shirt. He brought a faint sharp aroma of vomit, quickly dispelled by the air conditioning.

He sat heavily behind the desk and shook his head. "Never had that happen to me before. Never."

"I'm sorry."

"So don't be sorry. How could you know? When was this taken?" He was studying the picture carefully.

"Last April."

"Where is he now?"

"I have absolutely no idea."

"I think, why I threw up, we were always a close family, me and my two sisters. This man isn't any Evan Lawrence. His name is Jerry Tobin. Everybody working here at the time liked him. That was five years ago. And I have thought about the whole thing ten thousand times. Doris, she was my kid sister, she fell head over heels. What can you do? I didn't want her marrying any con artist like Jerry Tobin. He was very slick. He could really close a sale. Hell, Dorrie hadn't turned twenty-one even. But she got her money when she was eighteen. We all did. That was the way Poppa's will worked. I told her that she was going to have to wait a year and see if she still loved Jerry enough to marry him. She was furious. She didn't want to wait. She was pretty. And she wasn't thinking straight because good old Jerry Tobin had gotten into her pants, and she couldn't get enough of it. They called from the bank and said they had tried to keep her from cleaning out her accounts, but they had no legal way to stop her. She didn't come back home, not ever again. She was dead by evening of the next day. Down near Kerrville, just past a little town named Ingram, on a back road. It was her car, her white Buick. She was driving. They missed a turn and went off the road and hit a live oak a kind of glancing blow. It threw him clear when the car rolled. They think she was knocked out. They couldn't tell because the car burned. It burned her all to hell. They had to identify her from dental work to be sure. People saw the fire and stopped. Jerry Tobin was face down on a stony bank, all scuffed up. He didn't come to until he was in the ambulance. He came to the funeral service here in Dallas. He cried like a baby. He still had some small bandages on. But she was dead. Where was the money? It had burned up with her and her luggage and clothes and car, and his luggage and clothes. Too bad. All gone."

"Much?"

"Depends on who is counting. Two hundred and twenty something thousand. I didn't buy it. I didn't buy the story. I drove way down there and looked at where it happened. I looked at what was left of the car. There was a police investigation. They cleared him. Dorrie'd had a couple of minor accidents and a whole bundle of moving vehicle violations. She always drove too fast. He knew that. Everything fitted together. I hired private investigators. I wanted them to find him loaded with money. I wanted to get the whole thing opened up. But all of a sudden he just took off. He left a note on my desk. *There are too many sad memories around here, Marty. I can't take it any longer. Goodbye and good luck.*"

He tried to smile.

"I thought I was past being really hurt about it and then I saw that face, that goddam smirk of his, and it got to me. Why do you want to find him?"

"Maybe the same kind of thing. A little bigger stake. And more risk."

"How much bigger?"

"Half again."

He whistled without making a sound. "Maybe there's some law about using a false name."

"And maybe he had it legally changed. If I can't locate him, what difference does it make?"

"She was so alive! Look, if he did it twice, then he killed them both."

"Just an assumption, Marty."

"You sound like some kind of lawyer. You know what I did? When they weren't finding out anything about him—those investigators I was paying—I asked one of them if he knew of a good safe way to find somebody who'd be willing to kill Tobin. It made the investigator very nervous. He didn't seem to want to ask around. I was going to try some other way of finding somebody when all of a sudden Tobin took off. I am not a violent-type guy, as you can probably guess, McGee. But she was my kid sister, and that son of a bitch came into her life and ended it. Maybe it happened just like he said. So what? He was still to blame, wasn't he? I'm not hurting for money. I could hire the best there is." He tried to force a laugh, but his eyes filled with tears and he hopped up and stared out his window. "We were always such a close family," he said in a hoarse voice.

"Did you try to trace him?"

"For a while. It's a big country. Even back then all the rules were beginning to break down. You know, about new identities. People drifting all over, calling themselves anything at all, buying new names with driving licenses and passports and the whole thing. They say you can trace people through social security numbers. If a person stayed put, maybe you could. But a drifter can invent a new number for every job he has. I traced down the number Jerry gave when we hired him. It took months for the report to come back through the local office. It was a number issued to a woman with an Italian name."

"Was he a good salesman?"

"I don't know how he'd have done in the market we got now, but five–six years ago he was a killer. He could close a deal while the next guy would just be getting around to showing the bathrooms. I would say he cleared somewhere in the low six figures in the time he was here."

"Would you know about him getting ripped off by somebody with a tax-shelter scam?"

"Jerry? Ripped off? Not likely."

"Buying a bunch of Bibles to donate them later to schools and churches for four times what he paid?"

"No way at all. He had a good business head. Very very sharp. I've got some pretty good moves myself. But I think he could have come up with better ones. I kept telling him I should open a branch of Eagle in Fort Worth and he could run it, but he didn't want any part of it. He said he was lazy. I don't think so. I think it was something about the exposure, about attracting too much attention to himself."

"Did he get into any kind of trouble while he worked for you?"

"Not money trouble. And not really what you'd call touble. We were peddling a development called Crestwinds, and we put together a model house with the contractor and some decorators. During open house the salesmen had to take turns manning the place. So they had keys. One of our saleswomen went back after hours one night looking for a gold earring she could have lost there, and she found Jerry in the sack with the wife of the contractor. It was a second wife, a young one. That was before he took aim at my sister Doris. The woman that found them raised hell, and I told Jerry to find a better place for his fun and games. It didn't happen again, at least that I know of."

Finally there was no more information to be gained. He was dispirited, quite unlike the mood he'd been in when I arrived.

As I was getting ready to leave he gave me his card. "Look, stay in touch, Trav. You get a line on him and need any kind of help at all, phone me. Okay? A promise?"

"Sure."

"What is inside the head of a man like that? I mean, assuming he killed Doris or any other girl, what's the point?"

"I read somewhere that the average bank robbery nets eighteen hundred dollars. That could have something to do with it."

"But he couldn't have been hurting for money. He made good money. He didn't have a lot of expensive habits."

His last question was, "Where do you go from here?"

"When did the accident happen?"

It took him a moment to count it out. "In May. A Saturday, the twenty-first. Five years and two months ago."

"Did the press cover it?"

"Yes. On Monday morning. It didn't make the Sunday papers."

"So from here I go and look up the report."

"I came across the clippings a year or so ago and wondered why I was saving them. I tossed them out."

eleven

Wednesday the twenty-first of July in Naples was one of those rare mouse-mist days of summer, a heavy overcast, no wind, and an invasion of almost invisible bugs from the swamps and inlets, driving the tourists off the beach in front of the Eden Beach Hotel and its bungalows, sending them into the lounges for listless sessions of Scrabble or backgammon or into their rooms for the dubious diversion of daytime television.

Even though Annie Renzetti had been free of her fifty-three proctologists since Monday, she did not seem to be unwinding completely. I sensed a reserve. I roamed the area while she did her office work. Even though we had been circumspect for over a year, it is just not possible to conceal a relationship in a hotel setting. She was the boss lady, and I was "him." I was her "him," my status known to the bookkeepers, the room maids, the dishwashers, the bartenders, the waitresses, the girls at the desk, the grounds keepers, the pool sweeper, the beach tenders, the lifeguards, the tennis pro, and the in-house maintenance men. So I was conscious, and had been for some time, of a discontinuous but consistent appraisal.

Gossip can exist only when the relationship gossiped about can have some effect upon the community, good or bad. What are they *really* like when they're together? Do they say anything about us? Will they break up? Will that change her? Will somebody else come along? What will that do to the situation here? What does he/she see in her/him?

She was the queen bee of the hotel and I was the prince consort, the sporadic visitor, and a source of some concern and uncertainty to them. By instinct Annie had fastened upon a very good personnel management technique. She treated every employee with courtesy, fairness, and impartiality. She pitched in on any kind of unpleasant work when there was an emergency. She did not make a confidant of any employee and thus kept a certain distance from them all. She listened to complaints, prowled the whole area at unexpected times, rewarded top performance with raises, and fired the lazy, the indifferent, the thieves, and the liars. I was proud of the job she was doing, and at the same time felt a little uncomfortable with it. She was a paragon. And she was making a hell of a lot of money for the chain.

I bought myself a Blood Mary at the pool bar and borrowed some of the bartender's Cutter's. He was stiff and formal with me. "Yes, sir. Celery, sir?" The safest place to keep me was at full arm's length. It can make a person lonesome.

I went back to her cabaña, the last one in the row, up on six-foot pilings, let myself in, positioned myself in the middle of her small living room, and tried to undo some of the damage of too many days spent sitting in cars and offices and airplanes. One very sound rule for the care of the body is always to keep in mind what it was designed to do. The body was shaped by the need to run long distances on resilient turf, to run very fast for short distances, to climb trees, and to carry loads back to the cave, so any persistent exercise you do which is not a logical part of that ancient series of uses is, in general, bad for the body. A succession of deep knee bends is destructive, in time. As are too many pushups. As is selective muscle development through weight-lifting. As is jogging on hard surfaces. A couple of years of such jogging and you are very likely never to walk in comfort again. Man is a walking animal, perfectly designed for it. The only more efficient human energy use is the bicycle.

So what I am after when I have been too sedentary, and feeling bad because of it, is limberness. The unstretched tendons try to lock in place, resisting extension and contraction both. Stretch slowly like a cat awakening. Then twist and bend slowly, as far as you can, in any position where you can feel the muscles pulling. Hold that position, then push it a little farther. Hold it, then push again. Loosen all the fibers in that fashion, slowly and without great strain, until you have limbered your entire body. Then play the Chinese morning game of imitation slow-motion combat, striking the long slow blow, balancing on one leg, retreating, defending, striking again. Then it is time to take the long slow swim along the beach, breaking it up with little speed sprints. Crawl, breaststroke, backstroke, working the muscles you've limbered up.

Anne Renzetti came back to the cabaña after I had finished my swim and my shower and had stretched out on the long padded window seat in the living room to scan a magazine called *Motel and Hotel Management Practice*. It said the shape of the soap makes a big difference in how long it lasts.

As she was apologizing for having to take so long over her management chores, I scooped her up. She clung in warmth and fragrance, with a soft and smiling mouth, and I backed to the couch and sat with her, holding her on my lap, holding her close—a small and tidy woman, as electrically alive as a basket of eels.

A long time later, as the sun was dipping down into the red-brown smog that now greases the edge of the sky all along our coasts, I made us our drinks and we took them out onto the shallow porch, in the deck chairs side by side.

"I flew into Tampa," I said, "got a connection to Fort Myers, and picked up a rental car there and drove down."

"Down I-Seventy-five?"

"No, down the old coast road, the Tamiami Trail. An exercise in masochism. I get the feeling that if I'm away for three days, I can see the difference."

"Maybe you can. My company subscribes to a service for me, and the last issue had an article about Florida population. We're getting a thousand new residents a day. Permanent residents. A little family every six minutes. In the public restaurants of Florida, one and a half million people can have a sit-down meal at the same time."

"No more. Please."

"We're the seventh largest state. We get thirty-eight million tourists a year."

"And the rivers and the swamps are dying, the birds are dying, the fish are dying. They're paving the whole state. And the people who give a damn can't be heard. The developers make big campaign contributions. And there isn't enough public money to treat the sewage."

"Poor *bay*bee!"

"Poor Florida. Everything is going to stop working all at once. Then watch the exodus. Okay, coming down that way this morning depressed me. But you cured the depression. You're a natural resource they can't drain and pave."

"You say lovely things. Where's Meyer? What did you find out?"

So I told her the whole thing. It was pitch-black night before I finished. She hadn't seen the photographs of Evan Lawrence, a.k.a. Jerry Tobin, and she wanted to see the Xerox copy of the news story, reproduced from microfilm. We went in and turned on the lights. I fixed fresh drinks while she studied the clipping and the photo.

"She was a very pretty girl, wasn't she?"

"Yes indeed she was. They played down the angle that she was probably running away with Evan Lawrence."

"Was she?"

"Her big brother, Marty, thinks so."

I gave her the drink and sat near her. She kept looking at Evan Lawrence's face in the color enlargement, her expression odd.

"What's the matter, Annie?"

"What I was going to say before, out on the deck there when you told me all about it, I was going to say I couldn't make it sound like something that really happened, those two things, those two women. It seems so sort of pointless. I mean, they both adored him, right? What was the need? Suppose he was with them for years and years and got tired of them. Like taking out insurance on the wife. That sort of dirty thing. But, looking at him . . ."

"Looking at him what?"

"I can sort of understand. I think this is a kind of man most women never get to see even once in their lives. I knew one like that when I was very young. He used to come to our house. I was about thirteen. He used to bring his wife. She didn't have very much English. I think she was Hungarian. He was trying to make a deal with my father. He wanted a tract of land my father had inherited. He wanted to build some kind of factory on it, and he was trying to get my father to take a stock interest instead of demanding cash for the land. I heard years later that if my father had taken the stock interest, he would have become a very rich person in a very short time. I looked at that man with the Hungarian wife and I fell madly, totally in love with him."

"Why?"

"How do I know? I looked at him and I saw strength and kindness and gentleness and love and understanding. I saw right away that he would know every thought and emotion I might have without my having to tell him. I looked at him and something inside me melted. There is something very much like that in this man's face."

"I can't see it."

"Another woman would."

"So why does what you see in his face make it easier for you to understand what we think he did?"

"That man I fell in love with? He turned out to be very corrupt. He cheated his associates. His wife drowned mysteriously in a boating mishap in California. When he was arrested, he posted bail and disappeared. I've heard he is living in Turkey. They have no extradition. He had everything and he threw it away. Just like this person here, whatever his name is."

"Maybe Meyer will come up with a better name through the university records."

"Have you wondered if this person might be insane?" she asked.

"I've thought about it."

"If a person has built up enough of a structure of delusion, the things they do only make sense as they relate to the delusion. What is he, about forty? Or a little more. He may have been doing this sort of thing for years."

"Without attracting a lot of attention?"

"A little here, a little there. But he keeps moving on."

"What kind of a delusion would make a man kill women who have fallen deeply in love with him?"

"Punishing them for loving somebody he knows is unworthy of love?"

"Come *on* Annie!"

"So he's schizo. The lover and the killer. There are mental disorders a lot wilder than that."

We left it there. I put the picture and the clipping back in my case. We had a late supper in a private corner of the lounge.

"Okay," I said finally. "What have you got on your mind?"

"Does it show? I didn't want it to show."

"Annie, about one minute ago I said that these tiny potatoes are really delicious. And you smiled and said they surely are. And they happen to be sautéed scallops."

"It's not *fair,* damn you, to do it that way. That's entrapment."

"What's going on?"

"I wasn't ready to tell you yet. I've been summoned to Chicago. I go up Thursday night and come back Saturday."

"What's going on?"

"A friend in Chicago gave me a tiny clue over the phone."

"Such as?"

"Do you remember, when I first went with the company I was secretary to a Mr. Luddwick?"

"Then he was transferred to Hawaii?"

"Right. And his replacement got into a one-car accident driving down here, and by the time he was recovered enough to take over this hotel, I was doing so well they decided to let me run it."

"And you've been doing well ever since."

"They must think so. The executive vice-president, Mr. Minter, has had a heart attack and he's taking early retirement. So they're bringing Al Luddwick back from Hawaii to take over. That leaves Hawaii open. It's brand new and twice the size of this one. And lots more money."

I frowned at her. "They're going to offer it to *you?*"

"Why not? I don't mind saying I am doing a hell of a job. All they have to do is look at the ratios. Every computer study they run tells them I'm doing a hell of a job."

"At least it's nice to be asked."

"I'm not sure I'm going to be asked, Travis. So far, it's just a rumor."

"But if they ask you, you wouldn't take it, would you?"

"Why the hell wouldn't I?"

"What about us?"

"Good grief, Travis, what *about* us? You don't understand how these things work, do you? Right now, I'm red hot. Suppose they offered it and I turned it down. What would that tell them about me? Oh, they'd probably keep me on here, but they'd be . . . dubious about me. Maybe I was scared to try something bigger. Maybe I have some kind of action going on the side, down here, and they better do some more auditing. The instant I say no, I stop being Golden Girl."

"So who needs to be Golden Girl? What's wrong with the life you have?"

"How can you be so chauvinistic stupid?"

"Hey, wait a minute!"

"I mean it. Look, when I think of that much bigger a job, I get flutters in my stomach and I can't take a deep breath. My God, honey, that is the direction of the stock options, the bonuses, the eventual seat on the Board. Look, I have something I can do damn well. I love the work. I love the challenge. What am I supposed to do, cut myself back like pruning a bush so I can be your convenient little shack job?" She thumped her breastbone with her knuckles. "I am me in my own right. What do you do in Florida that is so damned important anyway? Of course I don't want to lose you. Why can't you ship the *Busted Flush* out to the islands as deck cargo? You could have a better life out there than you have here. Those good old buddy boys of yours around Bahia Mar would forget you in three months. What would you be giving up compared with what you're asking me to give up?"

The food was good, but the appetite came to a dead halt. We went for a walk. We took the quarrel up and down the beach. The breeze had come up, out of the west, shoving the bugs inland. The waves slapped on the starlit sand.

We took the quarrel, unresolved, to bed, both of us secretly hoping that lovemaking would provide a solution somehow. It was a gentler interlude than ever before. There seemed in it elements of sadness, of regret and farewell. Afterward I kissed her moist eyes and tasted the salt, asked her why she wept.

"For what might have been, I guess."

"Such as?"

"Had we been younger. I don't know. At my age with this pelvic structure, having a baby would be a very dangerous thing. And you're past changing, McGee. You're past having tots around. But even if I were younger and wanted to risk it, the thing I talked about before would make me wary."

"What was that?"

"The way you keep some important part of yourself hidden away. The reserve I can't break through. Maybe you were different a dozen years ago. Maybe then you could give all the way. With me, I get the feeling you are a user, not a giver."

"And you feel like someone who is only used?"

"No, dear. Not that harsh. I don't have the right words. What I do know is that I have more energies than you can waste. I can't use all of myself with you because neither you nor the years will let that happen. But I can use all of myself in my work. Believe me, I'm not motivated by trying to make a lot of money, or be important, or force people to respect me. I want to do what I do because it is tricky work, and when it goes well I feel a very intense satisfaction. Can you understand all that?"

"I can try."

She made a sound in the darkness almost like a laugh. "Oh, my darling, this has been good. I needed you. I needed more of you than you were willing to give, but it was damn good nonetheless. And now we've bitched it all up for fair."

"How so?"

"If they offer me the job, I'll take it. But if the rumor is wrong, and they don't offer it to me, and I stay here, I don't want this relationship with you to continue."

"Why not?"

"The fact you could ask that question is one of the reasons."

"Maybe I'm not very bright."

"Okay, you are a no-win situation for me. You unfocus my attention on my work. You create little problems with the hotel employees. Some of them think they can get a little smart-ass, as if they have something they can use against me in some way, and I have to smack them down. After you have been here, my bed is always too empty for night after night. Yet when I know you are on your way over, I feel a funny resentment. As if I'm some kind of chattel. You and my work overlap in a way that makes me irritable. Can you understand?"

"I think maybe I'm beginning to. Maybe we can leave it that you can come over to Lauderdale whenever."

"I don't think so. Thank you, but I don't think that would be wise. Besides, I really do expect to get the position in Hawaii."

She turned her head and looked at her bedside clock. Ten past three.

"Travis?"

I slipped my arms around her and pulled her closer.

"Travis, do me a favor."

"Sure."

"Just get up and get dressed and get in your little rented car and go home."

When I started to speak she pressed two fingers against my lips.

"Please, dear. I want to cry in peace. I want to cry for a long long time, and then sleep like death. Please go. Please don't say anything. We've said it all."

And so I dressed in darkness, picked up my gear, let myself out, making certain the door was locked. One of her alert security guards checked me, grunting recognition after putting his flashlight on my face.

And here is how it was for me, as I droned across Alligator Alley in the little tin car.

I told myself there was no understanding women. I told myself she didn't understand what she was throwing away. I told myself I would probably read about her in the papers, years hence, a hard-bitten little gray-haired woman who had been made head of something or other.

I felt lost and lonesome and, in a curious way, unworthy. I still kept telling myself there was no understanding them.

But honesty cannot be indefinitely suppressed. Yes, I knew exactly what she meant. I knew exactly why she had made her decision, and I was forced to admit that no matter what I thought of it, it was the right decision for Anne Renzetti.

Then came the hard part. I had suffered loss. I had been rejected. I was the lover cast out. I was alone. And when I tried to plumb the depths of my grief and my loss, I came finally upon a small ugly morsel way down in the bottom of my soul. It was a little round object, like a head with a grinning face. It said ugly things to me. It kept telling me I was relieved. I strained for the crocodile tears, but the little face grinned and grinned. It shamed me.

And as I unlocked my houseboat and got ready to go back to bed, I realized that Annie had perhaps suspected that the little ugly feeling of relief and release would be there. We are all, says Meyer, in one way or another, large or small, hidden or revealed, rotten at the core.

Goodbye, Annie girl. I loved you as much as I can love. And I will feel an aching need for you for a long time.

So what if I did put the *Flush* aboard a freighter as deck cargo and go out to the islands? New place. Cleaner skies. Hadn't I been saying sour things about all of Florida going down the drain under the polluting weight of an unending invasion of new residents?

Florida was second rate, flashy and cheap, tacky and noisy. The water supply was failing. The developers were moving in on the marshlands and estuaries, pleading new economic growth. The commercial fishermen were an endangered species. Miami was the world's murder capital. Phosphate and fruit trucks were pounding the tired old roads to rubble. Droughts of increasing severity were browning the landscape. Wary folks stayed off the unlighted beaches and dimly lighted streets at night, fearing the minority knife, the ethnic club, the bullet from the stolen gun.

And yet . . . and yet. . . .

There would be a time again when I would canoe down the Withlacoochee, adrift in a slow current, seeing the morning mist rising at the base of the limestone buttes, seeing the sudden heart-stopping dip and wheel of a flight of birds of incredible whiteness.

On an unknown day down the road ahead, I would see that slow slide of the gator down the mudbank into the pond, see his eye knobs watching me, see a dance cloud of a billion gnats in the ray of sun coming through Spanish moss.

And once again maybe I would be wading and spincasting a pass at dawn, in an intense, misty, windless silence, and suddenly hear the loud hissy gasp of a porpoise coming up for air just a few feet behind me, startling me out of my wits, and see his benign, enigmatic smile as he sounded again.

Wild orchids, gnarls of cypress knees, circlets of sun slanting down onto green marsh water, a half acre of wind moving across the grass flats, fading and dying, throaty gossip of wild turkeys, fading life of a boated tarpon, angelfish—batting their eyelashes—moving coy and elusive between the sea fans, the full, constant, mind-warping, roaring, whistling scream of full hurricane.

Tacky though it might be, its fate uncertain, too much of its destiny in the hands of men whose sole thought was grab the money and run, cheap little city politicians with blow-dried hair, ice-eyed old men from the North with devout claims about their duties to their shareholders, big-rumped good old boys from the cattle counties with their fingers in the till right up to their cologned armpits—it was still my place in the world. It is where I am and where I will stay, right up to the point where the Neptune Society sprinkles me into the dilute sewage off the Fun Coast.

It has too many magic moments that make up for all the rest of it. Too many flashes of a pure delight.

I realized there was no point in trying to sleep. I dug out the tallest glass I owned, found four oranges in the cold locker that had no soft spots, made a tall mourner's breakfast of juice, cracked ice, and Boodles gin, and took it up to my fly bridge forward of the sun deck, swiveled my captain's chair, and put my heels on the starboard side of the control panel. The promise of dawn was a salmon thread over by the Bahamas.

I realized that Annie might never be aboard again, and there was a sudden sickening wrenching sense of loss, a kind of vivid despair. Loss with no dilution of relief.

When the drink was half gone my phone began ringing. I hurried on down, knowing who it was, hoping she wouldn't give up. She was still there.

"Yes?"

"Look. Not like this."

I exhaled a long breath. "You're right. Not like this, Annie."

"Because, plus the rest, we were friends."

"*Are* friends," I said.

"And we keep the friends part."

"You let me know what they say in Chicago."

"I will."

"I hope they offer it and you take it and work your tail off."

"Thank you. But of course it will take some time to turn this over to somebody else. Properly. So . . ."

"We'll see each other again."

"So there'll be time to end this a little better than we did tonight. I was rotten. I'm sorry."

"We're both sorry."

"How come two people can be more than the sum of the two individuals, and then so much less than the sum?"

"Comes of being some kind of human person, Annie."

"Okay, I had to call. Good night or good morning or whatever. Were you asleep?"

"I was topside with a cold drink, thinking long sorry thoughts and watching for the dawn. You?"

"I went down and sat at the water's edge. Long sad thoughts. So I finally had to call."

"Good luck to you, friend."

"Good luck to both of us," she said and hung up.

I went back and nursed the rest of the drink, finishing it when the sun came up into the smutch, oozing red, bulging with the promise of angry burns on the young white hide of the visitors, and another deepening of the tan on the spare leathery bodies of the lizardlike octogenarians on their retirement terraces. I went down and fell into sleep, using it like a giant Band-aid. When the phone woke me at noon I felt an unlikely confusion, a sense of not knowing who I was or where.

twelve

"Where are you?" I asked Meyer.

"In a Holiday Inn in Austin. What I have to report is nothing to report. Except eyestrain." He sounded tired and discouraged.

"You got my message?"

"About the name Jerry Tobin. Yes. My friend is on a sabbatical, but the graduate student who works for him had your letter here for me. I would say it helps confirm what we already suspected."

"I agree."

"Travis, I selected the seven most likely years, making the best possible estimate of the man's age. I found that the Office of the Director of Development and Endowment has a library facility, and they were kind enough to provide me with adequate space and access to their complete collection of yearbooks, from the university facility here and also from the branches in Arlington, Dallas, and El Paso. They also have yearbooks from every other facility in the state. So I can state that the man did not graduate from any division of the University of Texas, or from Texas Christian in Fort Worth, Texas Tech in Lubbock, Texas Wesleyan in Fort Worth, Texas Southern in Houston, Texas Eastern in Tyler, Texas Lutheran in Seguin, Texas A and I at Kingsville, Texas A and M at College Station and Prairie View, East Texas Baptist at Marshall, East Texas State at Commerce, North Texas State at Denton, or West Texas State at Canyon. Or the University of Dallas at Irving."

"Did you—"

"Let me finish. I found lots of people named Lawrence and lots of people named Tobin. I could not match them up in any productive way. I made the assumption that he may have attended without graduating, so I have been poring over the group photographs in all the yearbooks, one hundred and twenty-five, to be precise. One from

East Texas Baptist, an unlikely place and an unlikely year, was missing. If it is possible to wear out a rather large magnifying glass, I have done so. I have had the picture of the man at hand to constantly refresh my memory. Have you ever realized how much most young men look like one another? Just as we, I suppose, look rather alike to them. I have made some reference notes as to certain possibles. Such and such an institution, yearbook for such and such a year, page fifty-six, football squad, second row from rear, fifth fellow from the left. There are about fifteen possibles, and I want to go back to them once I have gotten some transparent plastic for overlays, and a grease pencil to add facial hair in the same pattern as the possibles. I don't expect to be able to eliminate them all. Whatever number is left out of the fifteen, I will assemble vital statistics for each."

"That sounds like a lot of drudgery."

"It is, it is. Research is part of my basic training. The accumulation of facts. One expects it to be dull. When enough facts are assembled, a conclusion can be drawn. That's the interesting part."

"Have we got a choice of conclusions?"

"I will find him, and we will learn who he really is, or was. I will not find him and we can conclude he did not graduate from a Texas institution and probably did not attend one or, if he did, was inactive in extracurricular activities."

"You find that exciting?"

"Interesting, I said. My impression of him was that he had some education. A smattering. About what you'd get if you graduated from a state university after attending on an athletic scholarship, or if you had gone to one of the technical schools."

"How soon will you be done?"

"I might finish up tomorrow. I would be done by now if they'd let me work evenings. But they close up at five, lock the doors, and set the alarms."

"Makes for long evenings."

"Travis, I have learned a very curious thing about television. The sponsors seem to be paying advertising agencies to create commercial spots which criticize competing products. The Lincoln is better than the Cadillac. California Cellars is better than Gallo or Inglenook or Almadén. Headache remedies, stomach acid remedies, deodorants— all of them are claiming to be better or stronger or more lasting."

"So?"

I heard the little sniffing sound he makes when he is impatient at not being understood. "Travis, as an economist with a reasonable grasp on reality, I can tell you that the manufacturers who permit such obvious nonsense are guilty of monumental stupidity. One expects a kind of fumbling inanity from advertising account executives, but not from the men who are paying the bills."

"I'm not following."

"Merchants from the days of prehistory have known that the practice of knocking the product or service of the competition is self-defeating. When Jones, Smith, and Brown own stores on Main Street, and each tells customers that the other two merchants are thieves, within a reasonable period of time it will occur to the customers that all three are selling inferior goods and performing inferior services, and so their businesses will inevitably decline. And, on television, the average consumer pays so little attention to commercials, I would suspect that when a competing product is mentioned by name, it is lodged as firmly in consciousness as the name being advertised. I am sorry to bring it up, but I am appalled at such expensive stupidity. It could only occur in a culture based upon administration by consensus, by committee. One can express resentment only by never buying a product which is held up as being better than another competing product. If enough of us would do that. . . . Forgive the digression. What about Hack's boat?"

"I walked down and took a look. It isn't back in the slip yet. I asked around and they said it was still at the yard."

"How's Anne?"

"Just fine and dandy."

"Is something wrong?"

"I said fine and dandy. What's wrong with that?"

"A forced blitheness. A hollow cheer."

"She's going to be offered a better job, she thinks. Running a much bigger complex in Hawaii."

"And if it is offered, she'll take it."

"Yes."

"Hence the hollow cheer?"

"I guess so."

"I plan to catch a midday flight back to Houston Saturday. Would it be convenient for you to—"

"I'll be there in the afternoon, and see you at the apartment."

"Find out when your flight will be in and call me back, and we can probably meet at the airport."

By four o'clock on an almost bearable Saturday afternoon, we were back in the apartment. The interior air smelled hot, stale, and lifeless. Meyer turned on the air conditioning. The emptiness of the place was a further confirmation of the death of the niece. There was a collection of small pottery cats on a bookshelf, a closet still packed with her clothes.

Meyer had bought himself a shirt in Austin. Gray, in a western cut, with short sleeves and pearl buttons. His black pelt curled up out of the open neck. He sat and read the Xerox copy of the clipping about the death of Miss Doris Eagle.

"No doubt of its being the same man?" he asked.

"None. It really hit Eagle very hard."

"And so that man is out there somewhere," Meyer said, with an all-inclusive wave of his arm. "Eating, sleeping, washing his hands, thinking his thoughts, remembering his women. Let me show you what I've got."

He had narrowed it down to four faces and had photocopies of the groups in which they appeared.

"I tried to get the original negatives," he said, "but because year-books are not reordered or reprinted, after the press run the artwork and photographic work and dummy pages are discarded. I've circled the possibles in red grease pencil. Look at them through the glass. You have to think of them as being Evan Lawrence, twenty years earlier. These seem to match the coloring, shape of the head, placement of the ears and eyes."

I looked at the four. A baseball squad, an intramural track team, members of the theatrical club, and the members of a fraternity. I looked up at Meyer standing over me. "These could all be the same person."

He handed me four file cards. Warren W. Wyatt from Lubbock, Cody T. W. Pittler from Eagle Pass, Coy Lee Rodefer from Corpus Christi, and B. J. Broome from Waco.

"Those were their addresses when they enrolled. Not one of these four got a degree from the universities they were attending when the photographs were taken. If the pictures were larger and clearer, maybe I could eliminate one, two, or all of them. Incidentally, all four went to the University of Texas—Wyatt at Austin, Pittler at El Paso, Rodefer at Austin, and Broome at Arlington. And there is no guarantee that the people in the pictures are correctly identified by name. The lists of names can be incorrect due to transpositions, deletions, and so forth. For example, in this fraternity picture there are thirty-two faces, thirty-three names."

"And maybe he didn't go there."

"I'm inclined to believe he did. Or at least had some connection with it. If I went around saying I went to the University of Heidelberg, sooner or later I would come upon someone who either went there or who knew the city well. It's easier to know than to lie. Dumb persons tell dumb lies. Evan Lawrence didn't strike me as being dumb."

"And he could be one of these four?"

"Say at twenty-to-one odds. Or more. But what were the odds against your learning that he probably was not aboard the *Keynes?* What were the odds against that woman from Venice coming along with her camera and taking a picture which happened to show with sufficient clarity Pogo's left hand? Odds such as that are beyond calculation. Except for coincidence, we would have believed him blown to bits, even after finding out about Norma emptying out her trust. What do we do next, Travis? You're better at this sort of thing than I am. Do we start checking these people out?"

"I think I'd rather see about those Japanese stone lanterns. He said he worked for a man named Guffey who had a place north of Harlingen. He gave the impression it was after he got out of school, but a lot longer ago than when he worked for Eagle Realty. Remember, he said that they won't be needing any Japanese stone lanterns down in that end of Texas for a long time."

"Look for the lanterns?" he said, eyebrows high.

"They're conspicuous. A ranch wife would probably put one in her flower garden. Coarse gray stone, and they usually come in three parts. The four legs, and then the middle part where the candle or light bulb goes—it usually has four openings, about fist size—and then an ornate cap on top, like a pagoda roof, too heavy for anything but a hurricane to blow off. They'd still be at the places where he sold them. Harlingen sounds likely enough; I'll assume Guffey was a name he made up at the moment. But if we go poking around the back roads, we want to try to be a little less conspicuous. What's her van look like? Roger Windham said it was old."

And it was. A heavy-duty GM originally painted a dark blue. Where the paint hadn't been knocked off by the stones of rough roads and the branches of overgrown trails, it was a faded patchy blue. Where it had been knocked off, it was rust. Big steel-belted Michelins, eight ply. I rolled the door up and tried it. The battery was weak, and I didn't think it would ever catch, but it finally did, ragged at first, and then with a healthy roar. The speedometer said five thousand and something, and, guessing it at ten or eleven years old, I didn't know whether it had been all the way around once or twice. It had a dual battery system, a cot, a DC icebox, heavy-duty air conditioning, and a wooden crate of tools. It had an empty water tank, a tiny sink, and a Porta-Pottie.

We went out while the motor was still running and took it ten miles west and ten miles back to give the alternator a chance to pick the batteries up. It was almost full of gas in both tanks, and the oil was up to the line, and the batteries needed no water. But it was loud and rough, with a slight tendency to wander.

After we got back, Meyer said we probably should ask Windham if it was all right to use it, to take it down past Victoria and Corpus Christi into the valley. The papers on it were in the side pocket. The owner was Norma Greene, not Norma Lawrence. He said he had the lawyer's home number.

He caught Windham just as he was heading out for a cocktail party. Windham told Meyer that it was his truck to do with as he pleased, but there might be a question of insurance. The insured was deceased. And insurance companies, in the event of accident, leap upon any excuse to refuse to accept a claim. Just drive very very carefully until Monday afternoon or, better yet, not at all, and by that time he'd have it covered.

Meyer said it would probably be better not to drive it at all. He was tired. His eyes were tired. His mind felt fatigued. He said he felt older than usual. There was little daylight left. He fell asleep in a chair. I thought of going out and getting something to eat, but realized I would set off the alarm system if I went out without knowing the right numbers to punch into the control panel. I went foraging through the cupboards and icebox. I found some wine and some vodka under the sink, a can of chili in the cupboard, and a wrapped slab of rat cheese in the refrigerator. Had a vodka on the rocks, heated the chili with a lot of thin slices of cheese. Roused Meyer and we ate same, in silence. He trudged up to bed. I cleaned up, looked around, and found a paperback by Stephen King about a big weird dog. Took it to bed and read a lot longer than I'd planned to. Very scary dog. Very scary writer. Wondered if he would be able to guess what kind of person Evan Lawrence was: as scary as King's dog, but in a different way.

I kept trying not to think about Anne Renzetti, but the instant I turned the light out, there she was. The thought that kept flashing on and off right in the front of my mind was YOU BLEW IT. YOU BLEW IT. Later on there was another sign, farther back and not as bright, which kept saying YOU'LL NEVER GET A BETTER SHOT AT IT.

At what? Home and fireside? A riding mower for Christmas? A golden retriever who'd ride with his head out the car window, panting?

As the old spinach eater said, "I yam what I yam."

thirteen

There was some red tape to be arranged about the estate and the vehicle registration, so we didn't get out of town in the van until so late on Monday, the twenty-sixth, we got only as far as a place called Robstown, about ten miles west of the Corpus Christi city line. We holed up at a motel on the far side of Robstown, on U.S. 77, and as soon as we got in the room, Meyer started looking up Rodefer in the Corpus Christi phone book.

He found nine Rodefers, but none of them were Coy Lee or C. L. or even C. So Meyer wanted to go right down the list. "We're right near the city. Why not? Why does it have to be lanterns first when we can eliminate this one right away? Or maybe find out it is the right one."

There was no answer at the first Rodefer. As he started to call the next one, I realized I should be doing it. To his obvious relief I took the phone and placed the second call.

"Hello?" A female voice, hesitant, neither young nor old.

"This Miz Rodefer?"

"Well . . . the way you say it, it isn't Rod, it's like Road."

"Ro-defer. Sure, I *knew* that. It's just, I guess, ma'am, I haven't rightly said it in so long, I said it wrong. Mebbe you can h'ep me, ma'am. Long long time back I went to school up to Austin with Coy Lee Rodefer, and I'm over here in a motel next to Robstown, and I was looking in the book to see if old Coy Lee was in the book and he isn't. But there is a bunch of Rodefers and I thought, Well, why not take a chance and see if he's related to them, and so they'd know where he is today. Him and me were on the same runnin' team together."

"Coy Lee, he's my husband's first cousin! What did you say your name is?"

"Travis McGee, ma'am. Just passin' through the area."

"Well, if you were up there in the college with him, then you'd know why he had to drop out."

"I just purely don't know, Miz Rodefer. You see I had to drop out too on account of bad sickness in the family, and I had to go home to take care. I've always promised myself I'd go back someday and finish up, but I somehow just never did."

"What happened was he got so tired and run down and wore out, they thought up there he had that . . . what do they call it? That kissing sickness. I can't think of the name."

"It doesn't come to me either right at the moment."

"Anyway, after they gave him a lot of blood tests it turned out he had the leukemia."

"That's too bad! He was such a strong fella."

"He came on back here and moved into his old room with his folks. He was in and out of the hospital I can't remember how many times. He'd go into revision . . . that doesn't sound right."

"Is it remission, ma'am?"

"That's it! Anyway, it was pure hell on his mama, and I think it was what really turned his daddy to drink. His daddy was my Ben's father's brother. He didn't last a year after Coy Lee died."

"Oh, he died!"

"They both did, Coy Lee and his daddy, not quite a year to the day. His daddy died drunk, rolling the pickup over hisself at three o'clock in the morning. With Coy Lee it was pitiful. He went down to no more than ninety pounds, and he died in the hospital with his mama holding his hand and telling him everything was going to be real fine. I'd just started going with Ben, and he was broke up about it more than I realized he would be. It's sure some terrible sickness, but I hear they can do a lot more for people that get it than they used to be able to do. The thing that was so pitiful was it was the only child they had. His mama she married a man with seven grown children about two years after Coy Lee's daddy killed hisself. What I'll do, I'll tell her a fellow that was a friend of Coy Lee's up in Austin, he called to locate Coy Lee, and I had to tell you what happened to him."

"You tell his mama he was a good boy. He was a good friend, and I'm sure sorry to hear what happened. You tell her that everybody that knew him up there in Austin, they liked him just fine."

"She'll be glad to hear that, and I'll be telling her tomorrow."

"Thanks for helping me out."

"Sorry it had to be such bad news. But that's how it goes."

"It surely does. Good evenin'."

Meyer had been sitting close on the side of my bed to hear both sides of the conversation. He moved away, shaking his head, as I hung up.

No matter how many times you do it, how many times you pretend to be someone you aren't, and you get the good-hearted cooperation of some trusting person, you feel a little bit soiled. There is no smart-ass pleasure to be gained from misleading the innocent. In the country places of the Sun Belt, friendship has a lot of meaning. And when you want to know something, you find out the quickest way you can, even to trading on something that never existed.

We looked into the motel restaurant and decided to try almost anything else we could find. We drove over into the city and found a steak house where they guaranteed they would not, under any circumstances, fry the steak. Over coffee Meyer finally said, "That was depressing, talking to that woman."

"You didn't know old Coy Lee good as I did."

"No jokes, hmm?"

"No good jokes, at least."

"I was wondering what we would do. Suppose we found him in Corpus Christi? What if he was Evan Lawrence and Jerry Tobin and Coy Lee Rodefer? And we appear in front of him in these indigenous clothes, these big hats and twill pants and funny shirts. What then?"

"We try not to appear in front of him at any time."

"Just locate him?"

"And bring him to justice. Like they used to say in the series there with Marshal Dillon. *Gunsmoke*."

"Isn't that going to be exceedingly difficult, Travis?"

"If we never get any more evidence than we have now, which is next door to nothing at all, exceedingly is a mild word."

"So what then?"

"Meyer, for God's sake, we can't lay it all out in advance. We'll play it by ear. Maybe he has been messed up in other things. We might stumble across something that can be proved against him. He seems to like killing women. For money. Maybe he was clumsier some time we don't yet know about. Martin Eagle would like to know where he is, if and when we find him. I just have the feeling that the farther down the back trail we go, the more we'll learn. I am not going to sneak up on the ridge and dry-gulch him. As far as we know right now, he isn't wanted by anybody for anything. Maybe he *didn't* kill four people. Maybe somebody set the charge to kill him, thinking he'd be on your boat that day. Maybe he *was* on the boat. You're supposed to be the logical one, not me."

He managed a smile. "I'm not doing very well, am I? I can't seem to think about it. I want him shot. I want him dead."

Early the next day we were well down into the Valley of the Rio Grande. We went on into Harlingen, which had every fast-food chain either of us had ever heard of, and a lot we hadn't. We found a place to stop and look at the map. The likely counties were Willacy, Hidalgo, Starr, Zapata, Jim Hogg, Brooks, and Kenedy. Lots of grove land down in the valley, more big vegetable farms and ranchlands as you went north.

If this was the area where Evan Lawrence a.k.a. Jerry Tobin peddled his thirty tons of Japanese stone lanterns, they were going to be right out in the weather in plain sight, if you could get close enough to the house. And that was a problem. Out in the ranch and farm country, the houses and barns and sheds were a couple of hundred yards down narrow private lanes.

We needed some kind of a cover story to avoid being shot for trespass. If we got the necessary gear to look like surveyers, we would probably be shot for surveying. Meyer finally came up with something suitable. It involved finding a specimen net for capturing insects and rigging up a specimen box.

We drove up to Raymondville and turned left on State Road 186. By the time we hit the third farm, he had the routine under control.

"Madam, we are working on a project for Texas A and I up in Kingsville. There has been an infestation of Brown Recluse spiders, or fiddlebacks as they are sometimes called. We'd like your permission to check around the foundations of your house and around your outbuildings. We don't have to go inside any building, and we will not damage any plantings. It is a small drab-looking spider with an oblong body. The bite can cause fever, nausea, cramps, and ulceration at the location of the bite. If we pick any up here, we will let you know."

The old blue van looked plausible, and soon we were sweaty enough to look plausible. There were no refusals. The people were not exactly bursting with friendship and good-will, but Meyer's fussy professorial manner seemed to allay most of their suspicion.

We wandered the little roads, country roads, 1017 and 681, and went through towns named Puerto Rico, San Isidro, Agua Nueva, Viboras, Robberson, Guerra. I lost track of the number of stops we made. No stone lanterns. We had a bad sandwich and orange pop in a place named Premont, and an hour later we came upon the first stone lantern. It stood in the front yard of a small white farmhouse just north of a town named Rios, on County Road 1329.

A little round woman with a lot of gold in her smile gave us permission. By prearrangement, Meyer went about his net work, and I said, "Couldn't help noticing your stone lantern there. I had a friend who used to sell those. Maybe you bought it from him."

"Oh, no! We are being here only seis year. Eet wass here."

"Have other people got them too?"

"Very pretty."

"Yes, they are. Anybody else have one that you know?"

She beamed and waved a chubby arm that included the whole world north and west of Rios. "Minny minny peoples haff," she said.

We headed north and turned west at the first intersection. We were in stone lantern country. At the third lantern stop, we encountered a man who had bought one.

"Hell, it must have been fifteen, seventeen years back, she got me to buy that sucker. Young fellow selling them from an old pickup. Real nice young fellow to talk to. The big ones were forty-two dollars cash money, and the little ones were thirty-five. She had to have the big one, naturally. She loved that fool thing. She'd run out on warm nights and put a candle in it, then stand inside and look at it through the screen. It made her happy to see it out there. I used to kid her, saying you could buy a lot of oil lamps and light bulbs for that forty-two dollars."

He was a stringy man in his fifties, baked dry, straw hat tilted forward, his eyes the same washed-out blue as his work shirt. His big hands were permanently curled by hard labor, and the veins in his leathery forearms were fat and blue.

"Do you think she'd remember the salesman's name?"

"Allie died six years ago, friend. On a rainy June day just one day after her forty-fourth birthday. I took her a present but she didn't know me. She didn't know anything at all by then. She was never real well. She didn't have a good heart or good kidneys or good lungs, and they all seemed to go bad at the same time. Don't know why I go on like this. Man doesn't see people all day, he tends to talk their ear off."

"Did you happen to see the salesman?"

"Not up close. Saw him standing there when she came to me to get the money. I thought you fellows were after some kind of spider, but you sound like you're after that lantern salesman."

I laughed in a jolly hollow manner and said, "Two birds with one stone." At that point Meyer came trotting up to us, holding a twist of the netting with great care.

"This is a fiddleback," he said nervously.

"It sure is," I said, and we transferred it to our improvised specimen box. It seemed slow and lethargic. Meyer took out his notebook and wrote down the time and place.

"Could you describe the lantern salesman?" I asked the man.

"Hell, he looked like any other young Anglo around here. But he sure could talk Mexican. I heard him and Allie jabbering away like crazy. I met Allie when I was working down in Vera Cruz a long time back. Prettiest thing I ever saw in my life. I never could get my mouth around that Mexican talk. God knows I tried. She was a real smart woman. Trouble was, I had things to say to her that I never really could say, because she just never did get to have that much American."

"Where did he work out from?"

"I can tell you that. The one she wanted, it had a kind of a gouge in the top of it, into the stone. So he went right away and got a new top. Very obliging of him. He said it was a little less than fifty-mile round trip. He had his stock at a place north of Freer, off State Road Sixteen."

Meyer said, "You have a remarkable memory, sir."

The man smiled and shook his head. "Not really. Out here there aren't so many stopping by you can't remember them all. And Allie did talk to him a long time. I guess it made me kind of curious to look him over good."

We told him how much we appreciated his help. He seemed a little disconsolate at having us go. It meant company was leaving. The land around his buildings looked reasonably tidy, but the quick glance I had at the interior showed a fat brown dog stretched out on a welter of newspapers, and a young turkey pecking at something on the floor beyond it.

A couple of miles down the road, I stopped and Meyer dumped out the Brown Recluse. When he got back in, I asked him if he'd stomped it. He said that he had thought of it but decided that the spider had its rights, and had played its part in a charade reasonably well and at the right time, and anyway it was part of the scheme of things, just like the snail darter, the snow goose, and the ACLU. I reminded him that they were poisonous, and he said that you usually have to provoke something in nature to get it to bite. You have to threaten it or make it think it is threatened. Western sheep ranchers are poisonous, he said, because they believe they are threatened by coyotes, when all scientific data from reliable sources indicate otherwise. Wolves never chased the Russian sleighs, he said. A tarantula bite is less bothersome than a beesting, he said. The more precarious the existence of all living creatures on the planet becomes, he said, the more valuable is each individual morsel of life. I told him he seemed to be getting one hell of a long way from stomping or not stomping a little brown insect, and he told me that the spider is not an insect at all but an eight-legged predacious arachnid of the order Araneae. I asked him if his veneration for life extended all the way from brown spiders to Evan Lawrence; he too was part of the scheme of things. Meyer told me that I had a tendency to put discussions on an emotional basis, thus depriving them of all intellectual interest. I told him I was sure lucky to have him along to straighten me out on all these things.

He studied his notes and said, "Of the four students who could have been Evan Lawrence, we have eliminated one: Rodefer. Of the remaining three, the one most likely to be fluent in Spanish is Cody T. W. Pittler. Eagle Pass was his home town, apparently. On the border. And he went to the branch of the University of Texas at El Paso, also on the border. That, of course, does not eliminate Wyatt and Broome. Nor does it mean that any one of the remaining three could have been Evan Lawrence. All it does mean is that if it took an equal amount of effort to check out Wyatt, Pittler, and Broome, it would be logical to try Pittler first."

"I think Allie was probably a pretty nice woman."

"We should inquire in Freer about a Mr. Guffey, if indeed there is one."

"And change our act, I think."

"To what?" he asked me.

"We don't have to have an act to go around asking where the Guffey place is. And when and if we find it, we'll think of something."

fourteen

Freer was an intersection of three numbered highways. It looked flat and spread-out, with maybe two or three thousand people in it. On the edge of town I saw a farm equipment and supply agency, with a colorful row of tractors out by the shoulder.

I found some shade to park in and went inside. There was a small office and display room, with a maintenance floor out behind it. Meyer wandered over to the line of tractors and stood there, studying them, his cowboy straw shoved to the back of his head, kitchen match in the corner of his mouth, thumbs hooked into the side pockets of his ranch pants. He looked almost—not quite—authentic. But I was glad to see him improvising. He was beginning, in small ways, to enjoy the small arts of deception. As in the old days, before Dirty Bob.

I sauntered in and angled obliquely over to two men leaning against a monstrous piece of yellow equipment. I had no idea what it could be used for. It looked designed for the uprooting of trees and the mashing of small buildings. One was old, dressed in a yellow jump suit. He was the shape of a toby mug, had wild white hair sticking out in all directions, and wore a red embroidered *Bunky* over his left breast pocket. His face was almost as red as his embroidery.

The other man was swarthy and much younger, and huge. Size of a nose guard. Six-seven, maybe, and two sixty, thereabouts. He had a round amiable face and a nose that had been mashed almost flat.

As I came closer I heard Bunky say, "Now I'm not trying to tell you the bank will go for it, Miguel. You know how the times are. What I can't do, honest to God, is go on the paper with you. We're up to our eyeballs on the building here and the floor stock. I know you got a good record, and I'm sure that counts with the bank. But you should go talk to them first. I gave you the figures, the allowance and all."

Miguel muttered something I couldn't hear. They shook hands and Miguel left.

Bunky watched him go and then shook his head, smiled at me, shrugged. "What happens to too many of these farmers, they turn into machinery junkies. They get three dollars ahead, they want to go deep in hock to buy something about half again too big for the piece they're working. Bigger tires. Sit higher. A hundred more horse-power. Then suppose they drop the support level on his crop. He can't meet the payments on all that equipment, and pretty soon he gets foreclosed and loses the land too. And everybody from John Deere to International Harvester helps push them into bigger stuff. Fancy advertising. Know the smartest man in the county? Old Lopez. He's down on the Benavides Road. He's older than me, which means older than God himself. Old Lopez has got three husky sons. He had tractors and cultivators and all that shit. But when the gas price jumped out of sight—it takes eighty gallons to work one acre of land —he sat down on his porch a whole day thinking it over. And then he went right back to the way he used to do it. He works his spread with six mules. He drives the county agent crazy. He's making more money than anybody else in this part of Texas. Now he's got his land all free and clear. Doesn't owe a dime. You take Miguel there that just drove away. If he don't owe two hundred thousand right now today, I'll eat one of old Lopez's mules. Now wouldn't it be funny if you come in here to buy a thirty-thousand-dollar tractor and I turned you off before you could even ask? But I don't think so. You're no farmer. If you want to sell me something, forget it."

"No, sir. What we want to know is, would you know anybody around this area name of Guffey? A farmer, rancher, whatever."

He kneaded his pink chin. "Guffey? Guffey. Guffey. Last name?"

"Last name."

"Know anything else about him that could give me a hint?"

"A long time ago, more than fifteen years ago, he had a young fellow working for him who covered the whole area in a pickup truck, selling those stone Japanese garden lanterns that stand about so high."

"Well, hell yes! That was closer to twenty years ago. Two sizes. My Mabel bought two of the little ones for two corners of her rose garden, and I wired them for her and put the switch on the side porch. Pink bulbs she put in there. Turns them on these days only when company is coming after dark. Nice fellow sold them to us.

Obliging as could be. Toted them to right where she said to put them, and she changed her mind three times. Now who in the world was he working for? Let me think."

"I was told he lived right around here."

"Right around here can cover a lot of land, friend. It's starting to come back. He run off with the daughter. Crazy old coot bought tons of those lanterns. They came into Galveston by ship, and he freighted them on up here. What the *hell* was his name? Hold on, I know somebody that would know. I'll give them a ring."

He went back into the office, and I could see him in there through the glass, talking and laughing. He came out, shaking his head, after a very long conversation.

"There was a lot to that story that I'd forgot. I called a woman that remembers everything forever. Seems that over near Encinal, few miles east of the town on State Forty-four, there was a couple named Larker. She was close to thirty and he was closer to fifty. No kids. Mr. Larker, he worked in Encinal at the automobile agency there. His wife bought one of those lanterns when he wasn't home. And about two months later, he started coming down with the flu at work, and he headed on home, about a fifteen-minute drive, and when he put his car away, he saw that pickup with the stone lanterns in it parked behind a shed. There was a good enough wind blowing so nobody heard him drive in. He tippytoed to one window after another until he looked in the parlor and there they were on the carpet having at it, with her big long legs hooked over his shoulders, and her butt propped up on a pillow her mother had needlepointed for them for their fifth anniversary. Their two pair of pants had been flung aside, and he could hear Betsy Ann crying out over the sound of the wind. Hume Larker, he said afterward he just felt so terrible, what with having a chill from the wind blowing, teeth chattering, he just turned and sat down and leaned his back against the house and cried like a baby, sitting there hugging his knees. Then he got back into his car and drove out, and apparently they never noticed. He drove around for about an hour, and when he came back the truck was gone. Betsy Ann was in the kitchen, and she asked him why he was home so early and he said he was sick. He said he was going to go to bed, but before he went to bed he had one thing he wanted to do and he wanted her to watch him. She tagged along, looking puzzled, and he got a sledge out of the barn and went out to the kitchen garden and, with her watching, he sledged that stone lantern down into gravel. She didn't say a word and she didn't look at him. The next day and the next, he was too sick to go looking for the salesman. He had a high fever and he was out of his head part of the time. Nearly died, his sister told me. He sort of remembered hearing Betsy Ann yelling at somebody to go away. By the time he could rise up out of his bed and load the Remington and go looking for the salesman, the salesman had gone for good. And he had taken Walker Garvey's youngest daughter with him."

"Garvey?" I asked. I felt a presence behind my left shoulder and glanced back and saw Meyer there, listening with a rapt expression. I was glad to see him, because it was beginning to be too much to remember and repeat. But Meyer would remember it, word for word. He has the knack.

"Garvey, not Guffey," Bunky said. "Walker Garvey. Crazy stubborn old coot. Seven kids, all girls. They married and moved out soon as they could, until just Izzy was left. Isobelle. Jumpy little thing about sixteen when she left. Scrawny. Hardly even any boobs yet. Little old lively girl with buck teeth and hair so blond it looked white. Joe the salesman had a way with the ladies of all ages."

"Joe?"

"Wait a minute. It was Larry Joe. That's right. Larry Joe Harris."

"Is Mrs. Larker still in the area?"

"Last I heard. Hume had a stroke about three years ago and it was a bad one. Sixty-eight, I think he was. He lasted about three months. She sold the place to a family named Echeverría. She moved into Encinal, and I think she stays with her mother and takes care of her. The old lady is about eighty and got bad arthritis. You ask around Encinal for Betsy Ann Larker, somebody is bound to know her. Big tall pale woman."

"Is Walker Garvey still living?"

"He's been dead years. I can't even remember what he died of. He wasn't much loss to anybody."

"Where was his place?"

"Up near Cotulla. I think it's still in the family, one or the other of those daughters of his living there, but I don't know the name. I can tell you how to find it. The quickest way is take State Forty-four west to Encinal, get onto I-Thirty-five, and it's nearly thirty miles up to Cotulla. Get off the interstate there and take County Road Four Sixty-eight back southeast. It runs along parallel to the Nueces River. Four or five miles down that road you'll see a couple of houses and some sheds and so on set well back, on your right-hand side. They still call it the Garvey place, I think. Pretty good land there, a couple miles from the river.

"Gentlemen, a pleasure talking to you. Hope I've been of some help. It's coming up on closing time, and I don't stay around here one minute more than I need to."

We walked to the van. It was no longer in the shade, and hot enough inside to melt belt buckles. We talked it over and decided that the motel at Robstown had been comfortable enough and only about sixty miles away, so we decided to call it a day, but halfway there we came upon a motel in Alice that looked just about as good, and they had plenty of room, so we took a pair of singles out in the back wing of the place. The shower was a rusty trickle. The window air conditioners made a thumping roaring rattling sound, and the meat across the street was fried, but otherwise it was adequate. Good beds. Fresh clean linen.

Over a big country breakfast, Meyer said, "Larry Joe Harris. Same man?"

"Unless there's been a lot of people crisscrossing this part of Texas eighteen years ago, selling Japanese stone lanterns."

"That's sarcasm, I assume."

"I just think it's him. I have that gut feeling. The womanizing fits. And Guffey is close to Garvey. He tried to be too entertaining that night aboard the *Flush*. Told us too much, and gave us a good lead. What if he said he'd been selling lightning rods or weathervanes? We could have gone in circles without finding anything. We're narrowing it down."

"It might narrow down to the point where it disappears for good."

"You woke up cheery."

"Norma has been dead for twenty-three days. Did you wake up especially jovial?"

"I woke up trying to grab hold of a dream I had just had about Annie. She was on some sort of platform that was pulling away from me, and I was running, but the harder I ran, the farther away it got. She was waving and smiling. No, I am not especially jovial, and you are not particularly cheery. I feel as if my ordered life had suddenly turned random on me. The ground under my feet has shifted. I want everything to be as it was. But it won't be. Not ever again. Which do you like best, sincerity or sarcasm?"

He gave me a slow smile and the little blue eyes glinted. "On the whole, sarcasm is more becoming. Will we find Betsy Ann?"

"And we will show her the photograph."

We made the eighty miles to Encinal in an hour and a half. I was growing fond of the rugged old blue van. When it got up to speed, it was steady as the Orange Bowl.

I made my inquiries at a gas station just off the interchange. The attendant was a fat bald man in high-heeled boots. As he filled the tank he said, "Well, sure. I guess nearly everybody in town knows Betsy Ann." He looked at his watch. "She'll be going to work pretty soon now. She comes on at eleven and works lunch. You go down that street there, and turn right at the corner, and you'll see it on the right, with parking in front. Arturo's Restaurant. You should want to eat there, it's okay. But don't get the tacos. Get the chicken enchiladas. And they got draft beer."

We parked in front. There was only one other vehicle there, a dusty Datsun. There were beer signs in the windows, a rickety screen door, and three overhead fans down the narrow room. Booths on the right, counter on the left, tables in the back.

A tall woman in a waitress uniform was carrying a cup of coffee to a booth. She gave us a mechanical smile of welcome. She looked to be about fifty. She had long hair tinted an unnatural strawberry-blond shade and combed straight down in a young-girl style which emphasized rather than diminished the effect of the age lines in her pallid face. Under the blue uniform with its white cuffs on short sleeves, white collar, white trim on the pockets, her figure looked slim and attractive.

We took a table in the farthest corner. We had agreed that it would be best to get it over with before the restaurant filled up. She came back with menus. "The lunch special isn't ready yet, but he says it will be in another fifteen minutes. So if you want to have coffee while you wait. . . . The lunch special is a Spanish beef stew."

Meyer by preagreement took over. He is better than I am at this sort of thing. "May we ask you a personal question, Besty Ann?"

She frowned. "Do I know you? How do you know my name?"

"Believe me, we do not want to cause you any grief or any alarm. We want to be your friends."

"I don't understand. What do you want of me?"

"As I said, we want to ask you a personal question. We have to ask it, unfortunately."

"Who are you?"

"My name is Meyer. This is my friend, Travis McGee. We're from Florida. A man killed my niece three weeks ago. We have very little information about him. We're trying to find him by looking into his past."

She looked bewildered. "I don't know anybody killed anybody, mister. You've got the wrong person."

"Just tell us if this is the man you once knew as Larry Joe Harris." He slid the color print out of the folder as he spoke.

She stared at it and made a strange, loud, moaning cry and bent forward from the waist as though she had been struck in the stomach. She put her hand against her mouth.

A man in a white chef's hat came bursting through the swinging door out of the kitchen, a ten-inch knife in his hand.

"¡Que pasa!" he said. "Whassa matta, Betsy Ann?"

"Nothing. It's okay, Arturo."

"What do you mean, nothing?"

"Everything is okay, really."

He looked at her and at us with suspicion and went back to the kitchen. A young man with a beard was leaning out of a booth to look at us.

She tottered, then sat quickly in one of the other chairs at the table, eyes closed, and said, "Sorry. Sorry."

Meyer covered her hand with his. "I'm really sorry."

She took a deep breath and opened her eyes. "Where's the picture? I want to see it again. Thanks." She leaned over it and studied it. "He's kind of better looking than when he was young. I've told myself he died, or he would have got in touch somehow. But he didn't. I knew he never would. Sure, that's Larry Joe Harris. Is that all you want from me?"

"Yes. And we're grateful."

"He killed your niece?"

"It seems probable."

"It was eighteen years ago. How did you know about him and me?"

"We talked to some people over in Freer."

"Sure. That's where Hume's damn sister lives. That's the worst thing he ever did to me, telling his sister what happened with me and Larry Joe, telling her he looked through the window. I suppose you could say I did something bad to him too. All right. But telling his sister was like putting it on a billboard in living color in the middle of town. I just wasn't that kind of a person. I was twenty-three when I married Hume Larker and he was forty-three. I loved that man. You don't want to listen to all this dirty laundry."

"Betsy Ann, we want to learn as much as we can about Larry Joe Harris."

"He came by with those Japanese lanterns, and I thought they were just lovely. I got Hume to buy me one for the garden. I thought the salesman was a nice boy. I guessed he was twenty-two or twenty-three. He had a nice smile and he was polite. One morning around eleven o'clock, about a month later, he came by and asked me how I liked the lantern. I said I liked it fine. He said he sold lanterns and he read palms. I said that was nice, but I didn't have any money for palm reading. He said he would read mine free, right there in the doorway. So I held it out and he took me by the wrist and studied it and then smiled into my eyes and he said that he could read in my palm that I was soon to have a love affair. I said I was married. And he said it was going to happen very very soon. He just hung onto my wrist and smiled at me, and he walked me right back through my own house. And . . . it happened. I was like a person in a dream. You know those dreams where something is happening and you can't stop it? I wasn't that kind of a woman. He should have known that. But I guess he knew something else about me that I'd never known. He came back to the house eight more times while Hume was off working. I know the number because I counted. And we hardly ever had anything to say to each other. It was always just like the first time. I would say to myself I was going to tell him off next time he came by, and when that old pickup came banging into the drive I would get all pumped up to tell him no, I wouldn't, we shouldn't, but he would take my hand and I would go right along with him like some dumb kid. And I must have been years older than him then. He had power over me. I don't know what it was. When Hume went out to find him and kill him, I hoped he would, because Larry Joe had ruined my marriage. But Larry Joe had already took off with Izzy Garvey. Just a dumb little school kid, and she ran off with him, taking all the money Walker Garvey had hid in the house and just about everything else wasn't nailed down. Where is Larry Joe?"

"We don't know. Where did he come from originally?"

"Like I said, we hardly said a word to each other. All the rest of the time we lived there, people stared at me and whispered. That damned sister of Hume's. You're a nice man, Mr. Meyer. I'd tell you anything I know that would help. But I don't know anything. Every time I think about it, I feel so damn dumb. I could live a million years and still never know how that could happen to me that way. And the hell of it is, Mr. Meyer, if he came in right now and smiled at me and took me by the hand, I think he could lead me right off wherever he wanted."

"I do appreciate your being so open and honest with us."

"I hope you find him. You should do with him like they do with witches and vampires. Pound a stake right through his black heart."

"You have no idea where he went when he left?"

"No, and neither did the law. Walker Garvey called them in on it first thing. They left with over two thousand dollars from under a loose board in the floor of his closet, some watches and some guns, and some sterling silver flatware that had come down from Izzy's grandmother on her mother's side. And of course, the pickup truck, which was found, I heard, in Abilene weeks and weeks later."

"And the girl never came home?"

"Never even wrote."

A group of men came into the restaurant, talking loudly and laughing. She got up quickly.

"I don't know anything that would help you. Really. And I'd just as soon not talk about it any more."

"Thank you for everything you told us," Meyer said. "I know how hard it must have been for you, remembering it."

Her face softened. "It was a long long time ago." She hurried off to take orders from the new arrivals. When she came back toward the kitchen, we signaled to her and ordered the Spanish beef stew. When she waited on us she was polite but remote. It was as though the conversation never had happened.

fifteen

It was a quick twenty-eight miles to the Cotulla exit. In Cotulla—which looked to be twice the size of Freer—State Road 97 went straight, and we turned off on little old 468, narrow and lumpy.

We stopped twice to ask about the old Garvey place, and at the second stop we got explicit directions and were told to look for the name Statzer on the rural mailbox. That was one of old Garvey's daughters, they said. Christine.

The Statzer drive was about four hundred yards long, and the buildings were spread out on a long knoll. Kids and dogs came swarming out of the bushes. The dogs looked big and dangerous, but the little kids whapped them across the side of the nose and chased them back out of the way.

A chubby blond woman came out on the porch, shaded her eyes, and shouted, "Who you looking for?" She wore jeans and a T-shirt advertising Knotts Berry Farm.

"Christine Statzer?"

"That's me. What's it about?"

"Isobelle Garvey."

"Izzy?" She plunged down the three steps and came trotting to the car as we were getting out. "Is she alive? Where is she?" All the little kids were standing around, wide-eyed.

"I don't know where she is," Meyer said. "We came to ask about her."

The animation went out of her face. "So who is asking?"

"My name is Meyer. This is my associate, Mr. McGee. He is helping me look for the man we think married and then killed my niece. When he was using the name Larry Joe Harris, the same man is reported to have robbed your father and run away with your sister."

She tilted her head to the side and frowned. "Friend, that was eighteen damn years ago! That ain't exactly a red-hot trail you're following."

"The more we can learn about him, the better chance we have of finding him. We thought you might be willing to give us what help you can."

She shooed the children away and led us up onto the long deep porch. "They aren't all mine," she said. "Summertime, two of my sisters bring their kids up from Laredo for me to look after. It all evens out sooner or later. Set."

Meyer sat in a rocker. She sat on a bench and I sat on the porch railing. There was a mother cat with a basket of kittens under the bench. Three geese walked across the side yard, angling their heads to peer up at us.

"Papa didn't know a thing about Larry Joe. The way he found him, Papa went over there to Galveston when they wired him about those damn Jap lanterns coming in on a freighter. Do you know about the lanterns?"

"Your father got mad at a garden-supply dealer?" I said.

"Right. He got mad easy and often. He tried to import a dozen and then fifty, but thirty tons was the least he could take. He got the license and went ahead with it, and by the time they came in, he had almost forgot about them. So he went over and arranged for them to be trucked right here to the farm. On the way back, Papa picked up Larry Joe, hitchhiking, and got onto the problem of the thirteen hundred garden lanterns, all of them in three pieces, and this Larry Joe told him he could sell anything to anybody anywhere, and they struck a deal. I must say that everybody liked him. When I met him, I liked him fine. At that time I'd been married almost a year, and my first baby was beginning to show. You see, Izzy and me, we were the two youngest of the seven. And when I left the place to move in with Burt and his folks, just Izzy and Papa were left here."

Meyer slid the photograph out of his folder and handed it over to her. She studied it. "Must be real recent. He's forty here if he's a day. Fine-looking man. Who's that beyond him?"

"Norma. My niece."

"She's blurred but she looks pretty. Anyway, it looked like Papa had made a good choice, because Larry Joe surely unloaded those weird lanterns. He must have put ten thousand miles on that old pickup. The people that bought them made a real good buy, if you like that kind of thing. He got rid of all but about a dozen. They're still out there in one of the sheds, I think. I remember seeing them a couple of years back. Maybe Burt moved them, I don't know. Papa sicked the cops onto Larry Joe. I guess the trouble was that Papa always had too many deals going. He was always taking off to check out something he owned some kind of a piece of. And that meant that Izzy and Larry Joe were here alone probably once too often. We all really loved Izzy, all us sisters. She was the best of the lot, believe me. She was cute and warm and funny and loving. And just a kid. You know? Sixteen. Too young to really know what kind of man he was. After they'd been gone some time we heard of two situations where he was getting an extra bonus along with the pay for those lanterns. Some woman down near Encinal, and another one above Catarina. And if it came out there was two of them, you can be pretty sure there must have been ten more being so careful it never came out."

"Your father must have been very upset."

"He was like a crazy person. He never could figure out how Larry Joe knew about the money under the floor, because he'd never let on to any of us he kept that kind of cash money in the house. They took two gold watches out of Papa's desk, and they took the sterling silver flatware that came down from my grandma. And the pickup truck, which turned up in a used-car lot in Abilene weeks later. It turned Papa meaner than a snake. Not that he was exactly cheerful beforehand. He stayed sour until the day he died. Mom died when Izzy was three, wore down from having all us girls. Look, I'm telling you things. Tell me more about Larry Joe Harris."

"When he married my niece earlier this year, his name was Evan Lawrence. Five years ago, when he ran away with the sister of a real-estate broker in Dallas, his name was Jerry Tobin. She was killed in an accident near Ingram, when the car hit a tree and burned and he was thrown free. We don't know who he really is yet. We're trying to find out."

She got up suddenly and walked to the end of the porch. She stood by the railing with her back to us, then turned around and snuffled and knuckled her eyes.

"It fits too good," she said tearfully.

"How do you mean?" I asked.

She walked slowly back toward us and sat down. "Four years ago we had a rain here you wouldn't believe. A hurricane came in off the Gulf and must have dropped sixteen inches here on Webb County. There's a creek over there—you can't see it from here—it runs down into the Nueces and it's sometimes a trickle and sometimes dry. It was a river all by itself when that rain came, and it carved out new banks, and afterward one of my eldest sister's kids, she came running to the house talking about bones sticking out of the gravel bank. I went and looked and called the authorities. The experts dug it out. It had been buried near the creek about two or three feet down. They estimated it had been there ten to twenty years. The leg bones and one arm was gone, and so they couldn't tell how tall it had been. The experts from the state said it was a female from twelve to twenty years old. They found a couple of scraps of fabric. The trouble was that Izzy had never had any cavities that had to be filled, and she'd broken just one bone in her life, and that was a bone in her leg, and nobody ever found the leg bones. They had washed on down into the Nueces and washed away. The skull was stove in the back kind of like she'd been hit with the flat of a shovel. We sisters all got together and talked it over. Nobody could prove that the remains were Isobelle, and nobody could prove they weren't. And there was, of course, the note she left Papa. Something like, Please forgive us, we're in love, we're running off to get married, wish us happiness. We could understand running off, because every one of the rest of us couldn't hardly wait to get out of this house and away from him. We talked it over, and it just didn't seem natural he'd kill her before they even got started. Three of us out of six had met and talked to Larry Joe, and we all liked him. What we decided, there's a track where you can drive down and park in a grove by the creek, and couples sneak in there. So probably it was somebody else, we said. But we hadn't heard from her, not once in eighteen years, and we all loved her and she loved us all. And from what you tell me about him . . ."

She buried her face in her hands. She cried silently, shoulders shaking. Meyer hitched his rocker closer and patted her shoulder. He is a good patter. He isn't awkward about it. And, like the veterinary who can quiet jumpy animals with his touch, Meyer has good hands for patting and comforting.

She turned a streaming face toward him. "I think I knew it all along. I think I knew it even before the time it rained so hard." She hopped up and ran into the house, saying in a smothered voice, "I'll be back in a minute."

It was closer to ten. The geese went by again, looking us over with beady suspicion. A kitten crawled over the side of the basket and sprawled mewling on the porch floor. Meyer put it back where it belonged, and the mother cat seemed to smile at him.

The children came racing by, all yelling, the dogs in tongue-lolling pursuit. After the sound died, I could hear a meadowlark in the distance, an improbable sweetness.

She came out smiling and embarrassed. "It was a long time ago. I didn't expect it to break me up like that."

"We understand," Meyer said. "Can you tell us anything at all about the man which would help us look for him?"

"Like what kind of thing?"

"His likes, dislikes, skills, habits."

"Let me think. I saw him like three times, altogether it wouldn't be an hour. Papa said he was a real good shot with a rifle. I don't know how Papa found that out. Oh, and he spoke good Mexican. All of us down here in south Texas have some, but he had a lot more than most. I get along, but he went too fast for me. There's another thing, but I don't know as it means anything. We've always had dogs, and Izzy told me the dogs didn't like Larry Joe at all. The hair on their backs would stand right up. Izzy said it made him mad the dogs didn't like him. She said he liked to have everybody like him, everybody and everything."

She decided to show us the lanterns, and she walked out back to the sheds. We followed. She opened the third one and peered in and beckoned to us. When my eyes were used to the dim light inside the shed, I could see the dozen or so lanterns clumped close together in the corner, standing there like little stone dwarfs in conical hats. They were a murky green-brown, and the vines had grown in through the breaks and splits in the old boards and wound around them, in and out of the oval holes where the light would shine out of them at night.

"That's all there is left. He certainly sold one hell of a lot of stone lanterns. I didn't think anybody could sell that many. I thought it was another one of Papa's crazy ideas. You want a lantern?"

"No thanks," Meyer said hastily. "Nice of you to offer."

As she walked us to the car, she said, "If you should find him, could you let us know, me and my sisters? You write me and I'll tell them. My oldest sister named her youngest Isobelle. She's thirteen now, and she looks so much like Izzy used to, it breaks my heart to look at her."

As we went down the long drive I glanced in the rearview mirror and saw her back there, hands on her hips, a small plump figure in a wide rural land, encircled by kids and dogs.

"Eagle Pass?" I asked, glancing over at Meyer. He nodded agreement and sat there, arms folded, behind a wall of silence. When I came to a suitable place, I pulled over and looked at the map. Big Wells, Brundage, Crystal City. Maybe a hundred miles. A hundred miles of silence. A hundred years of solitude.

But it was only about thirty miles of silence. "Could you have believed this about him the night the four of us had dinner?"

"It would have taken some convincing," I replied.

"Yet now you believe he killed Izzy?"

"Of course. And Doris Eagle and Norma and maybe a few we haven't come across. Or more than a few."

"Motive?"

"I think my guess would be that he is a hunter. Women are the game he specializes in. He is a loner. A rare kind of loner, a man who seems affable, agreeable, gregarious, fun to have around. That is his act. That is his camouflage suit. That's the way he comes up on the blind side, upwind, every move calculated. Not every stalk has to end in death, Meyer. Betsy Ann was a practice stalk, no shell in the chamber. He got close enough to reach out and touch the game. The money is important to him only because it gives him the freedom to keep hunting. I have heard the same crap a couple of times from some of my delayed-development macho friends who go out and shoot things they have no intention of eating. 'My God, Travis, I was in love with that elk. The most beautiful damn thing you ever saw in your life. Stood there in the morning light, never knowing there was a soul within a mile of him. Raised his head and I put the slug just behind the shoulder, blew his brave heart to shreds. I tell you truly, I went up to him and squatted beside him, and I stroked his hide and I had tears in my eyes, he was so noble!'

"I think our buddy Larry Joe/Evan/Jerry must have some of the same bullshit running in his bloodstream. I think that when he mounts one of his victims-to-be, the idea that he is going to one day kill her dead gives him a bigger and better orgasm. In fact, he might be unable to make it unless he knows that's going to happen to her, at his hand. Murmurings of love on his lips, and murder in his damn black heart."

"Blackbeard," he said. "And other men down through history."

"Jack the Ripper?"

"No. That's quite a different motivation, I think. He wanted the world to know that murder had been done, that the evil women who sold their bodies had been punished by an agent of the Lord. We know of three possible victims of Larry Joe/Evan/Jerry spread over eighteen years. In no case was it labeled murder."

"So maybe that is part of the game."

"If it is, it requires that the game be played differently every time. Otherwise there is a pattern. . . . Hah!"

"Hah what?"

"Let me think a bit."

He thought for about twenty miles and finally said, "I thought I had an inspiration, but I can't make it work. It struck me that maybe he had a very good reason to eliminate Evan Lawrence, the name and the identity, along with Norma. What could that reason be? That possibly, as Evan Lawrence, the hunt had not gone too well with the victim he dispatched before he met Norma. Maybe there was a trail left which someone might be shrewd enough to follow—just as we're trying to follow him now—and if that did happen, it would end right there when the *John Maynard Keynes* blew up. A dead end. Justice done. But actually, it would be a convenience to him to drop an identity. I would imagine he had another one all set to slip into."

"He could buy identities in Miami as easy as he could buy explosives."

"Travis, there is one thing about him we should keep in mind. He does really look like a great many other forty-year-old men. Driving around Houston I saw at least a half dozen men who, on first glance, looked like Evan Lawrence. Average height, square face, tan, standard haircut, no distinguishing marks. A pleasant expression. Bigger hands than average, thicker through the neck and shoulders. Remember, I found a great many yearbook pictures which looked as if they could have been Evan Lawrence. I am saying that he can disappear into the people pool the way a trout can rise and gulp a bug and slide back down out of sight in the depths. Money makes the disappearance easier. Money diverts suspicion. Money can give a false impression of respectability."

"So what good are we going to do in Eagle Pass?"

"Maybe he started as Cody T. W. Pittler. And if so, maybe we can find out what turned him into a hunter."

"There we go again, Meyer. The old argument."

"Which one?"

"You start with the assumption that everybody is peachy, and then something comes along and warps them. You start with a concept of goodness, and so what we are supposed to do, as a society, is understand why they turn sour. Understand and try to heal. I start with the assumption that there is such a thing as evil which can exist without causation. The black heart which takes joy in being black. In almost every kind of herd animal, there is the phenomenon of the rogue."

"If he *is* Pittler, we'll find something unusual about his boyhood."

"You're sure of that?"

"Just as sure as I am that I learned some time ago what it was in your past that gives you a recurrent streak of paranoia."

"Now *hold* it!"

"Don't be insulted, Travis. That flaw is useful to you. It keeps you constantly suspicious. And thus it has probably kept you alive."

"Up till now."

sixteen

From Eagle Pass in Maverick County, across the river from Piedras Negras, the Rio Grande drops seven hundred and twenty-six feet in a few hundred miles until it flows into the Gulf below Brownsville at Brazos Island.

There is a deceptive illusion of lushness near the riverbanks, but for the most part it is a burned land of scraggly brush, dry hills, weed, lizard, cedar, and salty creek beds that slant down from the Anacacho Mountains to the north. To the northeast is Uvalde, where John Nance Garner lived and died in a broad and pretty valley, noted in his declining years only for his brief statement about the value of the office of the Vice-President of the United States. "It's about as much use as a pitcher of warm spit," he said.

Here all along the valley from Cameron and Willacy counties on the Gulf through Hidalgo, Starr, Zapata, Webb, Dimmit, Zavala, and Maverick, the American citizens of Mexican ancestry have, through the exercise of their right to vote, taken control of county functions: school boards, zoning, police and fire protection, road departments, library services, county welfare, and all the other boards and commissions which spring full grown from the over-fertilized minds of the political animals. This has been a slow and inevitable process for fifty years, and it is understandable that during this time most of the Anglos have been squeezed out of participation in county government. Some of those squeezed out were doubtless of exceptional competency. But so are some of the new ones. And the world keeps turning, and just as much money finds its way into the wrong pockets as under the old regime.

Sergeant Paul Sigiera saw us on Thursday morning at nine thirty after a twenty-minute wait in his outer office. There was room in his office for a gray steel desk, three straight-backed oak chairs without arms, and two green filing cabinets. He was in his thirties, in short-sleeved, sweat-darkened khakis. He had black bangs down almost to his eyebrows, anthracite eyes, and a desperado mustache. The small window was open and a big fan atop the file cabinets turned back and forth, back and forth, ruffling the corners of the papers on his desk and giving a recurrent illusion of comfort.

"Friends," he said in a Texican twang, "the goddarn compressor quit again, and it is hot as a fresh biscuit in heah. They don't fix it quick, I'm gonna assign me out to patrol and ride around with the cold air turned on high. Now what was it you wanted?"

"We're from Florida," I said. "My name is McGee and this is my friend Professor Meyer, a world-famous economist. Perhaps, Sergeant, you remember reading in the paper about Professor Meyer's boat being blown up in the Atlantic Ocean just off Fort Lauderdale on the fifth of this month."

"I maybe do remember something."

"Three people died and no bodies were recovered. We have been trying to trace the person responsible, and there is a faint chance that he may have lived here as a young man before he went off to the University of Texas. He may have even been born here. His name is, or was, Cody T. W. Pittler."

He studied us. His smile was amiable. "Before I come to my senses and come back home here, I worked Vice in Beaumont, and I saw the underside of everything, and I heard every scam known to mankind. You come on very smooth and reliable-like, just like every good scam does. So you fellas just empty out all the ID out of your wallets and pockets right here in front of me. Hang onto the money and the wallets, and I'll just poke around with the rest of it. Now if you'd just as soon *not* do that, you can get on up and leave and I'll go on to the next customer."

He took his time. He went through Meyer's little stack of paper and plastic first. "What were you doing in Canada, Professor?"

"Giving a series of lectures. My boat with my niece aboard was blown up while I was up there. The *Miami Herald* called me to tell me about it and ask questions. I flew back as soon as I could get a reservation."

"Who do you work for?"

"Myself. I give talks, do consulting work, write papers."

"What kind of address is this?"

"I have no address actually. That's the slip at Bahia Mar where my boat has been moored for quite a few years. I lived aboard."

"So your house got blown up."

"That's right."

"When I was a little kid my gramma's house burned up. She lost everything. For years after, she'd remember something and then start crying because she'd know it went up in flames too."

"It is . . . difficult," Meyer said.

"This credit card here. What's the limit on it?"

"Limit?"

"How much can you charge on it?"

"I don't really know. I think it's five thousand."

He looked at the picture on Meyer's driving license, holding it up as he looked carefully at Meyer. He nodded, pushed the little pile back toward Meyer, and began on mine.

He started with the license and the comparison, then read the license. "What does a salvage consultant do, McGee?"

"Advises people about how to go about salvaging something."

"Underwater?"

"Sometimes. And I do salvage work on a contingency basis, a percentage of recovery."

After a few more casual questions, he pushed my stack back and I stowed it away.

"Now let's get a couple of things straight that bother me some," he said. "You are coming down here into my back yard looking for somebody that killed three people."

"I guess you could put it that way," Meyer said.

"What other way is there, Professor? And so that makes you some kind of amateur detectives, don't it?"

"I guess we are doing what a detective would do."

"Why don't you leave it up to the people who know what the hell they're doing? You may be messing up a professional investigation. Ever think of that?"

"There isn't any investigation. At least, not in the way . . ." Meyer paused and shrugged and dug into his portfolio and took out the Xerox sheets of the clippings from the paper.

Sigiera read the account. "So this Pittler is some kind of terrorist?"

"We believe Pittler could be the Evan Lawrence that was reported killed in the explosion, along with his wife, who was my niece, and Captain Jenkins, my friend."

"No terrorists?"

"No terrorists," I said. "And three hundred thousand missing from the woman's estate, cleaned out before they went to Florida."

"It says here they were newlyweds."

"And so they were."

"How'd you people come up with that name?"

Meyer explained about the yearbooks, and the days of studying the pictures. He showed Sigiera the color print of Evan Lawrence. "Good-looking man. Doesn't mean much, though, does it? I caught me a guide last year, pretty as a movie actor. He'd led three groups of *braceros* across the river up near Quemado and killed them, every one, for the poor pitiful pesos they had left after paying him. Eleven bodies we found in a ditch with stones piled on them. And that killer had eyelashes you wouldn't believe, and if you looked right at him, he blushed." He pulled his wet shirt away from his chest, and said, "Question. What do you do if you find him?"

"Hold him for the authorities," I said.

"A salvage consultant doesn't have to do all that paperwork with licenses and all that, and he doesn't have to report to the law every time he enters a new territory. McGee, are you hired out to this professor?"

"We've been close friends for many years," Meyer said with enough indignation to be convincing.

Sigiera picked up the card with the name and address Meyer had gotten from the university records. "Set still," he said, and headed out of the room, leaving the door open.

He was gone almost forty minutes. Time dragged. The fan made a clicking sound. An insane mockingbird played its endless variations in a live oak outside the window. It was too hot for conversation.

When he did come back, it was obvious that something had sobered him. He had a file folder in his hand, a buff folder of the type where the sheets are fastened at the top with metal tabs that come up through two holes in the sheets and are bent over. The metal fasteners were rusty.

"Had to go over to the courthouse annex to get this," he explained. "There was a card on it here because it's still an open file. It's still an open file because I think we're looking for the same fella." He checked the name again. "Cody Tom Walker Pittler, who, if he's living, was forty-two years old the twenty-fourth of this month. And what we want him for, it happened twenty-two years ago last month. I was a little kid then, but I can remember hearing about it because it was something dirty. You know how little kids are. Everybody whispered about it that summer. First, let's double-check on him being the same one."

He slipped a photograph out of the file. A boy of about seventeen stood grinning at the camera. He was in football togs, helmet under his arm, hair tousled. The young Evan Lawrence, we agreed.

"High school," Sigiera said, "before he went away. Before he had the trouble."

He seemed thoughtful and in no hurry, and we made no attempt to push him. He flipped pages, read for long minutes.

He slapped the folder shut. "It's all in our damn cop language," he said. "The decedent, the angle of entry, the alleged this and that. Too many words. That's the trouble with the law lately. Too many words. Too many writs. Too many pleas. We can live with it. We have to live with it. But sometimes it gets a little scratchy.

"Here's what happened. Cody was apparently a normal kid. No juvenile record. No problems. His father, name of Bryce Pittler, owned a small contracting business that did foundations, put in septic tanks, and so on. Had a yard and a little warehouse and three transit-mix trucks. Worked hard at it and did okay. When Cody was about thirteen and his sister, Helen June, was eighteen, their mother died sudden. She caught the flu and it went into pneumonia and she tried to keep right on going no matter what, and they got her into the hospital too late. Bryce Pittler waited two years and then he married a twenty-five-year-old woman that worked in the office for him. Her name was Coralita Cardamone, half Mexican, half Italian, and she was supposed to be one very hot number around town at that time. If he hadn't up and married her so fast, his friends would maybe have had a chance to warn him off her. A year after they were married, that would be when Cody was sixteen or thereabouts, one of the big building supply outfits from Houston came down to all these little places along the river, buying up small contracting firms. They gave Bryce Pittler an offer he couldn't refuse, because it gave him a good piece of money, and they kept him on to run it the way he had before. They did that with the other outfits they bought, and some of the ex-owners turned out to be good managers and a lot didn't.

"Bryce Pittler turned out to be one of the good ones, so what they did after not too long was to make him a regional manager, covering all the way from Brownsville to El Paso. The daughter, Helen June, got married and moved out. Bryce Pittler had to be away three and four nights a week. That left Coralita and the kid alone in the house. I don't know how they got started, but bet your ass it wasn't the kid's idea. He thought his old man was absolute tops. They were close. But it was going on. They interrogated Coralita's best friend, a woman named"—he flipped the folder open, turned a few pages—"Leona Puckett, who said Coralita had told her about the whole affair. Leona said she had begged Coralita to stop with the kid because it was a mortal sin. Apparently when the kid got back after his first year in college, they picked right up again, just like they probably did whenever he came home for vacation. She was a very ripe woman, and they say she never got as much as she needed, and from what Leona reported, the kid was so well hung she just couldn't bring herself to give it up. So it was the old old story, except it was the traveling man that came home to find his wife in bed with his son. He heard them and went and got his pistol, the one he'd taught the boy to shoot. From the coroner's report, the woman was on top, and the headboard of the bed was against the wall opposite the kid's bedroom door. Maybe he didn't even know it was his son under there when he nailed her with one shot right to the base of the skull. She was instantly dead in mid-stroke. There were signs of a struggle. A chair tipped over. Bryce Pittler was on the floor, still alive, with a bullet that had gone through his lower right chest at an upward angle, nicked a big artery, and lodged against his spine. The pistol was near his right hand. The wound was consistent with what could have happened if they struggled for the gun. Pittler never came out of it. A neighbor walking his dog in the yard next door heard two shots, and then as he was wondering whether to phone it in, a car came roaring out of the drive and turned north. He phoned it in. Pittler died on the table. Never said a word. They had a double service. There was an all-points bulletin out. The law looked, but not very hard. I don't think the kid was running from us as much as he was running from what happened. I mean, that's about as rough as it can get for a kid. It's like in those old Greek plays. The neighbor recognized the profile of the kid driving the car as it passed the streetlight. And he hasn't been seen since. Here's a picture of the woman."

I looked at it and handed it to Meyer. Five-by-seven black-and-white glossy of a slender girl standing by a boat pulled up on a rocky beach. You could see the trees on the hazy far shore. She had turned to look back over her left shoulder, to smile at the camera. Her face looked small and sweet under the heavy weight of dark hair. Her smile was provocative. Her hips were rich and vital in taut white slacks below the narrowness of her waist. It was a starlet pose, hip-shot, canted. I wondered if Meyer was as surprised as I was to see how young she looked.

"So let's say Coralita started making it with the kid when he was seventeen. It wouldn't be any big problem to get him started. Kids that age don't think of very much else. So she would have him whenever she could when he was eighteen and nineteen and twenty. He must have felt real guilty about not being able to stop. A good strong boy that age could give Coralita a pretty good run. Maybe she tried to end it too. Who knows? But the old man would be away, and they would be alone in the house, eat supper, watch the TV, maybe try not to look at each other. Go to bed. Each one thinking of the other one in the other bedroom, both of them getting hornier and hornier. Both of them with the perfect excuse. What harm can one more time do? Who's to know? Then one or the other coming cat-foot down the dark hall, sliding warm into the bed, all arms and mouths and groans and shudders."

He shook his head.

"Human sexuality. A hell of an engine. Let it get out of control, and it can kill. You ever hear about the doctor that got asked to speak to the PTA about human sexuality? No? He went home and told his wife he was going to talk to the PTA and she said what about, and he didn't want to get into some kind of discussion with her about what he should or shouldn't say, so he told her he was going to talk to them about sailing. She was out of town the day he gave the speech, and when she got back a friend came running up to her and said, 'Mary, your husband gave the most wonderful talk to the PTA yesterday! You should be very proud of that man.' The wife stared at her and said, 'I don't understand. George just doesn't know anything about it. He only tried it twice in his life, and once he got motion sick and the second time his hat blew off.'"

After our dutiful and politic laughter, Meyer said, "What you are telling us about Cody and Coralita, Sergeant, is that you don't see them as evil people."

"What's evil? They got thrown together. She had the hots and he was just a kid. They were weak and they were stupid, and they happened to get caught. Maybe the best answer would have been if Bryce Pittler had killed them both and then himself. Not because of the punishment or anything like that, but just to keep from turning Cody loose on the world. You talk about psychology, I don't know shit from Shinola. All I know as a law officer is that there would be no way in God's world Cody T. W. Pittler could ever feel okay about himself. And the worst crimes I get are the ones done by people who are trying to punish themselves. I think they want to be dead, and they can't go at it direct, so they keep circling it, giving it a chance to happen."

All of a sudden there was a coughing roar that steadied into a loud hum, and cold air began coming out of the vents in the side wall. Paul

Sigiera jumped up and closed the small window. He went and stood in front of the vents and bared his chest and said, "Ahhhhh. Finally."

"We've taken up a lot of your time," Meyer said.

He turned and shrugged. "This is Thursday morning, friend. The quiet time. Last weekend's wars have been ironed out. The troops are regrouping. Tomorrow night there'll be some skirmishes, and by Saturday the fire fights will start and I'll be busy as a little dog in a big yard. This has been kinda interesting."

"For us too," I said. "One question. Did you develop a set of prints?"

"Sure did. Nice and clear. Beer bottle, bathroom glass, countertop, lots of good surfaces. They must have gotten a lot of sets of his and then picked the best and classified them and sent them in to FBI Central records. The theory is he gets picked up for something and the prints go in and they are cross-indexed in some damn way, and they identify him—sooner or later. It used to work better than it does now. But it didn't work too well, I hear, way back when."

"What happened to the car?"

"From the file they had hopes they could trace the kid that way. It was an almost new DeSoto, off white. It turned up finally near Alpine. It was at the bottom of a steep cliff out of sight of the highway. A backpacker reported it." He flipped the folder open again. "Says here they estimate it had been down there six weeks. I don't know how they worked that out. There was no body near it or in it. It was a place where there was a kind of scenic lookout, where he could have got out and pushed it and let it roll over the edge."

I looked questioningly at Meyer. He knew what I meant. He gave a shrug of acquiescence. "What if, using the name Larry Joe Harris, he killed a young girl over in Cotulla eighteen years ago? What if, five years ago, using the name Jerry Tobin, he ran off with a girl from Dallas and killed her in a fake automobile accident down in the hill country? What if, as Evan Lawrence, he married Professor Meyer's niece and blew her and two other people to bits. He made over two thousand dollars off the killing in Cotulla, two hundred thousand off the Dallas girl, three hundred thousand off his bride from Houston. What would you say to that?"

"Identification okay?"

"Through the picture we showed you. Total certainty."

"Like I said, I don't want to get artsy-fartsy fancy, like the psychiatrists in the courtroom. But isn't what he's doing, maybe, is killing Coralita over and over, killing his stepmother?"

"Punishing himself by killing her," Meyer said. "I could agree."

"So then there's more," Sigiera said. "It adds up to four years between Coralita and the girl in Cotulla, then a gap of twelve years?" He counted with his fingers, tapping them on the edge of his desk. "No, thirteen. Then five years until this one, this month. There'd be more in there. God only knows what his cycle is. If it's every two years, that makes three you know about and eight you don't."

"Women seem to be strongly attracted to him," Meyer said.

"Okay, he's a compulsive. You take a rapist. They go on and on until you catch them. But that's a crime of violence, not sex. They want to hurt and kill. This is different. He wants to love and be loved. He wants romance. He wants to heat somebody up until they're as hungry for it as Coralita was. Then he's got the excuse to punish himself and her for that kind of sex by killing her, depriving himself."

"Meyer and I had dinner with them aboard my houseboat."

"That's the first time you didn't throw in the word Professor, so now I'll buy the idea you're friends. Go ahead."

"I remarked afterward to Meyer there was a kind of almost tangible erotic tension between them, almost visible, like smoke in the air."

Sigiera shook his head slowly, making a bitter mouth under the droop of the mustache. "All the years," he said. "All the years on the run. Roaming among the women, all smiles. Taking little jobs and then moving on. Roaming and killing, and in pain all the time. By now he must be damn well expert at picking up new identities. It's never hard if you start with cash and with the smarts. But it can go wrong. Some little thing. He'd have to be ready at any time to fold the tent and run. I don't think a man can stand that much tension for too long."

"What do you mean?" I asked him.

"When you're a working lawman, you get used to every kind of criminal having a pattern. I got to know a very classy thief. I made a practically accidental collar when I was in Beaumont. He did rich people. Private homes. Coins and stamps and collectibles and jewelry. Portable stuff. He went to the big auctions in New York and Los Angeles. He got a line on his marks there. Would track one to, say, Atlanta. Research the house, the floor plan, the alarm system, the movements of the people who lived there. When the time was right and the house was empty, he'd park a rented van in the drive, with a sign he'd taped to the side saying BUGS-OFF INSECT CONTROL, and he'd walk in in his white suit carrying his spray equipment. Fifteen minutes after he'd bypassed the alarm system, he'd walk out with a pillowcase full of good stuff which he could fence for a very good score. Twice a year he did the same kind of job. I was cruising the neighborhood in an unmarked car, looking for an address of somebody we wanted a statement from. He had trouble busting into a safe and his time got so short he came out nervous, backed out of the blind driveway right into the side of my car. He thought I was a civilian. He came on very hard, but when I showed the badge and the gun he just wilted and sat down on the curbing. All the life went right out of him.

"While we were holding him, I used to go in and talk to him. Know what? He had a wife and kids in Cincinnati. He was an investment adviser. He had an office in a bank building. He belonged to a downtown club and a tennis club, the Junior Chamber and the Kiwanis. He did a lot of investment advising, and he was good at it. He washed his own money by feeding it in through the office, as consultant fees. He lived good. He had respectability. He told me that every time he made a good score and got back to home base with the money, he'd say to himself, Never again. He was safe. He could breathe. When he was out on a job, his wife and everybody else thought he was off taking a first-hand look at some of the companies where he was thinking of recommending the stock. He told me that he'd say never again, and in a couple of months it would start to build. He'd begin to get restless. And he'd remember how it was when he was inside a rich home. It was a kind of excitement he never could find anywhere else."

"I see what you mean," Meyer said. "This man Pittler might well have a base somewhere, a permanent identity he goes back to."

"I think he would have to have," Sigiera said. "A place to catch his breath. Stash money. Get his ducks in a row. Home base, where they don't know about his hobby."

"Would the sister know?" I asked.

"Who?"

"Helen June whatever."

"Good thought," he said. "They used to go grill her every few weeks until she moved away. She claimed she had never gotten a card or even a call from Cody. Let me see. Her married name ought to be in here someplace." He looked and grunted when he found it. "Mrs. Kermit Fox. Kermit was called Sonny. But this address is way out of date. Helen June got to be forty-seven by now. There must be somebody in town still sending her Christmas cards. Old Boomer might know. He's been working for the city for ninety-nine years. You like a little Mexican hot groceries? It's about that time."

He made a call, and then we went out to eat. It was a drive-in called Panchos. We sat at a table in the back. The specialty was chili with chunks of Chihuahua cheese melted in it and on it. Meyer, one of the world's great chili experts, was under close observation by Sigiera as he tasted it. Sigiera expected a gasp, tears, a mad grab at the ice water. Meyer smacked his lips, looked thoughtful, reached for the Tabasco bottle, put a dozen drops into the chili, stirred it well, tasted again, nodded at Sigiera, and said, "Just right, Paul."

"Professor, I'm beginning to like you."

He told us about the trials and foul-ups of working with the border patrol on immigration and drugs, and about his adventures as an undercover man in Beaumont.

We were on second coffees when an erect old man with ample belly, white mustache, white goatee, and a fifty-nine-gallon straw hat came to the table. Sigiera kicked a chair out for him. "Boomer, this here is McGee and this is the Professor. They're the ones want to know about Helen June Pittler Fox."

His handshake was big, dry, and muscular. He must have given his order on the way in. The waitress came with a glass of milk and a small order of tacos.

Boomer crunched a taco and washed it down with milk, wiped his mouth and whiskers, and said, "After Cody shot his step-ma and pa, about a year after, Sonny and Helen June moved clear out of the state. They moved on all the way up north. Sonny's folks had original moved down from there and he had some kin up there. Rome, New York. No point in giving you that address, because it isn't any good any more. Sonny and Helen June had but the one kid and it died in the first year from something wrong with its breathing. Sonny is the best auto mechanic I ever come across. He could make a living anyplace at all. They broke up. Can't say if there's a divorce. Anyway, she calls herself Helen June Fox and here's the address."

He put a scrap of envelope on the table. I held it so Meyer could read it as I did: Route 3, Box 810, Cold Brook, New York.

"Said to be someplace north of Utica," Boomer said.

"Long way to go to come up empty," Sigiera said.

"No place is too far," Meyer said. "And why empty?"

"Because most old cold leads turn out empty, that's all. The new hot ones pay off a lot more often."

We bought the lunch over Sigiera's protests, and we promised to let him know if we learned anything.

seventeen

They let us check out of the little motel north of Eagle Pass at three in the afternoon without paying for the extra night on the two rooms.

I estimated on the map that we were a little less than three hundred and fifty miles from Houston on Route 57, then I-35 and I-10, and so should make it back to the Houston apartment by midnight.

A brassy sun filled half the sky, and with the air on full blast it was still warm inside the van. At speed the van was just noisy enough to inhibit conversation. We were both involved in independent guesswork. When either of us came up with something, we would yell across to the other side of the seat to check it out.

"Hideout in Mexico?" Meyer shouted. "Got the language. Use the same papers going back and forth to the States. Change identity once he's across the border?"

"He was using Evan Lawrence down there, working with somebody named Willy in Cancún."

I glanced over at him. He looked disappointed.

Once, when we stopped for gas, he said, "If I had a hideout I would use trip wires and tin cans and cow bells to let me know if anybody was approaching."

"If we ever get close, we can expect that. And expect him to be dangerous."

"I still like the idea of Mexico. Maybe Evan Lawrence *is* his hideaway name."

"So why would he call attention to it by arranging to have himself killed?"

"I see what you mean. I'm not thinking well."

"We're doing okay. Thanks to you, we know the name he started with. And we know what started him."

"It seems incredible to me that we could have had dinner with him and Norma, and there wasn't the slightest hint of violence under that friendly face."

Then we were back on the highway, booming along through the end of the day, the sunset behind us, our shadow long, angling to one side or the other as the road changed subtle directions. I grunted and pulled into the next rest stop, parked with the motor running, and turned and faced Meyer. "We make it too complicated."

"How do you mean?"

"It just came to me. He had to destroy Evan Lawrence."

"Why?"

"The money."

Meyer frowned and then suddenly said, "Of course! It would be too risky to hang around as the mourning husband and wait for the legal procedures to clean up the details and hand over the money. When he talked Norma into gradually moving all the cash out of the trust, he knew he was going to stage a common disaster. Otherwise, if he could have risked staying right there, he would have left the money in the trust and it would have come to him on her death. But that would have meant a more careful research job on him by the law and the lawyers."

"Wouldn't you have inherited under the terms of the will?"

"Wouldn't it have been an easy job for him to get her to make a new will? And then that too would have been significant. You're right, Travis. Evan Lawrence was a temporary person. He could only last so long. How long was it, a half year maybe? And now he's back in his safe place. And sooner or later he'll come out again, as someone else. On the hunt. Prowling. Searching. Smiling."

Back up to speed, each of us thinking, adding up the little morsels we had discovered, from Christine Statzer, Martin Eagle, Betsy Ann Larker, Bunky, Boomer, Paul Sigiera. Like a child's game in the Sunday comics. Connect the dots and find the animal.

"Common disasters are hard to stage," Meyer shouted.

So I worked on that one, through the end of daylight into night, into late quarter-pounders at an almost deserted McDonald's at Seguin. "You can arrange it with fire," I said, "if you can find somebody approximately the right size. Hitchhiker. Backpacker. A transient is best, because he won't be missed for a long time, if ever. Chunk them both on the head, drive off the road into a tree, jumping free at the last minute, the way he probably did in Ingram. Then toss the match. Put your ring on his finger before you toss the match. Take off any rings he might have. Car fires are hot. Water is easier.

Overturned boat, drowned woman, man missing presumed dead. Explosives are good too, except it takes an awful lot. Send her up in a plane with a bomb in the luggage, after buying two tickets. Last-minute excuse. Join you later honey. But you kill a lot of other folk that way."

Suddenly a small elderly woman jumped up out of a booth across the way. I hadn't noticed her. She glared at me. "Monsters!" she said in a breathy whisper. "Monsters!" She scuttled out.

And Meyer started laughing. It was the first genuine laugh I had heard from him in a year. His eyes ran. He hugged his belly and groaned, "Oh, oh, oh." I levered him up and aimed him toward the car. He staggered with laughter. The little old lady might call the law, and it would be well to be up to speed in reasonable time.

On Friday morning at a travel agency in the shopping mall near Piney Village, we discovered that if you want to get to Utica, Houston isn't a good place to start from. Maybe there aren't any good places to start from. But they could get us to Syracuse by six that evening, with a long wait between flights at Atlanta.

A few minutes from Houston we came up through hot murky clouds into a bright white blaze of sunshine. At Atlanta we took a train from our gate back to the terminal. I wandered back and forth past a row of phone booths and finally went in and phoned Naples.

She answered on the first half of the first ring. "Yes?"

"Me," I said.

"Where are you?"

"Atlanta, heading north pretty soon. I wondered about the job."

"You didn't wonder enough to call me on Sunday, or Monday, or Tuesday, or—"

"I thought about it every day."

"I bet."

"I really did. We've been doing a lot of scuffling. Okay, tell me how it came out."

"The job was offered and the terms are marvelous. They gave me until Monday to think it over, so I did, and I phoned them and said yes."

"And if I had phoned Sunday?"

"McGee, I would like to stick you with it. I would like to tell you that if you'd called, maybe I would have said no. But it just ain't true, darlin'. I want that job so bad I can hardly breathe."

"When will you be leaving?"

"The man I'm training to replace me reported this morning. They want me in Maui on August fifteenth."

"How's the guy they sent?"

"Howard is a little bit slow to catch on, but once he has something firmly in mind, it stays there. I think he'll be okay. Cornell hotel school. They made him very well aware of the records I set here, so he knows he'd be a fool to make any big changes."

"Seems awful soon."

"It is soon. I've been a little bit depressed ever since I said yes, as a matter of fact. Not just about you but about the whole thing here. It's been a wonderful part of my life."

"Past tense."

"What's over, as they say, is over. How are you doing?"

"We learned the name he started with. Cody T. W. Pittler. And we think we know why he is a congenital murderer."

"More murders?"

"Lots we don't know about, probably."

"Do be careful, will you?"

"We may never get any closer to him than we are now. We're going up north to see his sister. She hasn't seen him in twenty-two years, probably. We think he has some safe place from which he ventures forth from time to time, to evil do. The great lover. He sets up passionate affairs with women and then does them in."

"At least they die happy. Sorry. That was bad taste."

"I encouraged it. I was giving it the light touch. But I don't feel light at all inside. I'm depressed by how soon it is going to be the middle of August."

"I'm glad, at least, that you finally called. I was beginning to get really annoyed with you."

"I've been basking in garden spots, like Freer, Encinal, Cotulla, and Eagle Pass."

"City life, huh? Excuse, Travis. I was on my way out when the phone rang. I'm to have a rum something with Howard by the pool, and we are going to talk about getting the east forty rezoned. We really need it if we're to have any room at all to grow here. Phone me, please, when you get back home. The minute you get home, okay?"

"Okay. Good luck with the rezoning."

"Good luck with your mass murderer, baby."

I hung up and went over to where Meyer was sitting. He was fatuously content. He had found a copy of *The Economist* on the newsstand and was learning all about economic crises in the NATO countries.

By the time we reached the Avis counter in the Syracuse airport, it was six thirty on a hot sticky Friday evening, the sun still high. We'd reserved the car in Atlanta, on Meyer's card, and it was waiting for us out in slot 20, a burgundy two-door with a drooped nose and a memory of cigar smoke inside. The Avis woman had given us instructions as to how to get on the Thruway. It was still bright daylight when we took the Utica exit and found, on the way toward downtown, an elderly and overpriced Howard Johnson motel. I could stomach the motel but not the restaurant, so Meyer studied the yellow pages. He has good instincts.

"What they seem to have the most of here is Italian," he said. "So one goes with the tide. Objection?"

"Not at all."

"Grimaldi's, I think. Let me see. Yes. Grimaldi's."

When we finally found it, the daylight was almost gone. It was on a corner, with a public park across from one side of it and some sort of yellow-brick public housing project across from the front entrance. We had a hard time finding a parking place. Meyer said that was a good sign. The doors opened onto smoke, loud talk, laughter, a general Thank God It's Friday flavor. The bar was off to the left, the dining area to the right. A slender, grave, dark-haired woman led us to a table for two against the far wall and gave us oversized menus. A small bald elderly waiter came trotting over and took our order for extra-dry martinis with twists. They came quickly. Meyer sipped, he smiled, he relaxed. "The food will be good," he said. "You never get a generous and delicious cocktail in a proper glass in a restaurant where the food is bad." Another Meyer dictum. They seem to work out.

And the veal piccata was indeed splendid, and went well with the Valpolicella.

Over coffee, Meyer said, "It's like coming back to life. All this. I was shut down for a year. Now there is a kind of internal pressure that every now and then pops another area of me wide open the way it once was. When I take pleasure in it, then I feel guilty that I owe this conditional resurrection to Norma."

"Conditional?"

"Of course. How long does it last? Only until the next animal gives me a choice between acting like a man or sitting on the floor and forgetting my name. At times I am anxious to find out, and at other times I hope there will never be another confrontation."

"You'll be fine."

"My words to myself exactly. Meyer, I say to myself, you'll be fine. Just fine." His smile was wry.

I looked around at the patrons of the restaurant and the bar. Politicos, many of them young. Lawyers and elected officials and appointees. Some with their wives or girls. It looked to me as if a lot of the city and county business might be transacted right here. They had a lot of energy, these Italianate young men, a feverish gregariousness. I wondered aloud why they seemed so frantic about having a good time.

Meyer studied the question and finally said, "It's energy without a productive outlet, I think. Most of these Mohawk Valley cities are dying, have been for years: Albany, Troy, Amsterdam, Utica, Syracuse, Rome. And so they made an industry out of government. State office buildings in the decaying downtowns. A proliferation of committees, surveys, advisory boards, commissions, legal actions, grants, welfare, zoning boards, road departments, health care groups . . . thousands upon thousands of people making a reasonably good living working for city, county, state, and federal governments in these dwindling cities, passing the same tax dollars back and forth. I think that man, by instinct, is productive. He wants to *make* something, a stone ax, a bigger cave, better arrows, whatever. But these bright and energetic men know in their hearts they are not *making* anything. They use every connection, every contact, every device, to stay within reach of public monies. Working within an abstraction is just not a totally honorable way of life. Hence the air of jumpy joy, the backslaps ringing too loudly, compliments too extravagant, toasts too ornate, marriages too brief, lawsuits too long-drawn, obligatory forms too complex and too long. Their city has gone stale, and as the light wanes, they dance."

"Very poetic, Professor."

"Valpolicella tends to do that to me."

"I've missed your impromptu lectures."

"Be careful what you say. I may try to make up for the lost year."

"I haven't missed them *that* much."

eighteen

After breakfast, the morning news on the car radio said that the high for the day was estimated to be one hundred and two degrees in downtown Utica, a record for the last day of July. I drove, following the directions given me at the motel desk when we checked out.

We headed out of the valley, up Deerfield Hill, past television towers, on a two-lane road so steep in places that the little dark-red car had a problem handling both the grade and the air conditioning, lugging down until it shifted itself into a lower gear. After the suburban houses came the small rundown farms, barns dark-gray and sagging, a few horses grazing. The farms were on a plateau where the road led straight into the distance, toward the misted foothills of the Adirondacks.

There was less traffic headed north than I expected. No doubt the vacation-bound had left the city on Friday. It was a little cooler on the plateau. We had merged with Route 8, and I wanted to get to the post office in Poland—as the man at the desk had suggested—to find out how I might find Mrs. Fox.

We came down off the plateau to run along a creek valley into Poland, a small commuter town with such large maples bordering the main street that they gave an illusion of coolness on this summer Saturday. Route 8 turned left by a tiny island of greenery in the middle of the village. Meyer spotted the post office ahead on the right, and I stayed at the wheel while he went in.

He came out quite soon and said, "We stay on Route Eight up through Cold Brook, another village the size of this one. And we'll see the name on a mailbox on the right side of the road, across from the house. The house is a mobile home. He said he thought it was gray and blue, but he wasn't sure. He guessed it at about ten miles past the far edge of Cold Brook. Strange thing, though."

"Such as?"

"He was reasonably cordial when I went to the window. But when I told him who I was trying to find, he got very short with me. Abrupt and impatient. He gave me the information and walked away. He registered disapproval of her, and of me for asking how to find her."

It was only two miles between villages, and I checked the speedometer when we left Cold Brook. Soon the road made a long curve up a gentle slope, and a sign at the top of the hill told us we had entered the Adirondack Park Preserve.

The man had underestimated by about three miles. When we came to her place, I began to understand why he had acted as he did. At one time evergreens had been planted in a long line, close together, along the left side of the road to provide, I guessed, a snow fence to keep the road clear in winter. The trees were very large. Several of them were gone, and her trailer sat in the gap about fifty feet from the road and parallel to it. It could have once been gray and blue. There was a big battered red-and-white four-wheel-drive Bronco on extra wide and extra tall tires parked in the dirt driveway headed out, leaving us no room to turn in.

I parked beyond her mailbox and we got out and stood there, stunned by the profusion of junk that filled the yard from fence to fence. Car parts, refrigerators, cargo trailers without wheels, stovewood, rolls of roofing paper, bed frames, broken rocking chairs, broken deck furniture, piles of cinder block, piles of roof tiles, a stack of full sheets of plywood, moldering away. Glass bottles, plastic bottles, cans, fenders, old washing machines, fencing wire, window frames, 55-gallon drums rust red, an old horse-drawn sleigh, crates half full of empty soft drink bottles, and many other bulky objects which did not seem to have had any useful purpose ever. The scene stunned the mind. It was impossible to take it all in at once. In a strange way it had an almost artistic impact, a new art form devised in three dimensions to show the collapse of western civilization. It made me think of an object I had seen in New York when a woman persuaded me to go with her to an exhibition at the Museum of Modern Art. That object was a realistic-looking plastic hamburger on a bun with an ooze of mustard, pickle, and catsup. It was ten feet in diameter and stood five feet high. This scene had that same total familiarity plus unreality.

"Maybe she's in violation of the zoning laws," Meyer murmured.

"If those are her own clothes hung out over there on the fence to dry, she is sizable."

We walked in, past the big vehicle. She must have seen us through the window. She opened the narrow door of the trailer and stepped down onto the top step of the three that led to the door. The trailer was up on cinder blocks.

"What are you looking for?"

"Mrs. Helen June Fox?"

"What do you want her for?"

She was a fairly tall woman. Her brown hair hung stringy straight, unbrushed. Her enormous breasts stretched the damp fabric of a pink T-shirt, sagging toward the protruding belly that bulged over the belt that held up her knee-length khaki shorts. She wore ragged white deck shoes, and there were scars and scratches on her plump white legs from insect bites. Her features were strong, the jaw heavy, the eyes muddy, unfriendly, and unwavering. The mouth was a little crescent, a tight inverted smile, like a bulldog. She and her clothing were smudged and stained. She was an untidy mess, and yet she radiated such a forceful presence that in some strange way she was almost attractive. She held herself well. One could see that twenty-five years ago she had been one hell of a woman, and she remembered how it had been and had retained the pattern of responding to admiration.

"Well?" she said. She finished the last of the beer from the can in her hand, crushed the aluminum, and flipped it out into the yard. It bounced behind a cinder block. "You government again? I told the last batch to get off my land and get off my ass or they'd be pickin' bird shot."

Meyer solved the problem. "Boomer told us where to find you." To my surprise and admiration, he managed to put just a little bit of south Texas in his speech.

Helen June grunted in surprise, came down the other two steps, and then sat heavily on the middle step. "That old fart still living?"

"Looks fine," I said.

"Always knew everything about everybody. I wonder who give him my address. Probably Auntie Minna. She always sends birthday money. She must be ninety by now."

"He didn't know if you were divorced from Sonny."

"He took off. I never bothered filing. Glad to get rid of the surly son of a bitch. What do you two want? You sure God aren't a matched set, are you. You look like some kind of bear, mister. A friendly bear. Cuddly. What's your name, dear?"

"Meyer. And he is McGee."

"We want to talk about your brother Cody," I said.

She got up and beckoned to us to follow her. We threaded our way through the tons of junk to an old picnic table with benches near the side fence, in the shade of a big spruce. We sat on one side and she sat facing us. She said, "We keep talking where we were, it could maybe wake up Jesse. He was out real late. He plays piano Friday nights. He gets ugly, you wake him up too soon. So what if I don't want to talk about my little brother? Did they catch him? Are you newspaper guys or cops?"

"He hasn't been caught," I said.

"Good. It wasn't his fault, any of it."

"Whose, then?"

"Boomer could have told you, you asked him. It was Coralita's fault, that little Eye-talian piece of ass. That was the worst mistake my daddy ever made in his whole life. He was a wonderful man. Everybody liked him. He was smart in business, but he was sure stupid about women. I was twenty when he married her. She was only five years older than me. She'd sure been busy. When I was in high school, the guys made jokes about her. Know what her nickname was? Gang-bang Cardamone. You don't get no nickname like that without making the effort. After Momma died, I spent two years trying to take her place around the house. I loved my daddy, and I did all the cooking and cleaning and dusting and bed-making and all. I studied recipe books. I kept everything shining for him. I was going to take care of him my whole life, and after two years he brought home that slut. He married her and brought her right into my house, right into my kitchen, right into his bed. I used to lie awake at night, and sometimes I could hear the two of them in there together, and I would think of the ways I could kill her without being caught. I had the feeling all the time that she knew exactly what I was thinking, and she was laughing at me. Most of the time she acted as if I wasn't there at all. But she certainly knew Cody was there. He was kind of an innocent kid. Younger really than his age. I tried to warn him about Coralita. I was afraid of what could happen, and I didn't want to hang around and watch. I got out by marrying Sonny Fox. Never did love him. What I loved was getting out of there, away from Coralita. So she wasn't getting enough, and she didn't dare go hunt for it because somebody would tell my daddy, and there was Cody right in the same house, safe as could be, and he would be too scared to talk, so she nailed him. I bet it was as easy as clubbing a bunny. She waggled that fine ass at him until he couldn't think about anything else, then I think what she must have done was slip into his bed while he was asleep, so he'd wake up so close to doing it he wouldn't be able to stop himself. And that one time would be all it would take to make it permanent. I just don't think she could have gotten him into it any other way. I used to think about that a lot. But that was a long time ago. Cody would never have been one to sneaky-cheat on his own daddy unless she worked him into it before he knew what was going on."

"What do you think happened that night Coralita was killed?" I asked.

"I told the stupid cops what must have happened. My daddy would never have shot Cody no matter what he did. The bed lamp was on, okay? He shot her in the back of the head, near the neck, and she died in one second. Cody heard the loud shot and he came scrambling out from under the body. When my daddy saw who it was, he couldn't shoot and so he turned the gun on himself to kill himself. That's what he would have done. And Cody saw what was going to happen and leaped for the gun, and my daddy kept trying to shoot himself, and while they struggled there, the gun went off and he did shoot himself. Cody thought he was dead and he took the car keys and ran down and got in that car and took off like a crazy person. They've never caught him and they never will."

"Why are you so sure that—" Meyer started to ask, but he was interrupted by a man yelling across the yard.

"Goddamn you, how the hell am I supposed to get my sleep with all this yattering going on?" He came down the steps out of the trailer, zipping the fly on his jeans. He wore black pointy cowboy boots. He was naked and brown from the waist up. He was slat thin, with bad posture. His chest was caved in, his shoulders thrust forward. He looked to be in his mid-thirties. With every move there was a ripple of small wiry muscles in his arms, torso, and shoulders. He had a long lean head, hollow cheeks, a thrusting lantern jaw, eyes deep under a shelf of brow.

"Who are these guys?" he demanded, coming across through the trash.

"We were just talking about my brother, Jesse. That's all."

"You woke me up!"

"We moved way over here so we wouldn't."

"You especially, Helen June, big mouth. Going on and on and on. You two. Git!"

She said in a nervous voice, "You better do like he says."

"But we haven't—"

"I mean it. I really mean it, McGee. You best leave."

The man reached the table and as Meyer stood up, Jesse grabbed his ear and yanked him back over the bench. The bench went down and Meyer fell on his back. I took a long step to the side, to reasonably open ground, and waited to see what he had in mind. He feinted at me with a long swinging left, and as I ducked to the left to avoid it, he went up into the air into a strange scissoring kick, and one of those boots whistled toward my mouth. I have a lot of quick. It's nothing I've earned or worked for, it's just that the hookup between senses, nerves, and muscles works faster than most. And adrenaline makes it work even faster. I saw the sole and heel of that boot, parallel to the ground, floating toward my teeth. The feint had moved me into the kick, and I moved back almost quickly enough. Not quite. The toe of the boot ticked the outside edge of my left ear and made it feel for a moment as if it had been torn off. He was having a big day on ears. The miss left him slightly off balance, but he recovered in the air, twisting like a cat, landing lightly.

One of those, I thought. Another one of those. They yell *Hah!* and try to chop you with the edge of the hand. About all I ever had of that came in basic training long ago. They want you to take your best shot, and then they use the momentum and leverage to fell you.

He moved warily, and I saw him gathering himself for another kick. When it started I moved back, and when the boot came at my throat I knocked it sky high with my forearm. Jesse landed hard on the nape of his neck. He rolled to the left and came to his feet again, too close to Meyer, who took the twenty-inch piece of two-by-four he had picked up out of the rubble and, holding it in both hands, swung at the back of Jesse's head. It went *ponk!* and Jesse sighed and looked far beyond me and collapsed slowly into a fetal position. As I moved toward him, Helen June yelled, "Don't stomp him, please. Don't hurt his hands! You better go right now while you can. Please."

She really meant it. I had begun to wonder how sane Jesse was. Or how sane either of them were.

"When will he be gone so we can talk?"

"Tomorrow evening."

So we left. I looked back. She was kneeling beside him, smoothing his lank hair back from his forehead.

After we had gone three miles back toward Cold Brook, I glanced in the rearview mirror and saw the red-and-white Bronco overtaking us, coming on at high speed. I made several guesses, all of them bad news as I floored the accelerator. The little car jumped out pretty good but, as I soon saw, not quite good enough. My speedometer said seventy-two on the flat, less uphill, more down. When he came up behind me and didn't smack into my rear end with his big steel bumper, I knew that he was waiting for enough clear vision ahead to come up beside me and edge me off the road. That gave me a better chance.

When the road was clear ahead, he came on up alongside. I could see him, sitting high and grinning. The instant he started to move in toward my front corner, I warned Meyer and hit the brakes hard. Jesse went shooting on ahead. The moment I slid to a full stop, I put it in reverse and backed it on up to speed, then banged the brakes again, turning the wheel hard right as I did so. The front end slid around beautifully and we rocked up onto two wheels momentarily, bounced back down, and I had it in gear and gaining speed, leaving a teenage pattern of black rubber on the pavement behind us.

I had come to my dead stop, and gone into reverse, right near the brink of that long upcurve to the left, that climbing curve a little way out of Cold Brook. Jesse had gone down the downhill curve to the right, out of sight. I kept looking back. No Jesse.

Meyer said, "I heard something back there."

"Such as."

"Well . . . a thud. A kind of crunch-thud noise."

At the end of a long straight stretch, I found an unmarked dirt lane. I turned in, went up a way, turned around, and came back to where I could park out of sight of the main road, yet see anything that sped past the leafy mouth of the lane.

Nothing came from the south. A bread truck and a pickup passed by from the north. After ten long minutes, we started up and headed south, after them.

From his tire marks and the location and condition of his vehicle, it was easy to see what had happened: an error of judgment. When I had outsmarted him again, it had made him very very angry. And in his rage he had tried to make a U-turn halfway down that slope. He probably knew his vehicle well enough so that, had he tried the same turn at the same speed on the flat, he would have had no problem. But on the slope, the inside wheels were at a slightly higher level, and about two thirds of the way around his U-turn, he lost it. The Bronco tipped over and rolled. It threw him out ahead of the roll, and rolled over him, and kept rolling until it wedged itself into a grove of small trees beyond the ditch.

He lay face down amid bits of glass and twisted little pieces of tarnished trim. His back was bloody. We parked beyond the bread truck and walked up to the scene. He had tried to make his turn where the curving downslope had been widened to three lanes to accommodate cars turning left into a side road. He was stretched out on the shoulder, face down, only his head on the paving. As we neared him, it looked as though his face had sunk into the concrete road surface as if into a liquid. The pool of red around his head revealed the basis of this curious and sickening illusion. Some part of the vehicle, probably one of the big tires, had rolled across the back of his head, and under the pressure the facial bones had given way, leaving the back of the skull undamaged. A spectator who had been headed north brought a frayed old blanket from his car trunk and spread it over the upper half of the body.

The pickup driver said to the bread-truck driver, "You know who it is, don't you?"

"I know who it was, pal. Crazy Jesse that played piano weekends up to Heneman's Grill. Moved in with the Fox woman last year. I said he was going to kill himself sooner or later the way he drove that souped-up Bronco."

There were seven of us standing there by now, and we all turned and looked down the hill slope to the southwest as we heard the distant keening of the ambulance siren, coming closer.

"No need to hurry," Bread truck said.

"Funny thing," Pickup said. "If they had put Jesse away for a couple of years for assaulting that Jamison kid, like they should have, instead of giving him probation, he wouldn't have been out getting himself killed today."

The Dodge ambulance pulled up, and two attendants ran to the body, slowed when they saw the blanket. One lifted it up, felt for a pulse in the neck, dropped it again, shrugged. The other strolled over to slide the body basket out of the back of the ambulance. A couple of northbound cars slowed for a look, then hurried on. A State Police sedan arrived. Meyer and I walked back to the rental and got in.

Meyer said, "If there is anything at all useful that she can tell us, we had better be the ones who tell her about Jesse."

"I want to thank you for thumping him."

"Not exactly a frontal assault. Not exactly meritorious. You would have taken care of the problem."

"Don't be too sure. He was reaching to unsnap that little knife case on his belt when you turned off his lights."

"I was too angry and too humiliated to stop to think about what I was doing. Look at my ear." He turned and looked to the rear so I could see his right ear. It was puffy and bright red.

I had turned back north, leaving the little roadside scene behind. I said, "I think you'll be better at talking to her. Okay?"

"If you wish."

He was silent until we turned into the dirt driveway, to park where the red-and-white Bronco had been. Then he said, "Stay in the car." A direct order. Unusual and unexpected.

She came out, trotting toward him when he was halfway to the trailer, her strong face vivid with the unasked question. The left side of her face was swollen and was turning dark. I heard her helpless cry. "I *tried* to stop him! I *tried*. I really *tried!*"

Then I could hear the murmur of his voice, explaining. She seemed to become a smaller person, to collapse in upon herself. He touched her shoulder and she turned into his arms. He patted her, comforted her. They walked together to the steps, his arm around her thick waist. He lowered her to a sitting position on the middle step, and she put her face down on her knees.

Meyer looked toward the car and made a small beckoning gesture. I got out and went to them. Her shoulders were shaking, but I could hear no audible sobbing. Finally she raised up and looked at both of us, tears running down her face, and tried to smile. "You'd miss even a lizard if you lived with it and fed it for over a year. He could be real sweet sometimes. I told him not to go after you and he knocked me down. Is the Bronco ruint?"

"It isn't very pretty," I said, "but I think it's just damage to the body. Frame, engine, wheels, and radiator should be okay."

"I'll have to see about getting it fixed up. I got to have a car, living way out here. I bought it for him. I traded my old car in on it, and it's in my name."

"Insurance?" Meyer asked.

"Only what they make you take out. I don't even know where they'll take the body. I haven't got any phone out here any more. It was a party line, and Jesse cussed the people who were talking when he wanted to use it, so they complained and one of them recorded what he said to them, and they came and took it out. I didn't know they could do that, but they can."

"We'll take you down to the village," Meyer said. "You can find out there, and make arrangements about the truck."

She wiped her eyes. "That would be a real help. I got to fix up a little." She struggled to her feet and went in and closed the door.

"What else do you think she can tell us?" I asked Meyer.

"I noticed something when we talked before. She said she was certain they would never catch him. There didn't seem to be any thought in her mind that he might be dead. It was a long time ago. If she had no word at all from him in all that time, she might believe he was dead. It would be a logical assumption. Certainly he had a better-than-average reason for suicide. But his possible death was no part of her monologue, Travis. So that seems to me reason to believe he has been in touch with her. I want to find out how. And when."

When she came out, ready to go, the change startled both of us. She wore a dark blue dress and carried a shiny blue shoulder bag. Her hair had been brushed, and she had managed to hide the deepening color of the bruise on her left cheek. She wore sandals with one-inch heels, and stockings which covered her scratched and bitten legs. She wore lipstick and some eye shadow. She looked slimmer and younger.

"Do you want to lock up?" Meyer asked.

She gave him a pitying look. "Who would look at my place and think there's anything worth stealing?" She patted the shoulder bag. "Anything worth stealing is in here."

Meyer folded the seat down and climbed into the back. She sat beside me. Meyer leaned over toward her and spoke to her. "How does Cody keep track of where you are?"

"I let—" She stopped abruptly.

"Who is it you let know? Who is the intermediary?"

"Damn you, Meyer. I thought you looked cuddly. You're a smart-ass son of a bitch. You tricked me." She worked herself around to face him. "You could set fire to my feet, I'd never tell you. You could pull out my fingernails, I wouldn't say a word."

"I don't think you know where Cody is."

"You're right! I don't have no idea at all."

"So you would write to this intermediary, or maybe phone when there's a change of address, and then when Cody phoned the intermediary he would get the information."

"Smart-ass!"

"He needs the address because he sends you money."

"Why would he do that?"

"You and he are family. He did a terrible thing. He wants to take care of you, so you'll think well of him. As you obviously do."

"He sends it because he's my kid brother and, until Coralita came along, we always looked out for each other. He doesn't have to *buy* my feeling for him."

"How does he send it?"

"He ties it onto a pigeon."

"Come on, Helen June," Meyer said in a wheedling tone. "If you don't know where he is, and I don't believe you do, then the way he sends the money can't tip us off as to where to find him. He's a very clever man. I'm just curious as to how he would go about sending cash to you. It must be cleverly done."

"He's smart."

"We know. He'd have to be to stay at liberty so long."

"I nearly messed up the first time he sent any. It was a kind of messy old package that came for me. I was still living with Sonny. Thank God he wasn't around when I opened it. On the outside it said BOOKS. My name was typed on the label. The return address was a box number in New Orleans. Inside were three paperback books with two rubber bands around them, one going one way and the other going the other way. I read the titles and decided it was some kind of sales gimmick. I'm no reader. Maybe the newspaper sometimes. So I unsnapped the rubber bands and leafed through the first one looking for the sales letter. And when I opened the second one, a bunch of hundred-dollar bills fell out onto the floor. There was forty of them. I damn near fainted. The middle book had been hollowed out, probably with a razor. Kind of a messy job. I guess it didn't have to be real neat. There was a typed note with it. And it said, 'Happy birthday, Helen June. Whenever you move, let so-and-so know right away. Get rid of this note and don't talk about the money.' Isn't that great? Here I am talking about the money."

"How many packages have you gotten?" Meyer asked.

"I don't know. What do you care? You with the IRS? Maybe a dozen, maybe more. They were mailed from Miami, Tampa, Houston, New Orleans, Los Angeles. Big cities. Sometimes with a little note. Birthday or Christmas or something. The biggest was eighty-five hundred. And the smallest was the first one. I never know when they're coming. He cares about me, that's all I know. That's all I care. It keeps me alive. I told you this just to show you that he's a good person."

When we got to the place where Jesse had died, a tow truck was backed up to the Bronco. The winch was grinding and they were gently picking it out of the small trees. There were no other cars there. Two little farm kids were watching.

Helen June got out and trotted to the tow truck. "This is my car!" she shouted over the sound of the winch. "Where are you going with it?"

He turned off the winch. "Hi, Helen June. Sorry about Jesse. His own damn fool fault. Bound to happen some day. We're taking it down to the Village Garage. Okay?"

"What's it costing me for you to take it, Jimmy?"

"Forty bucks, to you."

"Is that a discount or are you hiking the price?"

"A discount, damn it. Sixty otherwise."

"I got it right here and I want a receipt. Just a second."

She came back to the car.

"Thank you for coming to tell me, and thank you for the ride. I talked too damn much. I don't know what got into me. I don't tell people my private business. Not to a couple of strangers. Meyer, you came up on my blind side."

"I'm sorry that we . . . caused all this."

"If you hadn't it would have been somebody else. Or something else." Her mouth twisted, the smile bitter. "He was a real sorry man, but he was the only one I got."

"I know you don't want to talk about your brother," Meyer said, "but . . ."

"You are so right."

". . . you might want to see a recent picture of him."

She stared at him. "You got one? How?"

"It's back at the motel in Utica," he lied.

"I sure would like to see how Cody turned out," she said.

"It's a little past noon now," he said. "We could go get it and come back."

The Bronco had been plucked out of the shrubbery, and they had it ready to roll. "Hey, Helen June!"

She turned and yelled, "Hold it a minute, okay?"

She turned back to us.

"I hafta see about my car. I hafta find out where they took Jesse and tell his people. He's got folks in Gloversville. You want to come out to my place late this afternoon? Four thirty?"

When we agreed, she turned and loped off toward the tow truck in a clumsy, pigeon-toed trot.

As she climbed in, Meyer said, "I better come back alone. I think it will work better."

"Then we better check back into the motel." I headed south. "You got more than I ever thought you'd get."

"When people have something they don't want to think about, they'll talk about other things, sometimes too much. One time, long ago, I visited a friend in the hospital one afternoon and found out that they had told him that very morning he wasn't going to make it.

He babbled at me for two hours. He was quick and funny and intense. He told me the dirty details of his failed marriage. I suspected he had never intended to tell all that to anyone. It was a strange and uncomfortable period for me. Then he started to cry and ordered me out. I went to see him again, but he resented me because he had told me too much. I took advantage of the way she was feeling. She didn't want to think about Jesse."

Meyer left me in the motel with some magazines and the Saturday afternoon television. I took a late-afternoon walk, but the heat was still too intense. It made you feel as if you could not breathe deeply enough. I phoned Annie's private line, but there was no answer. I watched a portion of a bad ball game. I took a nap. I read the magazines. I tried television. Lawrence Welk had replaced the ball game. He had a batch of very old citizens there, playing old music very well on shiny horns. They had doubtless come out of the big band era and were happy to find work playing the same old stuff.

Meyer got in at ten fifteen. He looked grainy and old. I knew he'd tell me about it when he was ready, so I didn't push him. Inexpensive bourbon has its own aroma, and he smelled as if he'd had more than two. He took a shower and came out and stretched out on his bed, fingers laced behind his head.

"I think that what we had was a two-person wake, without the body. She thinks she's glad he's dead, but she isn't sure. She couldn't stop looking at the picture of the grown-up Cody. She said he had turned out to be a really good-looking man, like his father. I let her keep the picture. All right?"

"Of course. We've got three left. Anyway, why ask me? This is your parade."

"Every time I'd try to ease in on the identity of her correspondent in Eagle Pass, she'd sidestep. Nothing else was going to work. So I told her some stories. I told her all about Doris Eagle and Isobelle Garvey and Norma Lawrence. I told her about Larry Joe and Jerry and Evan. You see, Travis, Cody was her hero. The little brother, corrupted by the stepmother, had escaped and had made a successful life somewhere and was able to send money to his beloved big sister. She pictured him in a big house with a wife and kids and two cars. She couldn't stand what I was telling her. When she finally came to believe that the photograph she held in her hand had been positively identified by all concerned as Cody T. W. Pittler, her next line of defense was that Doris Eagle had died in a legitimate accident, that Izzy Garvey had gone off with Cody and run out on him later, and that he had been blown up aboard my boat. I asked her why all the names, and she said it was because the police still wanted him for what had happened at Eagle Pass. I had showed her the Doris Eagle clippings and the clippings about Norma's death. I told her about Norma's life, what kind of a woman she had been. She kept drinking. I kept drinking. We wept. I kept asking her why she wanted to protect such a man, even if he was her brother. She kept saying he was all the family she had.

"Finally she said that whenever she had changed her address, she had phoned the best friend she ever had, a woman in Eagle Pass named Clara Chappel. They had been all through the grades together back when she had been Clara Pitts. Because seating was alphabetical, they always sat near one another. They had double-dated, and they had both gotten drunk on tequila on the same date and lost their virginity the same night. They had been married at the same time, she to Sonny Fox, and Clara to Sid Chappel. Clara had always told her she wished Cody was a little older so she could marry him. She said she had moved seven times, since she had gone north with Sonny Fox, and had phoned Clara each time. Cody stayed in touch with Clara. She didn't know how. Clara never told her. She said it proved Cody was smart. He knew that if his sister knew how to get in touch with him, the police could find out from her. And she would never tell anyone about Clara. Then she seemed to realize she was telling me and shouldn't be. She drank more. It became difficult to understand what she was saying.

"At one point she led me out into that dreadful junkyard and reached into the bottom of an old iron stove and took out a tin candy box and opened it, shone the flashlight into it, onto a wad of hundred-dollar bills. Jesse had never found out about the money. She said he would have just taken it and left. She said Jesse wasn't good about money. Then she told me it had arrived early last month, early June. Seven thousand two hundred. You realize of course, Travis, that it was Norma's money. I told her it had been Norma's money. She wanted me to take it. I wouldn't. She put it back in the stove and clanged the old door. We were both crying. We supported each other back to the house. She said her head was aching terribly from being hit by Jesse. She called it his last love tap. She tripped on the top step and fell heavily into the trailer. I pulled her to her bed and lifted her onto it, half of her at a time. I drove back here with one eye shut so there would be one center line instead of two, one pair of oncoming headlights instead of two. It is a criminal act to drive in such a condition. I could have killed innocent people. I feel very sad and soiled and old. She really hasn't anything left now."

"I'll see if I can reach Paul Sigiera."

"You do that."

He kept his eyes shut while I tried. His breathing became heavier. He produced a long rattling snore. I finally reached Sigiera despite the efforts of two other officers on duty.

"Ah so," he said. "The Consultant and the Professor. What are you all consulting and professing?"

"Cody sends money to his sister at irregular intervals. Cash. From four to ten thousand in hundreds. Over a dozen shipments since he took off. He keeps track of her through a woman named Clara Chappel. She used to be Clara Pitts. Married to a Sid or Sidney Chappel. She phones Clara her changes of address and Clara relays them to Cody. So you know a Chappel family?"

"Hope to spit. There is no place in Maverick County high enough to stand on and see everything Sid Chappel owns."

"I have the feeling that when sister Helen June sobers up tomorrow, she is going to get to a phone and let Clara know that McGee and Meyer know about Cody's pipeline. So I thought if you got to Clara Chappel first—"

"And leaned on her? You've got to be kidding. Maybe I can do it with footwork and fancy talk. How's Helen June?"

"Living among junk with a piano player until today; then he rolled his Bronco over on himself and squashed his head."

"Just a coincidence?"

"You could call it that."

"Why in hell did Helen June tell you people anything?"

"The Professor talked nice to her. And she was in kind of a shocked condition. I would appreciate it if you would do what you can and let me know."

I gave him my phone number aboard the *Flush*. He said he would give it a try, but not right now, not on a Saturday night. There was too much action going on among the lower classes, such as cops, he said. Meyer slept on. I walked to the restaurant and had a bowl of chowder and a hot dog. A leggy sixteen-year-old girl with blond hair black at the roots, wearing a quarter pound of eye makeup, gave me the fixed challenging stare of the seasoned hooker while she ate her strawberry cone. There's no VD any more. Now it is all STD, Sexually Transmitted Diseases, and there are a lot more of them than there used to be, and a lot more people have them than used to, and some of them are resistant to all known antibiotics. I walked back through the hot night, thinking sad bad thoughts.

nineteen

When we finally got into Lauderdale, late on Sunday afternoon, after bad flight connections, I took a long hot shower and then phoned Annie. She sounded cross and overworked. The comptroller was down from Chicago. There were conferences about updating the computer system.

"Try me tomorrow," she said. "I don't know what tomorrow will be like, but it won't be any worse than today. Any luck on your quest?"

"Quest? Nice word for a series of blind alleys. I got kicked in the ear. Otherwise fine. Take care of yourself. Happy computing."

When I tried her on Monday on her private line, I got a solemn and heavy masculine voice saying, "Eden Beach, Howard Pine speaking."

"May I speak to Anne Renzetti, please?"

"I'm the new manager. Perhaps I can help you."

"This is personal, thanks."

"Oh. She flew back up to Chicago this morning out of Fort Myers with the comptroller. I would say she'll probably be back Wednesday. But it might be Thursday. I can give you a number where—"

"No thanks. I'll try again."

Meyer had gone over to B-80 to look at the thirty-one-foot Rawson. After that he had an appointment with the insurance agent. Then he was going to go buy clothes. And get a haircut.

I roamed around the houseboat, seeking out small chores, trying not to notice the big ones that needed doing. Restless, restless. I knew too much about Cody T. W. Pittler, and at the same time not nearly enough. I wanted to bounce what we knew about him off some knowledgeable person, and I suddenly realized that the ideal person would be Laura Honneker. About eleven years ago, after she had been practicing her profession of psychiatry in Fort Lauderdale for a little over two years, an unstable patient had broken into her office and made off with a batch of patient files. Though in the files she had referred to the patients by initials other than their own, she had foolishly left her cross-index in the same file cabinet and he had taken that too.

Her patients had begun to complain. They were outraged at the calls they were receiving from the thief. Along with all the usual dirty words, he was telling them details of their lives known only to them and to Dr. Honneker.

She did not want to take the matter to the police. She did not want the responsibility of what that would do to the patient who had taken the files. A mutual friend told her about me, and she asked me to come see her. I explained that I attempted to recover things of value which could not be recovered in any normal manner, and I usually kept half the value. She said that in one sense the files had no value, but in another sense, if the misuse of them destroyed her in Fort Lauderdale professionally, they were very valuable. So we agreed that I would bill her according to the difficulty I encountered.

She was about my age, maybe two years younger. She was a big Norse-looking woman, fair and well scrubbed, with a trick of establishing very direct eye contact, her eyes a skeptic green. She was tall and aglow with health. I found out that she ran miles on the beach at first light every day, back when it wasn't dangerous.

I phoned in and brought her crazy man to the office the next day, files and all. He was a heavy little man who believed the world was out to get him, and the best defense was to be offensive. He sat in the corner like a naughty child while she went through the files to be certain they were all there. She asked me if it had been a lot of trouble, and I smiled at the heavy little man and said, "No trouble at all."

She ordered him into the next room, and he trudged in and closed the door without making a sound.

"What would be a fair fee for your trouble, Mr. McGee?" she had asked.

The question seemed to be put in a challenging way. So I had replied, "We should set up an appointment and negotiate it, don't you think?"

"What did you have in mind?"

"We could negotiate over dinner."

She thought that over, smiled, agreed. We set a date. I picked her up at her place. It was a pleasant evening. We had a lot of attitudes in common. The way we negotiated it, she bought the dinner and I bought the wine. I sensed that she had all her defenses ready in case I threatened to presume too much. When we said good night at her door, I said I would give her a ring sometime. She said that would be nice. But we both knew it wouldn't happen.

About six months later I went to a big party at a conspicuously large and expensive house on the bay. I do not generally go to cocktail parties. I forget why I went to that one. Some people named Hunter gave the party. I arrived late and found, among the celebrants, one Dr. Laura Honneker, solemnly, quietly smashed. She walked and talked very very carefully. She told me in a slow and precise speech pattern that she did not drink, but that the previous night, at 3:00 A.M., a woman she thought she was helping had put the bedside gun in her mouth and pulled the trigger, thus awakening her husband in the ugliest possible way. So she had decided to have a cocktail. Or two.

I soon discovered she had been targeted by Ron Robinette, who was then living aboard a half million worth of motor sailer over at Bahia Mar, with an income from mysterious sources. He was big and ruddy with hair dyed black, teeth capped white, a lot of chest hair showing, and a constant smile underneath his little mean eyes. He hovered close and managed to keep touching her, establishing management and control. I saw him muttering into her ear and saw her shaking her head no. But Robinette manages to score in situations much less promising than this one.

So I worked it out and went over to them and said, "Time we took off, Laura honey, or we'll be late for dinner with the others."

"Others?" she said.

I got her by the elbow, and she resisted for just a moment and then came along, docile and unsteady.

"Now *hold* it, McGee," Robinette said, following closely. He put his hand on my shoulder.

I spun, shrugging his hand off, and said, "Screw around with me, Ronnie, and I'll do exactly what I did last time."

He tried to bring himself up to the point of actual resistance, but his memory was too good. He shrugged and gave me an evil look and turned away. Ten seconds after I handed her into the passenger side of my old Rolls pickup, she passed out. I wanted to take her to her place, but I couldn't rouse her. I rifled her purse and found her apartment keys, but they had no number on them. I knew the building but not the number. So I took her back to the *Busted Flush,* toted her aboard—she was a considerable burden—and laid her down on the bed in the spare cabin. I eased her shoes off. She was so slack

I wondered if she had something else beside too much booze, some kind of illness. I took her pulse. It was a heavy, slow *ta-bump, ta-bump, ta-bump*. She didn't feel feverish. So I left her there. I fixed myself a light supper and then read until after eleven.

Before I went to bed, I looked in at her. She had pulled her dress off and dropped it on the floor. I put a blanket over her and left a robe and a disposable toilet kit on the chair near the bed.

By midmorning, when I was on the second half of the paper and the second cup of coffee, I heard the shower. Soon she came out wearing the robe, her head wrapped in a white towel.

She said she felt rotten. She turned gray at the offer of eggs and settled for coffee, black. She seemed very ill at ease. Finally she said, "What am I doing here anyway?"

"Nursing a hangover, I think," I told her. And I told her about snatching her away from one Ron Robinette, thinking to drive her home, but having her pass out on me.

"Robinette. Big fellow with a red face. Smiles a lot?"

"The same."

"What was wrong with him taking me home?"

"I thought you deserved better. After all, you are an old acquaintance of mine, right? And Robinette has a case of what you professional people call satyriasis. You'd have been screwed lame by now, conscious or unconscious, sitting, kneeling, lying down, or standing on one leg. You'd walk funny for a week. And I didn't touch you, except to tote you from my pickup to your bed."

I felt a lot of tension go out of her, tension and suspicion. "Oh," she said. "And thanks. Who took my dress off?"

"It had to be you, because it wasn't me, Laura."

"I can't even remember," she said. "I guess you saved me from an ugly experience, which would have been my own fool fault. I was depressed. I hardly ever drink. I had some martinis. Then things got kind of blurred. It isn't fair. A man can get depressed and drink too much and he . . . he isn't vulnerable the way a woman is."

When her hair was reasonably dry, she combed it out, went in and dressed, and I drove her back to her car. Before she got out of Miss Agnes, she frowned at me and said, "If you hadn't known me at all, would you have rescued me from that man?"

"I doubt it. I can't run around under the trees catching everything that falls out of the nests, Doctor. Why should I steer Robinette to somebody else who might have just as bad a time?"

"Then I'm very glad poor Mr. Finch broke into my files and you came to that party. Very glad." She leaned toward me and put a quick light shy kiss on the corner of my mouth. It was not invitational. It was the kiss a young girl gives her uncle at Christmas.

My upright behavior must have intrigued her, because she began to appear at the right places and right times with such uncanny accuracy that we drifted into an affair which lasted not more than a month and was called off by mutual consent. We were able to say the right things, do the right things, satisfy each other, enjoy each other, but there was something lacking. We were friends making love, not lovers making love. The bodies functioned, but the hearts never took to the wild leaping. So it had a faint flavor of the mechanical, an aura of the incestuous. And, also, I had the feeling she was watching both of us with her professional eye, a surveillance guaranteed to chill any dalliance.

So now, needing advice, I phoned her office. The woman who answered told me the doctor was with a patient, but she could be disturbed if it was an emergency. I said it was a social call and left my name and number.

Laura called back twenty minutes later. "Travis! How good to hear your voice."

"I've been trying to remember when I saw you last. About four years ago, I think."

"Closer to five. We ran into each other at Sears. Housewares."

"It's been five years? How are you anyway?"

"One hundred forty and holding."

"Married yet?"

"Almost was, but I backed out at the very last moment, almost when he was putting the ring on me. Turned chicken. I know you aren't."

"How would you know that?"

"Let's just say that your social circles and my professional clients overlap a little here and there. And sometimes we talk about you."

"Favorably?"

"Sometimes, sure."

"The reason I called, I want to pick your doctor brains over dinner. I want to tell you what I know about someone, and you tell me what you can guess about him. I buy the food and the wine."

She said she was free that very evening, but she had some dictation to catch up on and had planned to stay in the office for a couple of hours after the last patient, so she thought she had better meet me at the restaurant. She named one of the new French ones. They are popping up all over Florida like toadstools after a rain. They vary from wretched to superb. The very best one I know, and I think it the best between Miami and New Orleans, is over on the west coast of Florida, at a shopping mall called Sarasota Square. It is outside the mall, in an area containing a K-Mart and a supermarket. It is called the Café La Chaumière and is owned and operated by an agreeable type named Alain who used to be a chef at the Rive Gauche in Washington. She said she would make the reservation.

When I got there at eight, they were all smiles when I said I was joining the Doctor Honneker. Would I go to the table? No, thank you, I would wait at this here little corner bar. She came in looking elegant in her office business suit. A little heftier in the hip, a trifle thicker around the waist, some horizontal lines across the throat and verticals bracketing the mouth. But a fine figure of a woman, with a lovely green-eyed smile.

I carried my drink to the table and we ordered her one. She told me her practice was booming, due mostly to having some luck with the nose-candy crowd: young lawyers, doctors, contractors, merchants, dentists, politicians. "I get them of course after they are finally willing to admit they are in serious trouble. So they are pretty well habituated by then, and very jumpy. Have you ever used it?"

"Tried it twice and didn't like it either time. The great big rush of confidence and well-being is just fine, but when it fades it's hard to remember just exactly what it was like. You just remember you felt real good, and now you don't feel so great."

"My reaction exactly. I've been having some luck with diet, drug therapy, and analysis. One thing I am sure of: when I have a patient who backslides and comes back to me six months later, there is a discernable diminution of intelligence and awareness. I'm administering standard intelligence measurements to all my cocaine patients now as standard procedure. If I can accumulate enough data, I'm going to try to do a paper on it."

Over the soup she asked me what I wanted to ask her. I had gone through some mental rehearsals. "Here is your hypothetical patient, Laura. He is now forty-two. When he was thirteen, his mother died suddenly. He had one sister, five years older. When he was fifteen his father married a twenty-five-year-old woman who worked in his office. She was a very sexy item, with a chronic case of the hots. The father was promoted to a job where he had to travel three and four days a week and stay away overnight. When he was seventeen, after his sister married and moved out, the patient was seduced by his stepmother and they entered into a relationship that lasted perhaps three years. Call it two years, plus the vacations when he came home from college when he was twenty."

"That's really a fairly common form of incest, Travis, and—"

"That's just part of it. After the end of his freshman year, the boy came home from college and they picked up where they left off. The father came home unexpectedly one night, heard them, listened at the bedroom door, got his gun, and stepped in and killed her with one shot to the back of the head, near the nape of the neck. From the evidence at the scene, the woman was on top, her feet toward the doorway. The boy squirmed out from under her, and we do not know what happened next. There was evidence of a struggle. So either the father tried to kill the boy or tried to kill himself. They fought for the gun and the father was shot. He died soon after they found him. A neighbor heard the two shots and saw the boy as he drove away in the father's car. The car was found weeks later at the bottom of a canyon, with nobody in it or near it."

She dropped her soup spoon into her shallow bowl and stared at me. "Good grief! What was the boy's relationship to his father?"

"The boy loved and respected his old man."

"Worser and worser. What kind of boy was he?"

"Standard issue. Athletic. Not a great student. Interested in theater, I guess. He was in the drama club. Reasonably good-looking. Big shoulders and hands."

"Are you quite sure he's alive?"

"It is a reasonable certainty."

"Is the sister alive?"

"Yes. He sends cash to her, secretly. He has a way of keeping track of where she is. He's sent her the better part of a hundred thousand dollars over the past fifteen years or so."

"Does she condone his behavior?"

"She says it was all the fault of the second wife."

"Is he still a fugitive?"

"Technically, I guess. Nobody is really looking for him for that early shooting."

"But they are looking for him for something else?"

"I'd rather not say yet. What would it do to a person, that kind of history?"

"I don't think . . . I don't believe anyone would be strong enough to walk away from something like that undamaged. If he loved his father, then he hated the stepmother. The long history of betraying his father every time they had a chance, that isn't something he could get used to. It would just pile guilt upon guilt, higher and higher. He would have contempt for himself, for being unable to stop. He would feel weak and used and contemptible."

"How would it have ended if the old man hadn't caught them?"

"I don't know. I can guess. The stepmother was turned on by the danger of it, by the 'badness' of it. She was walking a very dangerous tightrope and knew it. One scenario would be for the boy to kill her, to strangle her or beat her to death. That would be an understandable way of seeking punishment for all his sinning. That would give them—meaning society—the excuse to jail him for life, put him away, out of touch with decent people. A less dramatic and probably more plausible reaction would be for the boy to just run away, leave it all behind. Killing himself would be one kind of running away. Killing himself and the woman must certainly have occurred to him as a way of expiating guilt and punishing both the guilty parties. Guilt is a powerful and frightening thing, Travis. He might just have disappeared into limbo. A wandering migrant worker. A future bum on a park bench somewhere. But when it was all taken out of his hands in such a gaudy brutal way, before he could plan and make expiation, I . . . I just can't predict the effect. I do have the gut feeling that this might be a terribly dangerous personality, a man completely dead inside. I think he would probably be ritualistic. He . . . he would want to take revenge on his own sexuality as being the agent that caused the trouble."

"How would he do that?"

"Self-mutilation would be understandable. Or total denial and deprivation."

"How would he react toward women?"

"Oh, God. That would be a bucket of worms. I think he would want to punish them for their sexuality, for being the symbol of the temptress. What are you getting at?"

"Try this. Would this be possible? For him to hunt down women, one after the other, young attractive women, seduce them, enchant them into a very physical and erotic affair, actually seem to love them, sometimes even marry them, and then kill them?"

For a moment she frowned, and then her eyes widened. "It would be ritualistic. He would be punishing her for her sexuality, and he would be punishing himself by depriving himself of her passion. It's intricate, Trav, but I could buy it. Yes. And he would acquire a very special knack of making himself attractive to women, of always saying the right thing, doing the right thing. He would have to keep changing his identity, wouldn't he?"

"I know the name he started with and three more, and know of three dead women."

We were side by side on a banquette. She grabbed me so strongly just above my right knee I could feel her nails through the fabric of my trousers. "My God, tell me about him! Tell me all about him!"

It took a long time. She asked questions. We suddenly stirred ourselves, realizing the check had been on the table for a long time and the waiters were circling at a discreet distance, coughing, and the place was absolutely empty except for us. So, in apology, I over-tipped, and she followed me in her car, back to the *Busted Flush* so we could keep the discussion going.

We sat in the lounge with cold beer in hand, and I said, "Maybe we won't ever find him, Meyer and I. But suppose we do. Suppose we find him and walk up to him. He is going to know us. How will he react?"

She took a long time thinking it over. She said, "You must realize that he has been wondering for years what he would do if that happened, if somebody was able to unmask him. Since you say he is likable and plausible, I think he will give you a totally fabricated account of what actually happened. He will make it sound real. He has depended on charm for a long time. I think you will have to pretend to believe him."

"Why?"

"He's a murderer, Travis. He has developed his capacity for violence. There will be no hesitation in him at all. Believing his story, you will have to maneuver him to a place and time where he can't hurt you and can't get away from you. Then and only then do you start casually dropping the names of the dead. Not accusatory. Affable. Almost laughing at him. Doris Eagle. Isobelle Garvey. He will not know how much you know, and suddenly you will seem to be all-knowing. You will become the God-Daddy here to punish him at last, and I think he will come competely, totally apart, with no hope of ever putting himself together again. I have broken people that way so that I could put them back together again in a better pattern, with their help. The more you look amused at their lies, the wilder the lies become. And quite suddenly they break."

"And if he just denies it? Maybe I didn't get it across to you. This is a *very* plausible, likable man. If he can hold himself together, no jury will convict."

"If he just denies it, you must edge very very carefully into the Coralita situation."

"Why delicately?"

"There is such a phenomenon as denial. By now he may well have convinced himself that it didn't happen. Confrontation would reinforce the denial. You would have to ask him about little things. What color were Coralita's eyes? Can you think of the unimaginable hell it must have been for that boy when his father was home? To sit at dinner with his father and Coralita. To try not to look at Coralita's breasts and her hips and her mouth for fear his father would guess what was going on between them. To lie in bed and hear his father in another bedroom, perhaps in the same bed where he had had sex with Coralita. It must have been an unimaginable misery for the boy, and then to have it end with the death of both of them. . . ." She shook her head. "It would just be too uncomfortable for him to carry that around. It would be too vivid. And so the brain would wall it off. Be very careful with him if you find him. Don't give him any chance at all. People who are quite mad—a very unprofessional word —have enormous quickness and strength. We see a lot of it in mental hospitals. It will take four or five husky young attendants to overpower some frail little old man who has decided he does not want his medication."

After we had worn out the topic of Cody T. W. Pittler, his life and times, she cocked her head and said, "You seem troubled about something else too."

"I had no idea it showed."

"I'm a trained observer, and once upon a time I knew you pretty darn well."

"I remember. Well, I'm having a little trouble with my old lady, to put it in the chauvinist pig manner."

"The nice little hotel executive?"

"How do you know about *her?*"

"Somebody once defined gossip quite properly as emotional speculation. And I *am* interested in you and your life."

"She is being promoted and sent to Hawaii. End of whatever it is we've been having."

"An arrangement?"

"Good enough word, I guess. There was no abused party in the deal. It seemed okay for both of us."

"Do you think it should be more important to her than moving ahead in her job?"

"I don't know exactly what to think. I just feel sort of depressed about it."

"Do you love her?"

"What can I say? I feel very good being with her. I like to look at her. I like to listen to her talk. We have a lot of dumb little private personal games we play. When I'm away from her I miss her."

"How does she feel about you?"

"Sort of the same. But she says it has never been enough. She says she has never been able to really let go completely with me because I keep a certain distance from her. Perhaps I do. If so, maybe it's a flaw in my character. She says we're a convenience to each other, a handy shack job without complications or obligations, and she says that it is not a very noble preoccupation for either of us. She says that at first she thought it was going to be everything, because each time we were together, we got further and further into each other, into knowing and understanding. But it went only so far and then stopped. I did not stop anything on purpose. The accusation makes me feel . . . sort of puzzled and inadequate."

"Does she really want the job?"

"As badly, she says, as she ever wanted anything in her life."

"Why don't you follow her out there?"

"I belong right here."

"With all anchors set, all lines made fast?"

"I guess so."

"Want to marry her?"

"I don't want to marry anybody."

She smiled, hitched closer, took my hand in both of hers. "Hey, can you remember back eleven years?"

"Of course."

"We had the same problem, my dear, in a different degree. I really wanted to fall in love with you. I thought it would be good for me. Turned out we could love each other in a physical sense, but we couldn't fall in love. We fell into like, not love. And that isn't ever quite enough. Bawdy as we got at times, we were still, in an unfortunate sense, brother and sister. So we knocked it off. Without rancor. And I confess to a little sense of relief when it ended. I could stop pretending to be in love. Got a feeling of relief about her? Are you tucking it away, as an unworthy emotion? Is that making you a little ashamed of yourself, and is that why you feel depressed?"

"Doctor, you are too damned smart."

"Just be awfully awfully glad you and she had a good run at it. That's all. And be glad for her if she's getting what she wants. And for heaven's sake, don't try to punish her as she leaves, like a little kid who's losing all his candy."

"Am I like that?"

"You poor dummy, *everybody* is like that!"

So we kissed and I walked the doctor to her car, held the door open, and gave her a proprietary pat on the behind.

When I closed the door, she ran the window down and leaned to look up at me. "I don't want to make you angry."

"Then don't."

"Please, Travis. Don't obstruct. What I want to say, which may make the whole situation easier for you to understand, is that maybe your hotel executive friend has more capacity for genuine maturity than you have."

"Thanks a lot."

"It need not be an insult, if you don't take it as one. You have been living your life on your own terms. You need make only those concessions which please you. There are always funny friends, parties, beach girls, and the occasional dragon to go after. I don't pretend to know any of the circumstances that shaped you. I would guess that at some time during your formative years there was an incident that gave you a distaste for most kinds of permanence. None of us decide arbitrarily to be what we are. We just *are* what we are, through environment, heredity, and the quality of our mind and our emotions. Are you ashamed of what you are?"

"No, but . . ."

"And that, dear heart, has to be everybody's answer: No, but. . . . And I can finish your sentence. No, but I wish I were a better person."

"You too?"

She rested her hand on mine. "I've got your disease, Travis. That's why I chickened out on marriage. I didn't think I could handle the role. I know I couldn't. But I *do* get so awful damn lonely sometimes." Her hand tightened on mine.

"And they tell me it can get even lonelier."

"I know."

"So, Doctor Laura, after my bird has flown, maybe you could offer some physical comfort, and accept some."

"I think I would like that very much. It doesn't have to be a case of turning the clock back. Somebody to hang onto in the long long dark night, somebody warm, somebody breathing warmth against my flesh. Somebody giving a damn. Even just a little damn."

I bent clumsily through the window and kissed her mouth. When I straightened I thumped my head on the top of the opening. She laughed. I told her doctors should have more sympathy, and she laughed again and backed out and drove away.

Meyer arrived at a quarter past one, as I was getting ready for bed. "Who stays open this late?" I asked him. "Barbers or clothing stores?"

"Was I supposed to report?"

"Don't get stuffy. I just thought you might be here while I was out to dinner, to take any call that might come from Sigiera."

"I came back and dropped off the clothes I bought. And then I went back to that Rawson again. The old lady had me stay and eat with her. And we've been talking. Her name is Margaret Howey, and she is really a hell of a woman."

"Going to buy it?"

"What? The boat? Yes, of course. It's a good buy, and it's roomier than the *Keynes* was. The insurance will cover most of it."

"What are you going to call it?"

"Times have changed. Perceptions change. Fashions change. Also, a boat has to fit its name. I thought first it might be the *Adam Smith*. But Margaret and I decided that the *Thorstein Veblen* would be nice."

"The who?"

"Veblen died in 1929 at the age of seventy-two. He was an economist, and some of his theories became clouded by his sociological theories. His book *The Theory of the Leisure Class,* with its ideas about conspicuous consumption, had a vogue for a time. I have never been a Veblenian myself. But Margaret thinks it makes a neat name for a boat."

"Whatever Margaret thinks."

"It will be utterly meaningless to everyone who graduated from high school in the past twenty years. That's the nice part of it."

"What will you call it for short?"

"For short? The *Thorstein Veblen* is quite short enough."

When he is in that mood, there is nothing reasonable that you can say to him. He told me Margaret would move north in two weeks, and he could have possession on August sixteenth, and on that day he would move it to the berth where the *John Maynard Keynes* had always squatted, with its meager freeboard making it look underprivileged.

twenty

Tuesday, the third of August, was one of those rare Atlantic coast days with no wind at all. Every scrap of cloth on every boat docked at Bahia Mar hung limp as rejection. The endless midday traffic droned past the marina and motel, under the pedestrian bridge over to the beach, leaving an oppressive chemical stink in the air.

There was a sheen of oil on the boat basin. Compressors chugged, cooling stale air belowdecks. Brown girls lay stunned on open decks, sweat rolling off them. A ship's cat lay in the shade of a tarp aboard a nearby motor sailer, sleeping on its back with all four feet in the air.

Sigiera phoned at one fifteen.

"McGee? This here is your smart Texican law officer speaking."

"Glad to hear from you."

"Thought you might be. I didn't go bulling into this thing. What I did, I tried to think of the angles. I tried to add up everything I'd ever heard about the Chappel family, and I didn't move in on Mrs. Chappel until I had a real good angle to play. This is my angle. A bunch of good old boys are going to try to put Sid Chappel in the state legislature next chance. He's willing. God knows he's willing. He's taken to shaking hands with people on the street he doesn't hardly know.

"So I got out there this morning about ten, and Miz Clara was in the pool, and the maid took me out and left me. I can tell you, it's hard to believe she's got to be forty-seven if a day. Pretty little thing, built like a schoolgirl. I just come back from there."

"And?"

"Don't try to rush me along. In some cases it's smart to kind of hem and haw and beat around until they finally ask. And she did. She said she would sure like to know what I had on my mind. That's when you kind of blurt it out, like you just hated to say it. So I said I'd come to do her a favor. I said some political enemies of her husband had me checking out the old Cody Pittler file, because they had the idea of using it against him when he would up and run for office. She asked me what that could possibly mean to her. She said I should talk to Sid. And I told her I was talking to her because she was the one who kept in touch with Cody, as a favor to Helen June. I tell you, McGee, she came up out of that pool water like a porpoise. One minute she's in the water, and the next minute she's standing in front of me, sopping wet. She asked me where I'd heard a damn fool thing like that, and I said Helen June tended to talk when she had more than three, and she said some words about Helen June that I didn't think a lady like that would know. She knew lots of them, and how to hang them together in chunks."

"And so?"

"And so I asked her if she'd heard from Helen June lately, and she said she'd gotten a call yesterday in the afternoon, and she had written down what Helen June told her, and she had planned on driving the fifty-five miles up to Del Rio, like she usually did with messages for him, and mailing it from there. So I told her that what she could do would be give it to me quiet like, and if it ever came up, I would swear that she had been intercepting messages and turning them over to me, and it would turn back on whoever was after Sid's hide. And if she didn't want to—right here I slapped my pocket—I'd just have to hand her this here warrant—that I didn't have—and search the house. So she called me some of the names she called Helen June, and she was so darn cute, I was willing to forget the seventeen years she's got to have on me and tote her right over onto one of those big sun cots they got. And she knew what I had in mind and liked stirring me up that way, and pretty soon we both started to laughing. She went and got the letter, and I got it right here. The note inside was typed. It didn't say dear anything, and there was no name at the end. I'll read it to you."

"That would be nice."

" 'Two men came here with your recent picture, claiming you have been killing women for their money and using other names. One was a professor named Meyer and he is a very nice man. He said you blew up his niece named Norma in a boat with two other people. He said you killed somebody named Doris and somebody named Isabel and maybe more. They made me believe you really did. It makes me feel sick. If you are doing things like this, terrible things, then the police should stop you. The other man is a lot taller and he has sort of a mean look sometimes. And he can fight. Be careful. I tried not to tell them anything. They got my address from Boomer. I think you would remember him.'

"So I asked her if those were the exact words and she said they weren't. She said she had taken notes and then put it down in a better way than Helen June had told it. She said Helen June had cussed a lot. I suppose you want the address to where she was sending it."

"It would be nice."

"It was going to Señor Roberto Hoffmann, Apartado Postal Number seven one oh, Cancún, Quintana Roo, Mexico. Did you get that?"

"I wrote it down," I said, and read it back.

"Now what will you do?" he asked.

"We'll go down there and show the picture."

"Well, did I do good?"

"You were practically perfect."

"I hope you two know you are dealing with a flake, a weirdo."

"We know that. We plan to be very careful."

"Let me tell you something about old Mexico. If he's been down there a long time, with money to spend, then he is dug in, and he'll have some good Mexican connections. You try to put local law on him and you will be the ones on the inside, rattling the bars."

"What's to keep her from writing the same thing over again and mailing it?"

"She and me, we reached an understanding. I told her if she did that, I would go to Sid and tell him how she has been screwing around writing notes to a guy that is still wanted for killing his own father. And I would tell him she had been doing it behind his back. I took a chance there. Maybe she told Sid. But she hadn't, and it scared hell out of her. He is known as a hitter. Besides, she feels like Helen June betrayed her. They swore never to tell anybody. She looked like she'd like to kill Helen June. There's another thing too."

"Such as?"

"It was sort of play pretend for her. It took her back to when she was twenty and Cody was fifteen and she wished he was older, back to when she and Helen June were real close. She'd bought Helen June's idea of how it happened, Bryce Pittler trying to kill himself and finally shooting himself when they struggled for the gun. And all the trouble was on account of Bryce marrying that trashy little second wife, who got what she deserved. All she ever had to send before was addresses, and a note saying she and Helen June hoped he was okay. He had phoned her a couple of times, making sure she never told Helen June his address. But then all this comes up, the idea he could have been killing people. Little old Clara, she doesn't want any part of that kind of going on. That could be some kind of trouble that would hurt her husband and her and spoil the life they've built up. And Helen June had been kind of hysterical over the phone. That took the fun out of it too. Okay, I did good, but it was ready to come apart anyway. You two did even better up there. He kept his two lives fastened together with a very thin thread, McGee, and it took hard work and luck to even find out it existed."

"Thank you."

"There's an official file here needs closing. So you could let me know."

"Could you get an assignment to go down there with us?"

"You've got to be out of your mind! The budget we got, we're down three men here already, and it could be more. We stay on our side of the river and they stay on theirs. Sometimes they'll bring somebody to the middle of the bridge for us, and we do the same for them. But it doesn't happen often. When you go down there, walk easy. Get yourself a local and pay him good."

Meyer got back at two o'clock, and I told him the conversation I'd had with Paul Sigiera. He sat, utterly quiet, sorting it out after I'd finished.

"One thing we know," he said. "He couldn't be Roberto Hoffmann in Cancún and be Evan Lawrence in Cancún. There must be endless thousands of American tourists flowing through that place, but the Americans in permanent or semipermanent residence must be well known to each other and to the resident Mexicans. So we start with Evan Lawrence's friend Willy, who sells time shares in condominium apartments, and this Willy might know a local who will help us."

"I checked with Fran at Triple A Travel, and she said the best and quickest way to get there is go to Miami and take Mexicana. I think she said it leaves at four thirty. We can get a tourist card at the airline desk. Mexicana and Aero Mexico always say all flights are full, but they leave about two thirds full, except at Christmastime, including the standby people. Hot there, she said. Very very hot. We can try to set up a rental car in the Miami airport, but she said that hardly ever works too well. No problem with hotels at this time of year, she said. When do you want to go?"

"Right now," Meyer said.

As it turned out, we weren't able to leave until the next day, the fourth, a day of hot wind and rain that lasted all the way to the parking garage.

The severe young man at the airline desk took the cash money from Meyer for round-trip tickets. My protests did not work. Return trip unreserved. We were on standby for the flight to Cancún. We went downstairs to a bus which took us to a new terminal building, where we sat in plastic chairs in a broad vista of plastic and filled out the tourist permit forms. We had tried to look tourist. Mesh shirts, seersucker pants, sandals, the big ranch hats we'd picked up in Texas, battered carry-on bags. Meyer had a lot of funds strapped around his waist under his shirt, in a canvas money belt. Money, he has always said, solves the unanticipated problems. It won't buy happiness, but it will rent a fair share of it.

It was a one-class flight on a 727, with no room for my knees. The flight time was two hours and a bit, and the hard-working Mexican flight attendants served a meal. There was an hour time change, so it was only a little past five fifteen when we began our long curving descent into the Cancún airport. The pilot took us over the Cancún peninsula. It was a spectacular view, lowering clouds overhead, storms out at sea, and a long slant of golden sunshine striking the column of tall hotels along the beach.

Meyer, thorough as ever, had arranged to read up on the place, and he explained it to me en route. "It is that rarity," he said, "a totally artificial community, without a history, without traditions. Less than ten years ago there were about thirty-five people living in the mainland village of Cancún. Several narrow islands stretched out into the Gulf. Mexico needed hard dollars, so they took aerial photographs of the seacoast and decided that this would make an attractive resort. Now there are over fifty thousand permanent residents. They made low-interest loans to people who wanted to build hotels and resorts. They linked the islands with a causeway and bridges, built an airport, built a road down the coast to Chetumal, the capital of Quintana Roo, and the dollars do indeed flow in. There have been problems, of course: help for the hotels, food production, and transportation. Now they are getting small cruise ships and convoys of recreational vehicles and yachts and flocks of tour buses. It has become a popular resort for middle-class Mexicans and Americans. Lately there have been a lot of condominium developments scattered near the hotels."

I glanced at him. He had the window seat. He was staring straight ahead, expressionless. He sensed me looking at him and turned toward me.

"What are we doing, Travis? Just what in the name of hell are we trying to do?"

"We're trying to find the man who killed Norma. And we might even succeed."

"Then what?"

"There are no pamphlets about what to do. No instructions. He's one kind of hunter. I'm another. We can do a little diving around the reefs, maybe a little fishing, call it a day, and head for the barn. Maybe it's enough to know where he is."

There was an unexpectedly steely look in his small blue eyes. "Surely you jest, my friend. We owe something to his next ten years of victims, be they two, four, or twenty. We will find him. We will find a way to . . ." He hesitated. "All I can think of is a phrase I hear on television. A way to terminate him with prejudice."

The plane squealed its tires on the runway, taxied back to the small modern terminal building, and we climbed down the rolling stairs into twilight, sweat, far-off thunder, and the smell of something frying.

We all stood in line at tall narrow desks where immigration officers checked our passports, then stamped our signed permits and slid them back to us. There was a lot of bright fluorescence in the airport building, and large clocks which did not work. The passengers stood waiting by the stationary conveyor belt which would start up and bring their luggage out of the holes in the wall. Tour guides were herding their customers into small groups, shouting at them about which bus to take. "We all going to Hotel Presidente. You say that, eh? All now. Presidente!"

"Presidente!" they cried in ragged unison.

"Good! That where you going. Boos numero saventy-one!"

There was a guard by the glass doors. Nobody seemed to be going out into the main part of the terminal. I walked smiling toward him, Meyer behind me. I nodded and pushed the door open and he hesitated and backed out of the way. So much for bringing things into Mexico.

We came out into the rental car area. Some of the stations were closed. Hertz, Avis, Dollar, and Budget were open. We nailed down a three-year-old Plymouth at Budget, pronounced Bood-zhett. It had fifty-two thousand kilometers on it and had recently been painted a curious pink. The air conditioning made conversation impossible. When we had to confer, we turned it off.

It was about seventeen miles into downtown Cancún. We had to turn right before we got to the center of the city. We turned, as per instructions, at the Volkswagen garage and headed on out to the hotel district. It was a dark hot night and beginning to rain. The hotels were lighted like birthday cakes. I pulled into the Bojorquez, and then the Carrousel, waving away each time the bellhops who scurried out into the rain to take our luggage.

Farther along, the Dos Playas looked suitable. Not too fancy, not too grubby. For eighty dollars a night, summer rates, plus tax, about twenty-two hundred pesos, we got a small fourth-floor suite with kitchenette. If you put your cheek against the window you could see the Caribbean. If you slid the glass door open you could go out onto a miniature balcony and see a lot more of it, as well as a corner of the pool and some vacant lighted tennis courts, the lights glinting off the bounce of rain.

We had a big bedroom and a little bedroom. We matched, and Meyer won the little one. We went down to a busy bar. Most of the customers were Mexican tourists. There were a few senior citizens from the States, paired off, drinking tequila, going through the funny ceremony of the slice of lime between the fingers, the salt on the back of the hand. Lick the salt, toss down the shot, bit into the lime. This was creating a certain amount of amusement among the Mexicans, because the tequila they were drinking was a nice amber *anejo*, which is as smooth as bonded bourbon. The salt-and-lime bit is imperative only when drinking the coarsest kind of mescal, that second distillation from the maguey which tends to remove the plaque from your molars.

No Dos Equis at the bar, so we had a pair of Cervesa Negra Modela.

Meyer said, "He could walk in here, you know."

"Totally improbable. But remotely possible. Sure."

"And what do we do then?"

"We become thunderstruck. We stagger with the shock of it all. We point the quivering finger at him and say, 'B-b-but you're d-dead!'"

"And then it's his play?"

"Exactly right."

"I will have absolutely no trouble looking shocked."

We took a look at the menu and decided to try a place we had passed on the right-hand side about four hotels back: Carlos 'n' Charlie's. When we looked outside, the rain had stopped, so we walked it, on a curving path, quite wide, made of some kind of red tile blocks, between plantings that smelled like flowers and richness after the rain.

The restaurant smelled of good food, but the music was too loud. We were early. It was only seven. Mexicans eat at nine, and the tourists from Stateside soon catch the habit. The man who took us back to the table looked taken aback, astonished at his own bad guessing, and totally pleased when I dropped a hundred-peso note on him out of my beer change. He immediately moved us to a better table, by a window overlooking the lagoon, and snapped his fingers to bring a waiter on the run. He said the broiled fish was fresh and good, as were the tiny shrimp from Campeche. Shrimp cocktail, broiled fish, and a bottle of local white wine.

"Who are we supposed to be?" Meyer asked. "Just tourists?"

"What we are is refugees from the sorry real estate situation in Florida. We took a look at what was moving in Dallas and Houston, and a friend suggested we might make a connection down here, selling time sharing in the condos."

"What do you know about time sharing, Travis?"

"Only what I learned secondhand from Cody, when he was being Evan Lawrence."

"One of the sales arguments is that when you buy a week or two weeks' occupancy in a registered condominium, you can subscribe to a centralized computer service and through that service trade places and dates with some other time-share owner. But essentially, what you do is buy the right to inhabit your one fiftieth or one twenty-fifth share of an apartment for a specific week or two weeks for the rest of your life."

"Arguments against?"

"In a fifty-apartment building, half sold on two weeks, half on one week, you have eighteen hundred and seventy-five owners. That number of families can seriously damage the facilities available to everyone: pool, courts, beach, all common areas. The original owners, once all the time is sold, move on. It is up to the eighteen hundred and seventy-five owners to find somebody who will take charge of maintenance, rent the empties on due notice, and take care of the two weeks of close-down and refurbishing once a year. People resist any increase in assessments. People mistreat the furnishings and appliances. In theory it sounds attractive. In practice it can be extraordinarily messy."

"A ripoff?"

"In most cases. If you cannot sell an apartment to one owner for a hundred thousand dollars, you sell it to fifty owners for thirty-five hundred apiece. Can you imagine being the last one in line, before the annual facelifting, and half the families in there ahead of you had small children and puppies?"

"So we will be posing as con men."

"In a sense, yes. Cynicism will be more convincing than an air of earnest integrity."

When we were bowed out by the headwaiter, a small, dark, burly Mexican thrust a pamphlet at each of us. It was a single sheet, folded. It invited us to free drinks and snacks from four to six o'clock any day at the Azteca Royale, a brand-new apartment building designed for vacation sharing. Absolutely free, without obligation. On Fridays the freebies would include a ride in a launch around the Nichupte Lagoon. Come to the reception desk outside the public lounge near the model apartment.

"This is what we were talking about," Meyer said.

"And they will know Willy No-Last-Name."

"If Cody Pittler was not lying, Willy was selling time shares right here in Cancún the first two months of this year."

twenty-one

The Azteca Royale was under construction farther out along the island chain, out beyond the turnoff to the Hotel Camino Real, almost to the shopping plaza that served the hotel district, and not far from a convention center and a native crafts center.

In the morning we had ridden on out to the end to where a gate and a guard barred the way to the Club Mediterranee, bribed our way past the guard, bought twelve dollars' worth of beads, and sat at an outdoor bar with a good view of the pool, drinking a brace of rum punches while we admired the pleasantly tanned mammary equipment of the younger lady guests. The bartender took three one-dollar beads for each drink, so two apiece was all our beads would buy. Bright sun, dark shade, ample drinks, and firm bobbing boobs splashing around in the blue water tended to stimulate erotic imaginings. This was what vacations are for.

After a light lunch and a nap back at the Dos Playas, we were ready for the sales pitch. The public lounge with the model apartment beyond it was at the right, or east, side of the structure that was going up. It had little brown men crawling all over the reinforced concrete beams of the basic framework, hauling up buckets of this and that on frayed ropes, their muscular brown backs clenching and shining in the afternoon sunlight.

It was five after four. A handsome young man in an elegant linen suit sprang up from behind the reception desk, hand outstretched, smile wide. "Welcome!" he said. "Welcome! We have marvelous things to show you, gentlemen."

"Bet you do," I said.

He handed us each a batch of pamphlets and directed us into the lounge. It was large. There were little conversational islands of chairs placed on rugs at random around the large tiled floor. A maid in uniform, her eyes half closed, stood leaning against the wall behind an improvised bar, a long table covered with sheeting. Two more elegant men and two handsome young women were talking together. They all turned to stare at us, and after a murmured discussion, the taller and better looking of the two women came striding toward us, turning to pop her fingers at the maid and jolt her out of her trance.

"Welcome!" she said. "Welcome, gentlemans. Welcome to the luffly Azteca Royale!" She wore a white blouse with a little black string tie, and dark red slacks closely fitted. She had a fine walk and lots of eyelashes.

"What would you like for drinking, please?"

I had a small dull headache from the rum, and asked for a beer. She turned and said some machine-gun Spanish across the room to the maid, who delved into an ice chest and came on the run with two opened bottles of Carta Blanca and two frosty mugs. The girl asked our names and told us hers was Adela and looked down and pointed to her badge, which did indeed say Adela thereon. She guided us over to one of the little chair groups, and the maid put the beers, coasters, and paper napkins on the table. Adela said she was sorry she could not join us in a beer, but she would have a Fresca, and her steely look at the maid sent her scampering off to get it.

"So!" said Adela. "What do you say? Here is looking on you?"

"Looking on you," said Meyer, and we sipped.

"What a wonderful opportunity this is for you mens! Now we are having the preconstruction pricing. And we can offer some of the best times in the year. The Christmas and the New Year's is gone already. But there is a nice week from the middle end of January, or two weeks if you like that. Do you like that, Mr. Mickey?"

"McGee. Miss Adela, I think maybe we are here under false pretenses."

She looked blank. "What is this pretenses?"

"My partner here, Mr. Meyer, and I, we thought we might come down here and sell some of this time sharing to the tourists for you."

She stared at us and then shook her head slowly from side to side. "Oh, no! This is a most bad season for selling. More people selling than buying. You have no papers to work here?"

"No, we don't."

"It is very hard to get them. Very long time. You have to have a . . . how you say, *abogado?*"

"Lawyer," Meyer said.

"Yes, and is much, how you say, bite for you to get papers." She rubbed her thumb and two fingers together in the time-honored gesture which means bribery.

I smiled at her. "Now suppose I went right out and sold three weeks for you and came back with the people and you signed them up. Wouldn't you give me a little gift?"

She chewed at her underlip. "But I could cheat you, no?"

"A nice woman like you wouldn't cheat us."

"I am not the *jefe* here. I couldn't say. You have experience?"

"Mucho!" I said. "Millions. But maybe we ought to get in touch with a fellow I know down here who's in this line of work. Willy. I can't remember his last name."

"Willy?"

"Another friend named Evan Lawrence was working with him, and Evan didn't have any papers either."

"Oh, what you mean is Weelliam Doyle, from Yooston."

"That's who I mean."

"Oh, he is gone a long time, that one. Many weeks. Too damn bad. My fren' thinks he comes back. I don't think so. She's a very high-class lady even if she's Indio. She's still living in his place, waiting for Weelliam."

"Would she know where Evan Lawrence is?"

"Who can say? I do not see him any more either."

"Where can I find this woman? What's her name?"

"Barbara. Barbara Castillo. The place, it is down that way, toward the land. You will see it on the right hand. La Vista del Caribe. Apartments. His is ground floor on the front, no view. Ring the bell on Doyle." She looked at her watch. "But Barbara is not coming there yet from work. She is running a reservation computer at Hotel Camino Real every day. And waiting. Maybe after six, a little bit after."

"Thanks. Sorry we weren't in the market to buy."

She gave a shrug, made a funny little gesture with her hand. "So if it looked like you could buy, the other girl would be here, no? She is working longer than me."

We got to La Vista del Caribe shortly after six. It was already almost dark. I would never, by choice, live just over a time line, on the west side of the line. All year long, your days are too short.

There was no one at the desk. Little kids were racing up and down the corridors. We looked around the ground floor until we found the right place: number 103. He had cut down an engraved calling card to fit the name slot. William Devlin Doyle, Jr.

The bell was underneath the name slot. I pushed it three times without result. As we were discussing what to do next, the door suddenly opened. She was tall and slender. She wore a robe and held it closed around her with her left hand. Her smile of greeting disappeared abruptly. She wore a black shower cap. There were droplets of water on her face.

"I was . . . who are you?"

"We're from Houston, Miss Castillo. We're looking for Willy. My name is McGee and this is Meyer."

I was trying to look my ingratiating, foot-scuffing, aw-shucks best as she looked us over. "Come in, then. Please." She led us into the living room. It was a small room, the furniture spare and gleaming, two unusual primitive paintings on the white wall, a bookshelf with books, small pieces of sculpture, two masks.

"Please be seated. I will be with you in a few moments." She went down a short corridor off to the right. Ahead I could see through a pass-through arch into a white shiny kitchen.

I slowly let my breath out and said to Meyer, "Is that the most unusually beautiful woman you have ever seen?"

"Very unusual," he said.

When she finally came back out, I hopped up. She wore a long toga affair in a crude rough weave, in an oatmeal color, sleeveless, tied at the waist with a thick gold cord. She wore gold sandals. Her gleaming black hair was brushed long. She had a suggestion of a look I had seen on drawings of old Mayan carvings, the slant of forehead, imperial nose, firm lips, the very slightly recessive chin, the neck as long as the ancient Egyptians'. Her eyes were a large almond slant, the color of oiled anthracite. Her hair was long, coarse, black, and lustrous.

"Please be seated, Mr. McGee. May I get you gentlemen a drink?"

I said a beer would be fine if she had one. I didn't really want it. I just wanted to watch her move around. She seemed to glide. It was the color and texture of her skin that was so unusual, and so complimentary to the rest of her, to her features, her slenderness, her polite dignity. It was a flat dusky tan, all the same even shade, not a suntan but a natural tone, without flaw, with the look of silk.

She brought the beer to us in mugs, on a tray. She said she was having her third glass of iced tea. The air conditioning had broken in the offices of the Camino Real, and she was dehydrated. All she could think of, riding the bus home, was a long cool shower.

"You are from Canada?" Meyer asked.

She smiled at him. "You are very good with accents, I think. I was educated in Canada, Mr. Meyer. But I was born in a little village to the south of here called Noh-Bec. It's a Mayan village."

"So you are Mayan?" Meyer said.

"I suppose. If there are any true Mayans left. The Mayans were a quiet peace-loving people. Long ago the Toltecs, warlike Indians, came over from Mexico and conquered the Mayans and interbred with them. I would suppose there would be some Spanish blood as well. That is the rumor in my family."

"It's a long way from Noh-Bec to Canada," Meyer said.

She smiled again. "A leading comment? Why not. My father and mother went down to Chetumal when I was three. They worked in the home of a man named McKenzie. The McKenzie daughter and I became inseparable. We were the same age. When we were eight years old, with my father's permission, Mr. McKenzie sent the two of us up to Toronto to live with his aunt and go to school there. Eliza McKenzie is still my best friend. She's married and lives in Toronto and has two children."

"I lectured in Toronto in June," Meyer said, ignoring my glance of warning.

"How nice. Is it still beautiful?"

"Very."

"What did you lecture on?"

"Economics, to economists. Dry stuff."

She stared down into her glass for a moment and then lifted her head to stare directly at me. The impact of that look was astonishing.

"I do not know where William is. I do not know where he has gone or why he went."

"I don't understand," I said.

"Neither do I. I don't know what to think. His clothing is here. His papers and credit cards. We were happy here together. We were talking about marriage. We quarreled, of course. I think everyone does. I thought he was wasting his abilities on these time-share projects. It is not really completely honest work. One has to promise more than can be delivered, and then try not to come upon the angry buyers later on. He is really a charming man, and quite intelligent, and with a lot of energy. But he was making a lot of money. He said that when he had enough, we would go back to Houston and he would go into another kind of work. But when I asked him how much was enough, he could not name a figure."

"Where is the money?"

"In the Banco Peninsular. All of it. Earning big interest in a peso account. He was buying peso C.D.s, and he told me he would cash in before the next devaluation. Then we would leave." Her eyes filled. "I am so terribly worried," she said. "I saw him last on the sixth day of July, almost one month ago. It was a day like any other. I go to work first. When I came to the kitchen, he was in here talking on the telephone. I asked what it was and he said he had to go see someone, so on that day he left exactly when I did, and he drove me to the Camino Real. He kissed me goodbye and said we would have some fish for dinner. Our car is a gray Volkswagen. I have not seen that either. They say he tired of me and drove back to your country. I can tell you that is a lie. I am so terribly worried."

"Do you remember a man who worked with him called Evan Lawrence?"

"Of course. Why?"

"How long did he work with him?" I asked.

She frowned. "From Christmas last year. Maybe three months, maybe less. I told William it was against the law to have somebody working for you, a foreigner without papers. He said to me, 'Who will find out? Will you tell them? Will Evan? Will I? He is a very good salesman. He has made us a lot of money. He is very good selling to the rich widows, promising them nobody can ever be lonely in Cancún.' I just hoped he would go away, and he did. He met a woman, not very pretty, working for Pemex looking for oil, and he followed her back to Texas. I was glad."

She frowned, pausing for a moment.

"Nora? A name like that."

"Norma," I said.

"He must have followed her back and married her, because the newspapers from Florida said that he and his wife and another person had died in a boating accident, an explosion, in Florida. Perhaps they were on their wedding trip. Everyone here who had worked with him selling the time sharing was talking about it."

She looked at me with doubt and speculation.

"How did you know her name? What do you really want?" She straightened in her chair and looked sternly at me and then at Meyer. "You will please tell me what my William, your great friend, looks like. Every detail, please."

I smiled. "A nice man. Tall. Well built."

"Yes?"

"Dark hair."

She stood up quickly. "Dark hair? Dark hair? He has hair so red that the people here call him El Rojo, the red one. And his face and arms and shoulders are entirely freckled. So tell me why you are here or get out at once."

"We mean you no harm, Barbara," Meyer said. "Please believe us. We need your help, and maybe you need ours."

"I do not want soft soothing talk, Mr. Meyer."

"Norma was my niece. She died as you say, in that explosion on July fifth. The boat had a bomb aboard. Norma was a successful woman. She had quite a lot of money she had saved. It is all missing. Everyone was supposed to think that Evan Lawrence died when Norma did. But he didn't. He wasn't aboard. That's why we're here."

Her face was expressive. I could almost track the patterns of her mind from the changing expressions.

"But he seemed so very *nice!*" she said. "He made us all laugh."

Meyer said, "I don't want to be brutal, Barbara. I don't want to add to your pain. But it now looks as though William Doyle was the only person in Cancún who knew that Evan Lawrence lives down here, under another name and identity. I don't think the man you knew as Evan Lawrence could take that kind of risk. I think he did what he had to do, to protect his identity. That's who the phone call was from. That's where he went."

Her lovely face twisted and then went vacant. She was standing. She put her hands forward, as though to brace herself, and then began to crumple. I reached her in two strides before she fell, picked her up, and took her to the couch, surprised at the warm sturdy heft of her under the coarse fabric.

Meyer appeared at my elbow, with a cloth soaked in cold water. He placed its folded length across her forehead. "I'm so sorry," he said. "Maybe it was a wild guess, not true."

She opened her eyes. "I've known he is dead. I've known it since three o'clock that day. I was working. And suddenly there was an emptiness in my chest, as if the strings that hold my heart had been sliced through, and it sagged to a lower place. I was going to tell William about that strange feeling. I know that was when he died, and I know he died thinking of me, trying to tell me. I could not admit it to myself. Suddenly you made me able to admit it. Don't be sorry. I couldn't live in limbo forever. He left everything behind."

I moved away. Meyer eased himself down to sit on the floor beside the couch. He held her hand. "The dead have to leave everything and everybody behind. For some, it is the right time. For others ; . ."

"How could that shallow smiling man be so wicked?"

"He has been able to get away with being wicked because he does not look or act wicked. He has the gift of friendship. He inspires trust. My niece loved him and married him."

She tried to sit up and he touched her shoulder, urging her back. "Please," she said. "What is his other identity here? You said he is someone else here."

"We can get into that later."

"Could you please get the box of tissues in the kitchen?" I went out and got it and brought it to her. She blew her nose and she wiped her eyes, and she tried to smile. "Sometimes we laughed about what my babies would look like. Dark little Indios with red hair. I said we should hurry with them. I am twenty-seven. William was thirty-two. He had been married once. I had not."

She pushed Meyer's hand aside and sat up, swung her feet to the floor.

"So! I am *not* a weak person. I come from people who have survived everything. And I come from people who know violence. That is the Toltec heritage, not the Mayan. And I am not going to mourn my man in front of strangers."

"Who would like to be friends," Meyer said.

She studied him. "Very American. Instant friends. Like your instant foods. Heat and serve. The heart does not move so fast. You walk in here and destroy me. In the name of friendship?"

"But we only—"

"Do you have a car?"

"Yes," I said.

"I will not work tomorrow. In the name of this new friendship could you pick me up very very early? There's a place I want to be when the sun rises. We'll have to walk a distance in the dark. Perhaps at quarter to four? I will bring a good flashlight. And insect repellent. Wear shoes for walking, please. I'm not asking too much?"

Meyer beamed at her. "Not too much to ask of old friends."

twenty-two

When I pulled up to the entrance to La Vista del Caribe, Barbara was silhouetted against the dim interior lights. She came striding quickly to our pink automobile. Meyer had moved into the back. She slid in beside me and said, "I'm very grateful for this. I should never have asked."

"It's fine," I said. "It's okay. Where are we going?"

"Toward the airport, but don't turn off there. We go straight for many miles."

She had brought cups, a thermos of coffee, a dozen doughnuts. The road was straight. It was almost eerily straight under the overcast night. It had no shoulders. The jungle grew right to the edge of the pavement. She sat quietly beside me, half turned to lean against the door, blue-jeaned legs turned and pulled up, sharply bent knees angled toward me.

"If we could go a little bit faster?" she said at one point. This was after a big bus came booming up behind me, doing at least eighty on the two-lane road, and nearly blew me away when it went by.

She identified the turnoffs as we passed them. There were not many of them. "Puerto Morelos, for the truck ferry to Cozumel." And San Carlos, Punta Bete, Playa del Carmen, Xcaret, Pamul, Akumal, Xelha, Tulum. Finally, not far past Tulum, where she said there were Mayan ruins on the seashore, she told me to slow down and pointed out the right turn. More straight two-lane road. But the vines and bushes leaned so far out over the concrete, I drove down the middle. An animal scuttled out of the way. It seemed to be tan and had an awkward waddling gait. "Coatimundi," she said. "There are small villages here near the road. All dark at night. The children catch the coatimundi pups and make pets of them. But when they are grown they get angry quickly and bite."

"Where are we going?" Meyer asked.

"Now it is only perhaps ten miles. It is called Cobá. Great ruins, partially excavated."

We arrived at a large parking area. There was a shack where one was supposed to buy admission tickets. I locked the car and we followed her and the beam of the flashlight directed on the ground.

A man came wandering out of a dark structure behind the shack. "*¡Señora, señora, cerrado!*" he cried.

She put the light on him. As he stood blinking, bare to the waist, she said a single long sentence in a language unlike any I had ever heard before. It was full of snappings and pops and little coughs. He bowed and backed away and she began walking again, so swiftly I had to take a couple of running steps to catch up with her.

"Watch where you step," she said. "It is uneven here. There are pebbles and stones."

I would estimate we went two miles on a dark track wide enough in places for a car, through the jungle, through the keening, shrilling of a billion bugs, the caws of night birds, a thick stillness of the air. Toward the end she was almost running.

When she stopped abruptly, I stopped in time but Meyer ran into her and backed off apologizing. She ignored the apology. She gave me the flashlight. "Here I am going up that pyramid. I will not need the light. Please don't turn the light on me while I climb it. It will spoil my night vision. Please wait here. When it is time, I will call for you to come up."

I turned the light off. She went off into darkness. In a few minutes I could see that she had gone toward a huge bulk that loomed up out of the jungle, bigger than any cathedral. As my eyes became used to starlight, I saw how it projected up and up, blotting out a big segment of the starry sky, and I could make out the paleness of her white long-sleeved shirt, a tiny object a third of the way up, moving steadily. Meyer was still panting from the fast two-mile walk. We had, all three, forgotten the bug repellent. So we stood in the darkness, waved our arms, slapped our necks and foreheads. I broke some small leafy branches off a bush. When we whisked those around, it lessened the problem.

A rooster crowed nearby, and when I looked toward the summit of the pyramid, it was now outlined against gray instead of against a blackness with stars. It was not much later when I realized I could see the tree trunks and see Meyer's face. Looking at the summit, I thought I could see her up there, sitting on a flat place at the very top, her back toward us.

Morning bird sounds began. There was a gray morning light, and then a rosiness beyond the pyramid as the sun began to come up out of the sea. I could see her clearly then, with a spill of black hair down the back of the white shirt. Sunlight struck her, golden, setting her ablaze. Soon we could see it against the treetops to the left and right of the pyramid.

A small herd of turkeys came strolling out of the brush, gabbling softly among themselves, stopped aghast when they saw us, whirled, and went back to cover swiftly, looking back over their shoulders, telling each other how dangerous we were to turkey life everywhere.

We heard her faint cry and looked up and saw her standing, beckoning to us. My watch said she had been alone up there for a little more than an hour.

"She wants us to climb up there," I said.

"Up *that?*" Meyer said.

"Come on. Just don't look down."

"Dear God," he muttered, and came padding along behind me.

When we got to the base of it, we could no longer see her up there. I put the flashlight down and looked at the dimensions of the steps. They were about twenty inches high and only about eight to ten inches deep. So the way to go was almost on all fours, to lean into the slope and use the fingers on the steps for balance. I told Meyer this would be the best way, and I heard him sigh.

Once one was into the rhythm of it, it was not bad. The full heat of the day had not yet arrived. It was a long climb. I tried not to think about going down. I waited near the top until Meyer was on the same level, about six feet to my left. She bent and caught his hand and helped him up the final tall step. I scrambled up. She smiled at us. She encompassed all the world in one sweep of her arm and said, "Look! Just look!"

I did not feel at all comfortable about standing on that small flat top. It was only about four feet by eight feet, and it fell steeply away in all directions. We were so high above the jungle that it looked like a dark green shag rug. The sun was two widths above the horizon. She pointed and said, "See that little silvery glint out there, like a needle beyond the trees? That's the Caribbean. Over thirty miles from here. Look down that way. See? There is the pink car. It is so glorious up here in the morning!"

To my relief she sat down, legs hanging over the rubbly slope on the side opposite the one we had climbed. We sat on either side of her. She pointed out smaller pyramids that poked out of the trees.

I said, "Is it part of being Maya? I mean, to come here when someone has died?"

"Not really. I don't know. Maybe they did that. It all ended hundreds of years ago. By the time the Spaniards came, it was already over. Archaeologists make up stories about what it was like in the Mayan cities, trying to read old stelae and glyphs, and other archaeologists translate in some other way and make furious objections. We do know that the classical period ended five hundred years before the Spanish came. The Maya abandoned their cities and temples, moved away, went off into the jungles. Why? No one knows. They thought it was because the land would no longer produce. But that has been proven false. They dug channels through swamps, piled the muck on the center rows between the channels, grew water lilies, and racked them up onto the long mounds to decay there. It was sophisticated agriculture and very productive. Tikal was the greatest city of all, to the south of where we are, in Guatemala. Perhaps two hundred thousand people lived there. It was a center of commerce on the rivers and the sea. This Cobá was one of the strange old cities. Like Chichén, Uxmal, Palenque, Bonampak, Yaxchilan. I have been to the others, but it is only here in this place I feel . . . part of it. As if it pulls upon my heart. We were a bloody people long ago, even before the Toltec, with rites, ceremonies, processions, blood sacrifices. And we had measurements of time going back eight million years. I was in Canada when my father died. When I was able to come back, I came to this place as soon as I could, and I sat here at dawn and said his Mayan name one hundred times as the sun came up. They gave him the name Pedro Castillo because they could not say his real name."

When she said it, it sounded like "Pakal." But the P was more explosive than the P sound in English, and there was a coughing sound to the K. The L was odd, as if during it she moved her tongue from the back of the roof of her mouth toward the front, giving it the value of "ulla."

"It was believed that he was descended from priests. Some priests became kings and then became gods. He would have been seen as a tall man anywhere, but he was *very* tall for a Maya. And my Mayan name is . . ."

If I'd had to spell it, it would have been Alklashakeh. The vowels were purred, the sibilants rich.

"It is all over," she said, "and yet it isn't over. I do not know why I was moved to say his name, and William's name, one hundred times at dawn from here. But it made me feel better both times, as if they were afloat in death and I had moved them to a safe shore. Do you know that deep in the jungle there are small secret villages where men with guns still guard hidden idols from everyone except the deserving Maya? The holy figures sit there in the dark huts, remembering everything."

She shrugged off her sadness and asked us to swivel around to face in another direction, toward a small nearby body of water and a cluster of tile-roofed buildings.

"There is the hotel," she said. "There is a lake in front of it. See? And the old Mayan road went across that lake on a causeway, and it went all the way through the jungle, all the way to Chichén Itzá. It was wide enough for a carriage, but they did not have wheels, it is said. If they did not have wheels, then why does one ancient wall at Chichén clearly show the meshing of the cogs of three wheels as in the gears of some machine? If they did not have wheels, how is it so that a giant roller was found here at Cobá, weighing tons, and was used to crush and flatten the limestone out of which they built that road? It went off that way, beyond that lake, for fifty miles. It is not all narrow and rough. But it is a trail that goes from here to Chichén and from Chichén to Uxmal. We were not animals. There was a culture here."

Meyer shook his head. "I'm not ready for all that, Barbara. I am still trying to comprehend the thing I am sitting on here, to comprehend the skill and devotion and determination it took to raise up this gigantic pyramid. I was about to say in the middle of nowhere. For them it was perhaps the middle of the universe."

She looked questioningly at me. "Was it worth getting up in the middle of the night?"

"It was. It is."

"You came up the right way. Go down the same way now, backward. Look down between your thighs and around your hips to see the next steps. If any rock step wiggles, take your weight from it at once. Sometimes they fall. People fall with them. Tourists burst their brains on the stone. There is talk about making it forbidden to climb the pyramids. What is life if all risk is taken away? Go down now, if you are ready. There is only one more thing I want to say to myself here."

By the time we reached the bottom, with almost simultaneous sighs of relief, Barbara was on her way down, quick-moving, graceful, assured. She turned and jumped down the last few steps, dusted her hands, smiled at us.

She walked toward us in the bright shadow of morning, in a flow of side light, her skin the shade of coffee with cream, or of cinnamon, fine-grained, with a matte finish, flawless and lovely.

We walked back to the car slowly, and she told us what she knew of the place. We took a side trip down a narrow winding path to look at a stele, a huge one, broken into three parts and re-erected, protected by a thatched roof, the carving on it so worn it was almost invisible.

At the ticket shack, she called the man out and walked over to the side with him, talked to him, gave him some money. We got into the car and drove to the hotel we had seen from the top. It was by then seven fifteen and there were six Japanese in the dining room having an exotic breakfast of *huevos rancheros*. We sat where we could look out at a small garden. She insisted that it would be her treat.

"Now then," she said, as coffee cups were refilled, "you know the other name this person uses?"

"And a post office box number in Cancún," Meyer said. "Box seven ten."

"There is no mail delivery down the highway," she said. "You rent a box in whatever city you are near. And near can be eighty miles."

"In any direction?" Meyer asked.

"Only going south. Along the highway toward Mérida, for example, you would not go that far before you would get your mail in Valladolid. Tell me. What is his name?"

"Roberto Hoffmann."

She sat so very still I had the feeling she was not even breathing. Then she slumped. "For one moment I thought there was something I would remember about that name. All I know is that I have heard it. I do not know when or where. But it is a common name. Anyway, there will be no trouble finding him. No trouble at all, if such a person exists."

"What will make it easy?" Meyer asked.

"The Maya network. Listen, my friends. All up and down this coast and off into the deep jungle, the Maya do the hard work. A lot of Mexicans have come in to work at the hotels, but in some of them, like the Casa Maya, it will be all Maya workers from one village. There is one man who has a big ranch. He has important political jobs. He is like the *jefe* of all the Maya. He can spread the word that Barbara Castillo wants to know where is this Roberto Hoffmann. If he lives in Quintana Roo, someone will know him. There are lots of strangers now, houses being built, people coming from Venezuela and Honduras and Germany, building houses by the sea. But the

Maya do construction, make gardens, roads, string wires. Someone will know. I will leave the word with him on our way back. It is beyond the place I showed you, Akumal, but not far beyond. With a stone wall done in the old way."

"We have a photograph of him back at the hotel," I said.

"Good. Because how he looked is not very clear in my memory. He had . . . a nice ordinary look. Just one more pleasant person who smiled a great deal and said agreeable things. Are you sure?"

"Almost positive."

She pursed her lips in thought and then asked, "Why would such a man want to marry that woman, your niece, and then kill her?"

Meyer told her Cody Pittler's story. She understood at once. "Aha!" she said. "He is killing Coralita over and over and over. He is punishing them and himself for being evil. But that does not include killing my Willy."

"I would guess that—"

"We will find out," she said. "We will find out soon."

On the way back, we stopped at the ranch on the west side of the road. She walked from the driveway to the ranch house and was gone for about ten minutes. She came back and said, "He was not there, but I left a note. He will get word to me. I told him it is urgent."

twenty-three

There was no word from Barbara Castillo the rest of that day, or all day Saturday or Sunday. On Sunday evening when we came back to the hotel at nine, there was a note to come to her apartment.

As she held the door open and we walked in, once again I was aware of the physical impact of her. She had all the presence of one of the great actresses, along with such vitality you could almost feel the electricity. It was like walking under the power lines that march across a countryside. In the field under the lines you can feel the hair lift on the nape of your neck and the backs of your hands.

She wore white shorts and a red blouse, no jewelry at all. She was barefoot. I had noticed before that her hands and feet did not fit with the slenderness of the rest of her. They had a broad, sturdy look of strength and competence.

She clasped her hand around my wrist. Her hand was quite cold and damp. She tugged me toward the couch. I sat beside her, and Meyer sat in the nearest chair.

"I *know* about him!" she said. "Many many things. I showed Ramón the photograph you let me take, and it is the same, but with a mustache now, and the hair much darker."

"Who is Ramón?"

"Oh, a nice shy little man, very broad and strong, very polite. He is Maya. One of the *jefe*'s employees drove him in in a truck to tell me about the man he works for, Señor Hoffmann. He has worked for Señor Hoffmann for, he thinks, eight years. He went to work for him shortly after the big house was built, one year or maybe two afterwards. Remember I pointed out the road to Playa del Carmen, where one can go to Cozumel by passenger ferry or small airplane? To find Mr. Hoffmann, you go down almost to the water and turn left, to head back toward this direction. It is a public road and it goes for maybe a mile. At the end of it there is a big iron gate and a warning not to enter. Once you are through the gate, the driveway winds through some gardens and then comes to the house. It is a big house, with a beach in front of it and a lagoon beyond it, with a boathouse and garages and servants' rooms. Mr. Hoffmann is very rich, Ramón says. But compared to Ramón almost anybody would seem rich. I asked what kind of work Mr. Hoffmann does. Ramón said that he often goes on business trips and stays for a long time. Many months. He is a *residente*. He has the proper documents. He speaks Spanish as good as any Mexican, and better than most Maya. There are six servants, including Ramón. He has no woman, this Hoffmann. He does not have friends who visit him. He does not give parties. The only time he leaves his house and grounds is when he goes out in his boat to fish or into the jungle to hunt tigers. Or goes away on a trip. He has a big shortwave radio receiver and a big aerial. He listens to it a lot. Now he has a television set. Of course there is no station he can hear, but when he came back from the United States last year he brought American movies and a machine to play them over his television. Sometimes he lets the servants watch one. Oh, and he has an exercise room, with machines in it."

"Did you say tigers?" Meyer asked.

"Tigers? Oh, yes. They are big tawny jungle cats. Wildcats or panthers. Do you know that men used to gather chicle in the jungle to make chewing gum? They tapped trees. The men who gathered the chicle were called chicleros. They shot the panthers. Then it became possible to make the juice in a laboratory. No more chicleros. The chicle trails are overgrown. The panthers are returning. They used to say the panther is the second most dangerous creature you can meet in the jungle. The most dangerous, of course, was the chiclero. They were wild rough men. So he fishes and hunts and stays by himself."

"What about William Doyle?" I asked.

She put her cool hand back on my wrist and tightened her grasp. She looked down and spoke so softly Meyer leaned forward to hear her. "On that day William dropped me off, Ramón said a man came in a small gray automobile. I showed him a picture of Willy. Ramón said possibly it was the same man, but he could not tell, they all look so much alike to him. They went out fishing in the boat. Usually a servant named Perez went along when Hoffmann fished, but he did not go that day. When the boat came back, Hoffmann was alone. He said he had let his visitor ashore at the house of a friend, and he would come back for his car later on. And in the morning, the gray car was gone."

"I'm sorry."

She lifted her head to look at Meyer. "You were right. William must have known somehow, maybe by accident, that Hoffmann and Evan Lawrence were one and the same. It was not healthy to know that. William thought he was a friend."

"Hoffmann seems to have all the conveniences," I said.

"Oh, yes. Ramón says they have a good well, which is very unusual in this part of Yucatán. And there are two big generators which came in long ago by ship, and tanks which hold many gallons of diesel fuel. Thousands, Ramón said. But it is probably hundreds. Also there is a tank and a pump for the gasoline for the car and the boat. With our little car, all he had to do was take it out onto the highway and find a place to run it off the road into the jungle. The village people would soon take everything from it. What was left will rust away very quickly. He could walk back by night, ducking out of sight when traffic came. It is no problem for him. I loved the little car. It was like a fat friendly little dog. It tried hard but it could not run very fast."

"Does Ramón understand he is employed by a bad man?"

"He does not want to think that. But it doesn't matter what he thinks. He will do whatever his people tell him is necessary."

"The others too?"

"If they are all Maya. And if we ask them, through the *jefe*."

"If he goes hunting he has guns there," I said.

"I forgot. Many many guns. And there are burglar alarms, Ramón said. No one can approach the house at night, or come in the lagoon in a boat. A loud siren sounds. The children of the servants have set it off by accident, and they have been very frightened."

"And he is there now," Meyer said.

"Yes, of course. Ramón thinks it will be a long time before he goes away on a trip. Perhaps not until next year, not until the spring. Then he will probably leave from Cozumel, Ramón said. That is where he departs. Once a week Ramón comes to Cancún to look for mail in the box. Some years there are no letters for Don Roberto. Some years one or two."

She released my wrist. We sat there with our separate thoughts. We were together, but alone in our minds.

Meyer stood up and paced and came back to stand facing us, looking down. "One aspect of this keeps bothering me," he said. "And it goes right back to the beginning, back to Coralita. We have no proof of anything that happened that night. All we have is a commonly accepted hypothesis which has never been checked out with anyone who was there at the time."

"What are you talking about?" I asked him.

"There is a very wise British astronomer, Raymond Lyttleton, who has said that one must regard any hypothesis as though it were a bead which you can slide along a piece of wire. One end of the wire is marked 'zero,' for falsehood, and the other end is marked 'one,' for truth. One must never let the bead get to the absolute end of the wire, to either end, or it will fall off into irrationality. Move the bead along the wire this way and that, in accordance with inductive and deductive reasoning."

"Okay, where is your bead, Meyer?"

"One position of the bead is where Cody Pittler got out of bed and got his father's target pistol and shot Coralita in the back of the skull and waited to ambush his father. Then the struggle and the flight. That presupposes a murderous mind from the beginning, well concealed, awaiting any outlet. Another position adds an additional person to the mix, a young male friend of Cody's caught servicing the insatiable Coralita. Another position of the bead has the father coming home and getting into bed with Coralita, and having something she says confirm his suspicions about her and his son. So he gets up and dresses and gets the gun and kills her just as Cody comes home. I am saying that the people of Eagle Pass invented the circumstances of the murder which seemed to them to fit the situation. We know neither the truth nor the falsehood."

She jumped up and faced Meyer. "Why are you talking about all this? What difference does it make to anyone?" Her voice was loud and angry. "Don't you know what we are going to talk about now? We are going to talk about how to kill him."

"Barbara," I said, in what could have been construed as a patronizing tone.

She spun and bent to stare down at me. "Isn't that what we do? We kill him. We end his life."

I tried to look into her eyes, but there was no penetration in my stare. It bounced off shiny black polished gemstones.

"Young woman," Meyer said. "I am not going to be a party to killing that man unless and until I can communicate with him."

"What about? His movie collection? Which airline he likes?"

"About several hypotheses we have made about him. Before one shoots a fox in a henhouse, it is interesting to find out how many henhouses have been on his nightly route. I have more than an average curiosity about what makes the human animal react as he does. I do not think there have been many people who have adjusted so cleverly and carefully to a life of murder. I want to hear his views about himself."

She turned and dropped into the couch beside me. "And I do not care what he thinks about himself. Ask a cesspool why it makes bubbles! What I care about is how to kill him in such a way there will be no involvement of the police. None! There are two ways to do that. If he should disappear forever without any trace, it will be thought that perhaps he went on another trip and something happened to him there. If there is a body, then it should clearly be an accident."

"Going to his house is no good in either case."

"So," said Meyer, "it has to be when he goes to fish or to hunt. Or one waits until he travels."

"I will not wait for travel. I do not like the idea of the sea. It is all too open," she said.

"So how do we tell when and where he will go hunting?" I asked.

"He will hear of a great cat, a big one. The Maya guides sometimes make pad marks in the mud to play jokes on each other. They do it so well even the most expert are fooled."

"Where will this cat be?" I asked her.

She frowned, chin on fist, then brightened. "I think it will be near some cenotes. There is a trail off to the right before one gets to Playa Xelha. You cannot see it from the road. It is always marked with bits of red yard or ribbon tied high to the trees on the other side of the road. It goes in for more than a mile and then it comes to the old Maya trail from Cobá to Chichén. One turns right there on the Maya trail and goes perhaps three miles, then one leaves the Maya trail and goes west perhaps a half mile. There are big cenotes there, perhaps three or four. It is a good place for cat. It is wild there. Very thick. Very bad walking."

"Yes, but what are cenotes?" Meyer asked.

"I'm sorry, Mr. Meyer," she said. "This peninsula is all limestone, with a very thin coating of soil on top. In the heavy rains there are underground rivers, not very far down, which run to the sea. Long ago in many places the earth and limestone above the rivers collapsed in big potholes, fell into the rivers, and were washed away. What this leaves is a cenote. It is a deep round hole with sheer sides, or undercut sides. It would be usually a hundred or a hundred and fifty meters across and ten to thirty meters deep. In the dry season, there is no water at the bottom, or just a little. Where the river goes through at either side of this deep hole, there is a big cave, usually with a stagnant pool of water in the bottom. Drippings have made stalactites coming down from the roof. There are almost always bats, and bat dirt afloat on the pools. In the heavy rains the rivers swell and water rushes through. Some cenotes have a crumbled side so one can climb down easily and go into the cave if one wishes. Cats go down to drink from those where there are little streams. At Chichén there is a big deep cenote where the guides will tell you they threw virgins. What they threw in there were small children. They would throw one in at nightfall, and if he was still floating and living in the morning, hanging onto a steep side, they would bring him out, and from then on he could predict the weather in the next growing season."

I saw Meyer swallow. He cleared his throat and said, "Hoffmann would have guides."

"Yes. And they would know he was going in and not coming back out. They would not even need to be told why. They could go in and prepare the paw marks of a very big cat, then lead him to them and then track the imaginary cat over to the area of the cenotes. One of them is a sacred place. There is an old altar on the side near the cave, too high for water to wash it away."

"How soon would we do this?" I asked.

"I am not going back to my job until this is over. I have told them I have personal business. There is another girl they can use. She is not as quick as I am, but she will do. Often they hunt the jaguar, or panther, or puma, or wildcat—it has many names—by the light of the full moon. But I think that would be too dangerous. Too many things could go wrong. Sometimes the guides find a place where a big cat holes up in the daytime. Daytime would be best."

"Have you got it all figured out, Barbara?" Meyer asked.

"All but the end of it. We must go in with the guides the day before. It is very very bad walking. Believe me. We will find the right place and then they will bring him to us. Last night I dreamed he was on the ground and I slipped a knife into his belly. It went in like butter. But I could not pull it out. He was on the ground, smiling up at me, looking sleepy. I braced both feet and used both hands, but the knife would not come out. Then the handle of the knife was a snake and I jumped back and he started laughing and I woke up sweaty."

"What about weapons?" I asked.

"There will be guns for you two," she said. "I will tell the guides. We will find out which men Hoffmann has used, and the *jefe* will talk to them. It will all be arranged. I will leave a message and you can come here ready to go. You must have good strong shoes that come up high, to support your ankles. The trail is all loose rock as big as this."

She made a circle of thumbs and fingers big as a baseball.

"It will be steaming hot in there. You should wear clothing to absorb moisture, and maybe have a sweatband for your head and a light hat. We will need a great deal of water, so get something to carry water in. We will go in the afternoon and stay through the night. The guides will leave us there, wherever we decide. I will be the cat he has come to kill."

"Bedrolls?" Meyer asked.

"A light blanket only. Boughs can be cut. Bring a knife."

"Food?" I asked.

"I will arrange that. The guides will carry it. And a repellent for the insects. Each person should bring his own. And toilet tissue, and any medication you take. . . . You would know what you need for an overnight hike, the same as when you were little boys."

"Or little soldiers," I said.

"You were military?" she asked me.

"A long time back."

She went into a long brooding silence and held up a warning hand when Meyer started to speak.

"I think it will be possible to remove his rifle," she said. "If the guides could take him to a very difficult place where he had to climb up or down, one of them might take his rifle and then just melt off into the brush like magic, the way they can."

"Won't that alert him?"

"By that time, it will not matter, will it?" she asked.

Meyer was very quiet on the way back to the Dos Playas. He moved a chair onto our small balcony and sat with his feet up, braced against the railing. I opened two beers in our kitchenette and took them out. He thanked me and drank half of his before putting it down on the floor beside his chair.

"She thinks we should just blow him away," I said, turning to lean on the railing. "Did you see her eyes?"

"I did indeed. But she wants him to know why. They met. She is not a woman one would forget. If he gets a good look at her, then he'll know why. But I think she wants the satisfaction of a few words. I have a very ugly image of things to come, Travis."

"Such as?"

"I see us in a cave. Water is dripping. Cody Pittler is tied hand and foot. She is squatting beside him. She tells us to take a walk. We climb out of there and walk to where the guides are waiting. We all stand there and hear him screaming for a while, and then it stops, and she comes climbing out, looking tired but smiling."

"Was that on NBC or CBS?"

"Listen, I do not have any affection for Cody Pittler, God knows. And I am pragmatist enough to realize we can't get the law down here to do anything about him, and we can't get him back to Eagle Pass. I have just never directly killed anyone."

"This one should probably be indirect."

"Just the same," he said, picking up his beer and finishing it. "I don't know exactly how to think about it. How have you thought about it?"

"In the past? There has never been enough time to do much thinking."

"And afterward?"

"Kind of blah. Draggy. Tired and guilty and also a little bit jumpy. Takes about a week to go away. But the actual scene never really does go away. It's sort of like having a collection of color slides. Some nights the projector in your head shows them all. Meyer, just don't think about it. Let it happen. There is no little book of rules. No time outs. No offside. Just CYA. Cover your ass, because you can be certain the other guy will not feel that badly about you."

twenty-four

We waited a long time before we heard from her. We had a difficult time finding the kind of walking shoes she described. Everything else was easy. Meyer found shoes. I couldn't find a pair big enough until finally I found a pair a size and a half too big and too wide. But with two pair of heavy white orlon athletic socks, they felt snug enough, especially with the laces pulled tight. We found liter canteens in a downtown supermercado, on long straps, and bought two apiece. The Texas straws were too big for jungle walking, so we found baseball caps with Velcro bands which said Y-U-C-A-T-A-N in red across the front. Tennis shirts and tennis headbands and wrist bands were available, as were long lightweight cotton trousers. Small flashlights, repellent, waterproof matches.

I debated the choice of knives for a long time and at last bought two. They both folded. One went in a leather holster with a snap fastener on my belt, and the other went in the right-hand pocket. It had no case, and when I took it out exactly right, and flicked my wrist, the five-inch blade fell out and snapped into place.

Dressed for action, we looked like tourists waiting for a party boat. I got impatient and went over to her place twice, but she wasn't there. Meyer said she was doubtless doing everything she could. But Monday, Tuesday, Wednesday, Thursday, and Friday went by. On Saturday, August fourteenth, when we went down to breakfast, there was a small sealed envelope in the box. *Come here today at eleven this morning. B.*

We dressed in our jungle best. I had the car gassed and the oil checked. She was waiting for us outside the entrance, sitting on a bulky blue canvas pack. She hoisted it without effort and put it in the back beside Meyer. She seemed both intent and preoccupied as she looked us over, and gave a small nod. She wore a cotton T-shirt in a pale salmon color, baggy oyster-white slacks tucked into what looked to be L. L. Bean women's hiking boots. She had her black hair tied back and a white terry band around her forehead.

"You are late!" she said.

"By almost three minutes."

"If they should think we're not coming—"

"Don't get yourself in a nervous sweat," I told her. She flashed me a black and evil look out of the side of her eye.

"Have you got everything?" Meyer asked.

"Yes, but not in that pack. They have already taken some things out to where we are going."

I turned on the air conditioning, and that ended all conversation. I kept them too busy hanging on to think of talk anyway. The tires were the best-looking thing about the pink rental, so I had the satisfaction of making her yelp with alarm when I darted between an empty southbound fill truck and a full one coming the other way.

Almost an hour later she yelled to me to slow down. She leaned forward, looking high into the trees on the left. She told me where to pull as far over as I could. There was some semblance of shoulder there, gravelly and badly tilted. When we got out, three small men appeared out of the brush. She introduced them quickly. Jorge, Juan, and Miguel. They wore toe-thong sandals, dirty khaki shorts which looked too large for them, faded cotton shirts, and ragged straw hats. Jorge and Juan also wore small-caliber rifles strapped diagonally across their backs and machetes in scabbards on belts around their waists. They were solemn and their handshakes were utterly slack. They did not inspire a lot of confidence. Miguel wanted the car keys. He got in, and when I began to object he went roaring away, turning out almost directly in front of a maddened tourist bus. It blatted around him and went fartingly on its way toward Tulum.

She caught my arm and said, "It will be brought back when this is all over. Now we follow the boys."

And that was a very good trick indeed, following the boys and following her. It was a strange kind of jungle: scrub jungle. The soil could not support big trees. They ranged from sapling size to ball-bat size, and from ten feet tall to thirty feet. The cover was sparse. A lot of sun came down through the leaves. It was, as she had promised, a punishing trail. At first I tried to watch where I placed each foot, but that made the passage too slow. I finally decided to trust to the ankle support of the high shoes and let the stones underfoot roll as they pleased. Rain had washed all the soil from the trail, leaving loose rock. On either side, the terrain looked a lot better for walking, but it was a wilderness of tough vines that dropped from above, sprang up from below, and were hammocked from tree to tree. One would have to chop through them all to make a path.

It was incredibly hot in there. Though you could see off into the scrub jungle for maybe forty feet, there was no breeze at all. The air was as thick as pastry. The sweat began to pour. Jorge and Juan set a very fast pace, schlepping along in their dumb little sandals. They did not seem to sweat. I began to hate them. I wondered if Barbara was sweating. I lengthened my stride and caught up to her for a moment. Yes, she was. She was the winner of the international wet T-shirt award. But she flunked Miss Conviviality. Meyer, with shorter legs than mine and in not as good condition, had it the worst of all. He was panting and blowing and streaming. I had brought some salt tablets. I stopped, and Meyer and I took a good swig of cool water and a salt tablet each. They kept going, out of sight around a curve far ahead.

"Hold it!" I roared into the thick buggy silence of this third-rate jungle. There was no answer. So on we trudged, thrown off balance by the stones as they rolled, waving our arms to catch ourselves. Meyer said a few words I had never heard from him before. I discovered that there is a certain amount of sweat that begins below the forehead band and runs into the eyes. The wristlets took care of that for a time until they became too soggy.

I began to wonder if Cody Pittler had hired Barbara to take us into the wilderness and lose us for good.

They stood waiting for us where the trail converged with the old Mayan trail from Cobá to Chichén Itzá. Jorge and Juan squatted on their heels. Barbara leaned against a small tree. She took a look at me and decided that whatever she was going to say would not be appreciated.

"Now this way," she said. "Let's go."

"Can't you slow those dwarfs down?"

"Wherever there is a choice of directions, they'll wait."

"And you too?"

She gave me her obsidian stare and said, "Of course."

I had hoped that the old Mayan trail would be in better shape, but if anything it was worse. I finally settled into that hypnosis of physical effort which frees the mind to roam to better things. I stomped along until, not far ahead of me, I saw a better thing. Her baggy slacks had become as sopping wet as the T-shirt and clung to the alternate flexing and bunching of the round smooth musculature of her buttocks. Her hair was sweat-wet, flattened to her skull. I slowed and looked back. Meyer was out of sight. I stopped and saw him come around a bend. I caught up to Barbara, stopped her for a salt tablet and a slug of water. In the stillness I watched her throat work as she tilted the canteen. She exuded a warm murky scent of overheated woman. She smiled her thanks.

"You said it's a rough walk. Okay, it's rough. Do you have to be cross?"

"I'm not cross, Travis. Really. I'm just very very anxious that this works for us, that we kill him."

"Have you ever killed anybody?"

Her eyes changed. "No. I saw a person killed. When I was very small. He broke the law of the village. Have you ever killed anybody?"

"Not in cold blood. Not by trapping him, like this."

"Other ways, though."

I shrugged. "Self-defense."

"Many?"

"Not a lot."

"I heard it gets easier."

"I guess it depends on the person. From where I stand, you heard wrong."

"After I saw that person killed I had bad dreams and woke up screaming, night after night. Maybe I will after this, too. I don't care. I just don't care."

"When will he be coming in?"

"Tomorrow, earlier than we're arriving. Maybe ten thirty."

"Who brings him?"

"These same boys. They know this area. Miguel too."

Meyer came up to us, sighed, settled down on the curve of a fat root. He took a short drink, capped his canteen, and shook his head at us, smiling a sad and weary smile. He looked as though he had been dipped in fine oil. He gleamed. We talked for a little while and then went on together, better friends somehow.

At last we turned off the rock-strewn trail and angled off through the brush. The boys had their shining machetes out, and they cut through the vines with effortless twists of the wrist. I had hoped that it would slow them down so that we could keep up with them. I had finally realized that it was a childish game with them, to effortlessly outdistance the heaving sweating Yanquis.

Then they showed us another trick. Meyer and I were following Jorge. Barbara was off to the side, following Juan. Jorge would get a little ahead and then go around a tree in an unexpected direction.

Unless you noticed you would charge ahead and suddenly be wrapped in tough vines, held motionless. You had to back off and find where he had sliced through them. That took time. And by then he was farther ahead than ever, cutting tricky patterns through the undergrowth. So I roared at him with enough authority to stop him in his tracks. I told him that if he did not stay back so I could follow him, I would take his machete away from him, lop off his head, and kick it all the way back to the highway. He didn't understand a word, of course. But he understood the meaning. And from then on he kept looking back nervously, making certain Meyer and I were keeping up.

The second cenote we inspected looked about right. One wall had collapsed into rubble, so it was easy to clamber down to where the small stream flowed. It flowed through an area of flat rock. The flat rock extended into the mouth of the cave, with another flat shelf about three feet higher. It was astonishingly cool in the mouth of the cave. A breeze came blowing gently out of it. There seemed to be a kind of camping place on the higher flat rock, and just outside the mouth of the cave there was a big rusty iron kettle. Barbara explained that this had probably been a place where the chicleros met to boil down the gum they had tapped from the chicle trees. Juan had been carrying the blue pack. He put it down beside Barbara and went off to retrieve the stores they had brought in the previous day. While he was gone, Jorge made three fast trips off into the jungle, returning each time with a huge armload of boughs. Juan came back overburdened with goods. There was a small Primus stove, canned goods, a jug of water, bread, blankets, and two rifles wrapped in plastic and tied with twine.

He handed me one with a polite bow and smile. I undid it and found myself the proud possessor of a single-shot Montgomery Ward .22-caliber rifle. A friend of mine had had one just like it when I was a kid. It had been made by Stevens Arms up in Chicopee Falls, Massachusetts, back in the thirties. The front part of the foregrip was painted black. The blueing was pretty well gone. It was called a Frank Buck model, I remembered, but I couldn't remember who Frank Buck had been. I had the feeling he had gone to Africa to capture wild animals for American zoos. My friend's little rifle had been chambered for shorts. This one came with a small leather pouch tied to the bolt in which I found nine long-rifle shells. My face must have shown great dismay. He explained something very rapidly to Barbara and she said, "Juan says it is a very good gun. Very accurate. It belonged to his father. He treasures it."

I made myself smile. Meyer unwrapped the other one and handed it to me. It was a Remington 410 shotgun with four shells. All birdshot.

"We are a veritable arsenal of democracy," I said. "I think it would be useful if he left us his machete."

She took me seriously, and he did. And then they were gone. They disappeared without a sound.

"What are their orders?" I asked.

"They will bring Hoffmann here, but around to that side, where he cannot see that this is the easy side. It is steep, so one of them will go down first and ask Hoffmann to hand down the gun. The moment he reaches the bottom, the one with the gun will run over and up this slope and away. And the other will run back from the top of the slope. They will go down to the trail and wait there until we call. That will leave Hoffmann there at the foot of that steep slope. One of us can be here and another up over there where the brush is thick, looking down from hiding."

"Then what?"

"Where can he go? What can he do? If he tries to climb back out, you can shoot his leg. You seem to want to talk to him. That is all right. It won't matter by then. We can talk to him and you can hand me the gun and I will shoot him. I will walk closer to him and shoot him. Show me how to work the gun, Travis."

Meyer hitched himself back on the rock shelf, more deeply into the cave, folded his arms, and, with his back against damp rock, went to sleep. She had laid out the provisions and made the three blanket beds. I walked the area, climbed the steep slope, came around and came down the rubbly slope. I checked out the hiding place she had pointed to and I found a place that looked a little bit better. It was outside the smaller cave, at the opposite side of the cenote, where the water flowed in and disappeared. There was a jumble of big rounded boulders, some of them the size of sedans, with a good place of concealment behind them. I was about to suggest it as an alternate until I looked up and saw, about twenty-five feet overhead, how the land was undercut, tree roots hanging down. It looked as if the whole thing would come down. It was probably a lot more solidly set than it looked.

I hated the weapons, but the plan seemed reasonable. We ate some canned beef stew without much appetite. I stretched out and went to sleep. It was dusk when Barbara awakened me. "You must see this," she said. "Dear God, I have never seen anything like it."

The bats were leaving on their evening rounds. They had hung upside down all day and they were letting go and catching the air and darting out with that curious shifting tilting flight of the hungry bat. Hundreds of them. Thousands of them, long columns against the pale sky of evening. Meyer was watching in awe.

Bugs did not come into the cave in any great number. Barbara extracted a flat bottle from her pack, a pint of tequila. We passed it back and forth and moved toward the front of our cave and watched the stars come out. In the black velvet sky of full night, there was an incredible number of them. We finished the pint. She sat close to me and said, "You are so good to help me."

We ate with far better appetite than we had for the earlier meal. Our clothing was stale with dried sweat. Bugs screamed out in the brush. One had a whining noise that seemed to come from everywhere and bored through your ears into the center of your skull. There was a long spine-chilling scream in the night, not far away.

"Cat," Barbara whispered. "They're out hunting. They hunt the *esquintla.*"

"What is that?"

"A kind of giant rat. Quite fat and slow. They were put on earth to be food for the cats. They are a delicacy. Very delicious. They taste like pork."

"I must remember to have some someday."

"Want me to cook one for you?"

"Don't put yourself out on my account."

Later we heard some squealing which she identified as *esquintla.* Perhaps the big cat played with them a little before the kill. It is said that the adrenaline of fear tenderizes the meat. Everything has a purpose, as Meyer says. One needs merely to find out what it is.

The blankets were big enough to work like an envelope, over and under, and in the coolness the cover was welcome. We were close. At one point I could hear Meyer purring directly behind me while her breath, a sweetness flavored just slightly with tequila, touched my cheek with her every exhalation.

Tomorrow, I realized, would be the fifteenth. And suddenly I remembered Annie was leaving tomorrow for Hawaii. A great desolation moved across my mind, like a black storm coming across wide fields. It enveloped me, and I said her name without making a sound. I wondered if I would have to go to the top of the great pyramid at

Cobá and say her name a hundred times as dawn came. I reviewed every measured micro-inch of her, each cry and cadence, each sweet pressure. How big of a damn fool can one man be? No use hoping the job would fold, or that she would change her mind. No hope at all, at all.

twenty-five

We were up earlier than we needed to be, just after first light. After an improvised breakfast, we removed all visible traces of ourselves from the area outside the cave.

I took Meyer up to where he would lie in ambush and had him stretch out there, little shotgun at the ready, while I went down and climbed the steep slope and climbed back down again, trying to see any significant bit of him or his weapon. It was good concealment, and from there he commanded most of the cenote. I went back to where he was and made certain he knew how to operate the weapon, breaking it to extract the empty shell and insert the new one.

Because of the difficulty he would have getting into position, we decided it would be best if he established himself there a little before ten, ready with minimum motion to aim down from his thirty-foot-high vantage point.

Barbara and I were to remain in the cave, back in the shadows where we would be invisible to eyes adjusted to the glare of daylight. I would stand in a niche on the right side of the cave—right side facing out—near the entrance. From there I could see the steep slope down which he would climb, and would see Jorge or Juan catch the rifle and scoot across the floor of the cenote to the other side while Cody Pittler was halfway down the slope.

At ten thirty we became very tense, but there was another ten minutes of whispered conversation before Barbara Castillo silenced me and tilted her head, listening. As soon as I heard voices and a crackle of twigs, I suddenly felt we were doing this wrong, doing it badly. We were in a hole and he had the high ground. It was contrary to everything I had been taught long ago. I moved into the niche I had selected, and she moved deeper into the cave. I heard a quiet sloshing as she waded back into the edge of the pool.

Then they were visible up on the brink, speaking Spanish. Jorge pointed down and toward us, and I could imagine he was telling Cody Pittler that the great cat was holed up in the cave. Jorge swung over the edge and came lithely down, holding onto roots and onto the small bushes which had grown out of the steep fall of earth. He pushed himself away from the slope and dropped the last six feet, caught his balance, looked up and held his hands out, and called some instruction.

I held my breath. This was critical. I saw Pittler clearly as he lay on his belly, leaning down over the edge, holding the rifle at the horizontal, letting it go. Jorge caught it, by stock and foregrip, and stood there with it as Pittler started down. He wore pale khakis dark-sweated at waist, armpits, and collar, a tan bush hat with one side of the brim tacked up, à la Aussie, and rubber-soled hiking boots that had seen much wear.

When he was halfway down the slope, he looked back and down over his shoulder just in time to see Jorge light out in full gallop. There was no hesitation in Pittler. He pushed away from the steep slope, dropped fifteen feet, landed, and sprawled onto his butt, but while landing, he unsnapped the holster I had not seen, and without any scrambling haste, took out a long-barreled pistol and shot Jorge as he was starting up the rubbled slope a hundred feet away. Jorge took one more running stride and came tumbling over backward, throwing the rifle ten feet in the air. It landed near him. Jorge was on his back, slack face toward the cave, mouth half open, unhurried blood seeping from the corner of it, eyes almost closed.

Pittler looked back up at the silence at the top of the slope. He stood very still, listening. Then he began to walk carefully, slowly, across the floor of the cenote toward the body and the gun.

I should have put the pellet from the little gun into his right ear. It would have made a lot more sense. I put it into the meat of his right thigh. It made a pitiful snapping sound. He hissed with pain, fired two shots into the cave, and went on a hobbling, skipping run, faster than I would have believed possible, over to the bulwark of boulders and vaulted into the shelter behind them.

He knew he had been ambushed, and he had reacted swiftly and decisively. He had made the right moves. So he was in shelter now, waiting for what might come next, not knowing that Meyer was looking down at him from hiding.

He yelled a question in Spanish. Before I could motion back to her to be still, Barbara answered it in kind.

"For God's sake!" he cried. "Willy's damn woman. Barbara, honey, what have you got against old Evan?"

"You killed William!"

"Talk sense, honey. William got sick and tired of you. You were just a little bit too dark-colored for him. What I did, I helped him get back to the States, that's all. He's probably dating some little red-headed gal by now. Come on out and we'll talk it over."

"And maybe talk over your big house near Playa del Carmen, eh? And the name you have there? The Mr. Roberto Hoffmann who lives so quietly?"

There was a silence. Finally he said, "I'm very sorry you had to say that, Barbara. Very sorry. It means you're going to stay right here in this hole forever. I can't let you get away. Did Willy tell you? When he told me he hadn't told anyone at all, I believed him."

"What did you do to him?"

"I chunked him on the head, wired him to a lot of lead, and rolled him over the side of the boat. I guess in a way, honey, it was my fault. I went hunting too close to home. I didn't think until later on that after it was in the paper Evan Lawrence was dead, I'd have to stay nervous about him coming across me some day. Now Evan Lawrence can stay dead. No problem."

"No problem except me?"

"Except you and Juan."

"And me," I called to him.

"Who the hell are *you?*" he asked, with a small break in his voice.

"I'm here to ask you about Isobelle Garvey, Larry Joe. You recall her. Over near Cotulla, a long time ago. You buried her in the gravel, but floodwaters washed her out. Little bit of a thing. Too young for you. Didn't matter to you how young."

"I know that voice," he said. "Say some more."

"Sure, Jerry. Did you watch Doris Eagle burn up that night near Ingram?"

There was a long silence. "McGee?" he said, his voice not as audible as before. "Is that you, McGee?"

"I'm McGee. The problem is finding out who you are."

"I'm not any of those names you said. I'm not Jerry Tobin or Larry Joe Harris."

"I didn't mention their last names, pal."

"I'm not them, and I'm not Bill Mabry in Montana, or Carl Keith in Pasadena, or Max Triplett in Shreveport. I'm not any of those. They're gone, all of them. You don't understand. I'm Bob Hoffmann and I live near here. I live a quiet life down here in Yucatán. I don't have to worry about anything down here. You wouldn't understand how it is."

"Just the way Norma didn't understand."

"Didn't we have a good time that night, McGee? That was a great evening aboard your houseboat, it really was. I can remember, because I can still remember being Evan Lawrence. And he really loved that woman. When he first started making love to her she was cold as a fish. She was scared. She couldn't let herself go. But when Evan finally taught her to let herself go, she was a treasure. She was just about the all-time best. Evan was in hog heaven with that woman. When she was gone, he was gone. Is that so hard to understand?"

And he punctuated his question with a shot that clanged off the side of the old rusty iron kettle and ricocheted into my corner of the cave, smacked the wall near my temple, and stung me with rock dust. It set a few dozen bats to squeaky complaining. He had worked it all out while talking, guessing where I was from my voice. A trick-shot artist. I could see the small shiny groove in the red rust where the bare metal was exposed. Elementary logic told me that were I to move to where I could not see the kettle, the trick wouldn't work. I had a new load in the toy rifle. I dropped and edged to where an upjut of rock protected my head, but from where I could see, through a narrow chink, most of the rock jumble behind which he was hiding.

With the aid of some spit which I chewed into my dry mouth, I made a delayed bubbling moan. Barbara screamed and came running to me. I pushed her out of harm's way and whispered, "I just died."

"You killed him!" she yelled dramatically. "You killed McGee!"

I don't think it impressed Pittler, but it got to Meyer. "Cody Pittler!" he yelled. "Cody T. W. Pittler, look at me! You killed Coralita and you killed your own father who loved you. You killed Bryce Pittler. Look at me!"

There was the chunky little bam of the shotgun, and there were two snappy shots from Cody's handgun, and I saw the shotgun slide out of the brush at the top of the slope and fall through the sunlight, turning slowly, to clatter onto the rock below. My heart emptied. Poor Meyer. Friendship had brought him to the *Busted Flush* at just the right time for Dirty Bob to steal his pride and his sense of himself as a man. And now the fates and friendship had brought him to this sinkhole in the Yucatecan woodland to die at the hands of a madman —a very quick and able madman.

Pittler scampered out of hiding, ran to the shotgun and snatched it up, and ran back, limping badly. I tried a shot and knew as I pulled the trigger that I had missed him. I reloaded.

Pittler cursed, and I guessed he had discovered the limited possibilities of the new weapon. No possibilities at all, actually, except as a club. One used shell in the chamber.

Pittler yelled, much louder than was necessary. "My old man lives in Eagle Pass, Texas. Nobody killed him. Hear me? He ain't dead, God damn it! Don't try stuff like that."

"You've got your head all messed up, Cody!" I called. "You don't know who you are. You did that playacting in school and you forgot who you're supposed to be. You're crazy. Stick that gun in your mouth and save us the trouble."

He made an unintelligible howling sound, a ululation of pain and rage. And my eye caught movement above him, way up at ground level. It was Meyer, moving slowly from right to left. It was a blundering walk, and he was grasping small trees to pull himself along. He turned toward me, and he wore the mask of the young people who do pantomime in the streets. One half of his face was white, the other red, in an almost even division. And he smiled a ghastly smile.

I began talking loudly to Pittler to cover the sound Meyer had to be making, up there over his head. I told him he was a sick vulture, living on dead women. I told him lots of good things like that. And slowly, step by step, Meyer came out toward the lip of the overhang. Two small trees grew near the brink. Meyer grasped one in each hand, standing between them. And then, heavily, solemnly, he began to jump up and down. Three times. I ran to the mouth of the cave and aimed at the big boulders that hid Pittler, hoping to get him if he tried to run for it.

Somebody belted me on the outside of my upper left arm, just below the point of the shoulder, with a tack hammer. The arm was suddenly very tired. It sagged and I kept aiming and holding the gun with my right hand. Right after Meyer's third jump there was a grating sound, and then the whole landscape up there tilted and came down, gaining speed. Tons of rock and dirt and trees and roots and bushes. A vast piece of layer cake. A chunk of eternity. Meyer held to the two trees and rode it down. It filled and obliterated the area where Pittler crouched. When it hit bottom, Meyer was at a forty-five-degree angle, leaning forward. The impact jolted him loose and flung him forward on his face, and the spill of loose earth then covered him to the waist. His face was in the slow creek.

We ran to him. I had to work one-armed. Barbara Castillo was a marvel. She dug with both hands like a hasty dog, and together we pulled him out and dragged him past the creek and rolled him onto his back. The water had washed the blood off his face. It ran from a two inch groove over his right ear, persistently but not dangerously. He grunted and pushed us away and sat up. He stared at where Pittler had been. He did not try to talk. He merely pointed and raised his heavy eyebrows in question.

"Yep," I said. "He's under there."

There was a confusion of expressions on Meyer's face as he realized what he had done. There was awe, and concern, and a troubled wonderment. He is my friend. He is a man of peace and gentleness.

But he'd had a very bad year, and even though the end of the strange man called Pittler had been sudden and ghastly, in the doing of it, Meyer had restored his own pride and identity.

And finally the underlying emotion supplanted all the others, and his smile, a strangely sweet smile, won out, and spread slowly all over his face, proud and certain: the smile of a man who had suddenly been made whole again.

"When you felt it start to go, there was time to scramble back off it," I said. "You could have killed yourself."

"I had enough left to jump three times and that was it. Scramble back? Couldn't. You know, you think of weird things when you don't have anything left. I thought that if I was only wearing the right costume, you know, like a cape, I could spread my arms and fly out of here."

Barbara got a knife and cut up her spare shirt and bound his head, tightly enough to stop the bleeding. She used the rest of it on my upper arm. On her way back with the cloth she had squatted by Jorge and learned he was just as dead as he looked. The wound was at the base of the skull.

Juan reappeared. He looked sallow. He sat by Jorge, his lips moving. Then Barbara and Juan carried Jorge into the shelter of the cave, out of the sunlight. She talked with Juan and then told us it had been decided that some of his people would come out and get the body, and that we were leaving the supplies and stores for Jorge's family. There would be no fuss made about it, she said. Ramón would learn that Señor Hoffmann was never coming back from this trip. He would tell the others. Little by little, inconspicuously, they would strip the great house of everything they wanted. It might take months. And then they would disappear back into the jungle villages. Eventually the authorities would notice he was gone, the house empty and decaying. But nobody would really care very much.

Meyer said, "It offends my sense of neatness. Shouldn't we go to the house? Look for . . . I don't know. Proof? Money?"

"You couldn't go there, either of you. The servants wouldn't let you in. I could go there. Ramón would let me in. I could look around, I suppose."

"Maybe we should tell the authorities where he is," Meyer said. She stared at him. "Shot in the leg and buried alive? Both of you wounded? Do you want to spend two or three years here answering questions, living on tortillas and beans?"

"No," I said. "No way."

"Nor I," she said, with her habitual little air of formality.

Right at that moment I began to feel uncommonly hot and strangely remote. All colors were too bright. The sun hurt my eyes. I didn't start having the chills until we were halfway out of the jungle. Meyer had to drive.

Meyer headed back three days later, very nervous over taking back into the States the items Barbara had collected in Pittler-Hoffmann's house: a few thousand in U.S. currency, a stack of Mexican gold fifty-peso pieces, several diamond rings, and two expensive wristwatches. We had agreed among ourselves they should be sent to Helen June in upstate New York. No need to include any kind of a note. We believed she would understand from the contents that there would probably never be any more packages from her brother.

I thought I was recovering and would soon be well enough to travel, but the day after Meyer left the illness came back. Barbara Castillo moved me to her place, the better to look after me.

She had found no proof in the Hoffmann house. She had found no clue to where the rest of the money might be.

We didn't need the money, and we didn't need any more proof than we had.

twenty-six

Annie Renzetti phoned me from Hawaii at two o'clock on Sunday, September nineteenth.

"Isn't it pretty early there, kid?" I said.

"Sort of about eight. Morning on Sunday is my best office time. Catch up on stuff. Who was that who answered yesterday when I phoned?"

"Kind of a Maya princess type."

"A what?"

"A nice person. Barbara is a nice person. She's up here from Mexico on sort of a vacation. I keep talking her into making it a little bit longer."

"I'm glad you have a nice new friend, Travis."

"I'm glad you're glad. Next weekend we are having the great Meyer chili festival. On an empty sandspit way down Biscayne Bay."

"Gee, I wish I could make it."

"Wish you could too."

"How *is* Meyer?"

"In the very best of form. He has enlisted the services of a troop of young handsome women. They follow him around, helping him carry the provisions back to his new boat. Which, by the way, is a dandy. The *Veblen*. Built-in bookshelves, and his colleagues are helping him replace the library he lost."

"Did you really stop looking for Evan Lawrence?"

"Meyer and I had a moment of mature consideration when we wondered what we would do if we caught up with him. So we gave it up."

"That doesn't sound like either of you!"

"We're learning discretion late in life."

"Travis, there was a little paragraph in the *Advertiser* about the

HooBoy sinking. Wasn't that the name of Hack's boat? What happened?"

"Dave Jenkins waited until somebody finally showed up to claim the boat. They'd paid a lot of money to have it made much faster, and he'd had a verbal contract with Hack about what he would pay for it when it was done. Dave thought it might be something like that. He'd alerted the Coast Guard and their friends, and they came and put an automatic beacon in the hull that would broadcast for a long long time. So the men came and claimed it, paid off Dave, and arranged the title transfer, and three weeks later they caught it loaded with pot, hash, and coke. They had to make a hole in the hull before it stopped. And after they saw the load, they took the men off and let it go down."

"And you had nothing to do with that?"

"Annie, I don't want to have anything to do with anything like that. Boats sinking. People getting hurt. It's all behind me. Meyer is delighted that now we're both sedentary."

"Sedentary? You?"

"We're settling down a little, that's all."

"I don't think I like it."

"Well, Annie, you are out there in Hawaii earning your battle ribbons, and I am here admiring this year's crop of beach bunnies and dipping into a little Boodles on the rocks from time to time. Everybody seems in good form. We have a few laughs."

"You're going to make me homesick."

"How is it out there?"

"Same as last time. There's an awful lot of work. It isn't as much fun as it was in Naples. But . . . it's a bigger challenge. There are some chauvinists in the company who are hoping I'll fall on my face. I won't give them that little satisfaction, dammit. I just wanted to hear your voice, dear."

Barbara came in from the beach and came striding across the lounge to give me a quick kiss beside the eye before heading for her shower.

The conversation with Annie was soon over. It might be the last one, I thought as I hung up. There was a little edge of loss, but it had softened. It no longer bit.

I got up and stretched and wandered into the head, where Barbara was in the giant shower, singing. She has a nice voice but absolutely no sense of pitch or rhythm. Consequently whatever she sings sounds like "Home on the Range."

"Good swim?" I called.

"Just beautiful! Say, did you turn off the oven at the right time like I told you?"

"Of course."

"Who was that on the phone? The woman from yesterday?"

"Same one."

"I don't think I like her calling you. Her voice is too pretty. Is she as pretty as her voice?"

"She is in Hawaii, Bobs."

"Then okay. She can be pretty if she wants."

She had the shower turned high. I kicked off my sandals, dropped my shorts, peered cautiously around the curtain, then slid in behind her and grabbed her around the middle. She squealed and fought in a very satisfying way. So we had some good old scrubbing and soaping fun, and then some good old rinsing fun, and then outside the shower some great big towel fun before I picked her up and carried her off to bed, giving her head a slight thump on the doorframe in passing.

And once again, after love, I had the marvelous pleasure of burying my snout in the soft and fragrant texture of the side of her throat. In dusty tan tint and in taste and fragrance it reminded me of something, always had, ever since that night when in her apartment at La Vista del Caribe, my great shuddering and gasping and chattering of teeth had awakened her and she had come in from her bed nest on the couch to put more blankets on me. She called it a little jungle fever. I do not ever want to have a big jungle fever. When all other warming efforts failed, she had slipped in there with me, under all the blankets, to hold me tightly until all that kind of fever went away and an entirely different one began, over her dwindling objections. I did not mind when, later, after her breath had caught several times during one long audible inhalation, she cried "Weeeeleee." I did not mind being his surrogate that night, or having called him back to life for her for that one instant on the edge of release. But it never happened again. She never called his name again.

So suddenly I knew what was at the back of memory as I snuffed at her throat, eyes open to see the odd dusky-dark coloring.

"Cinnamon!" I said.

"What?"

"You smell like cinnamon and you have the right color. Cinnamon skin."

"My God, McGee, can't you come up with something more original?"

"I thought it was."

M35 She laughed. "It's a song, you idiot. *Piel Canela:* Cinnamon

Skin. They sing it all over Mexico. A love ballad, quite tender. You can ask any group of mariachis, and they will play it and sing it for you. Like this."

She sang it softly to me, but it sounded like "Home on the Range."

She dropped off to sleep and came awake with a start. "Oh!" she said. "I dreamed about that man again."

"Bad?"

"Not too bad this time. All that dirt and stone that came falling down, it made a pyramid, a perfect little pyramid, with him under it. Which makes sense."

"Sense?"

"Of course, McGee. That pyramid we climbed at Cobá? It is all a big tomb. There is somebody buried in there, maybe more than one. But they may never get to excavating, to looking inside."

"Why not?"

"For the same reason the Spanish left us all alone in Yucatán, why they didn't care to conquer us and civilize us and turn us into little brown Christians."

"Which is?"

"McGee, lovemaking must dim your wits. Because the Maya had no gold!"